THE RENEGADE GOD

MATT SPENCER

BACK ROADS CARNIVAL BOOKS,
BRATTLEBORO, VERMONT

BACK ROADS CARNIVAL BOOKS
mattspencerauthor.wordpress.com

Digital ISBN: 978-0-578-43945-7
Print ISBN: 978-0-578-43944-0

Copyright © 2019 by Matt Spencer
Cover art © 2019 by Luke Spooner

ALSO BY MATT SPENCER:

THE DESCHEMBINE TRILOGY

The Night and the Land
The Trail of the Beast
The Blazing Chief (forthcoming)

TALES OF OLD DESCHEMB

Changing of the Guards

OTHERS

Story Time with Crazy Uncle Matt
Cult of the Stars
Chapel of the Falcon
Summer Reaping on the Fields of Nowhere
The Drifting Soul

Ian,
This one's for you, brother

Acknowledgements

This book wouldn't exist if it weren't for Matthew Gomez and Cameron Mount at *Broadswords & Blasters*, and it wouldn't be what it is without the editorial help of Laura Janisieski and Garrett Cook.

Big shout-outs are also in order for Liam Barnett, Ian Bigelo, Luke Burke, Bill Hilburn, Sydney Isle, Audrey Maples, Emyli McGrath, Julian McTaggart, Lucia Morey, Luz Elena Morey and Dan Seitz.

THE RENEGADE GOD

PROLOGUE

Hasell dreamed that his wife was riding him, like she hadn't since they were a pair of mad young swamp-kids. She was young and gorgeous again, limber and brazen, her lush dark hair lashing, her plump, round tits bobbing in his face. He felt strong and manful, hard and wild, pumping his hips up against hers. When he looked up into her ecstatic face, though, he didn't see Ilda's soft brown eyes looking down at him. The eyes that stared out of her skull glowed bright yellow. Her teeth were sharp, and so were her nails…sharp like claws, or knives. When she ran them up and down his chest, they sliced deep. Bright blood welled up quickly and ran down his sides, pooling on the mattress around him. Except he wasn't lying on a bed anymore, but in slimy, festering mud. He sank deeper into it as Ilda's hips slammed down on his, taking him in deeper and deeper.

Her claws scraped down past his ribcage, sank into his belly, and ripped him wide open. Hasell screamed, but he didn't stop thrusting up into her, even as his guts boiled while she ripped them out of the bubbling cavity she'd made. Even this searing agony felt amazing, like he couldn't get enough of it, even as she caressed and licked his insides, draped them around her shoulders, bathing in his blood, throwing her head back ecstatically. As she came, she curled forward so those sharp teeth of hers bit deep into his windpipe and wrenched back –

Hasell thrashed awake, his heart hammering painfully. The sweat that soaked him didn't smell like his own or Ilda's, he noticed. He rolled over and saw that her side of the bed was empty. The light through the nearby window told him it was barely dawn. He let his pounding chest quiet before he dared move. No sir, he sure wasn't that young buck he'd been in the dream. Finally, he climbed creakily out of bed, pulled on his trousers under his long nightshirt, and went downstairs on shaky legs. Ilda wasn't in the kitchen, but he saw that she'd brewed up a pot of chicory, so he helped himself to a cup. He went out to the front room of the little roadside place they ran. She wasn't there either. The front door winked at him from the far end of the room, swinging open and shut in the morning wind.

When he went outside, he found Ilda standing alongside the building, staring out across the field that surrounded their place. It was a chilly morning. She'd had the sense to bundle up accordingly, unlike him.

He let out an audible "*Brrrrrrrrr*," hugged himself as he approached, and said, "So what's got you up so bright and early?" They oughtn't expect any travelers along this way for another couple of hours at least.

Ilda stared off into the crooked, vine-wrapped trees of the Trosolmarsh swamp that bordered the field. "The god of the swamp's coming back, very soon," she said in a weird, distant voice.

"Huh?"

Ilda jerked her head sideways and blinked rapidly at him, like he'd just snuck up on her. "I said there's a wagon coming, along the road. Sounds like it'll be here soon. Can't you hear it?"

He did, but he couldn't see it through the trees just yet. His eyes weren't what they used to be, but his ears were still as sharp as when he'd been a young tracker. "Yeah," he said, "but it's still a good ways off. That ain't what woke you so early."

"Something was howling like crazy out there, while it was still dark. That didn't wake you up, too?"

He shrugged and shook his head.

She continued, "Well, *some* critter was going crazy out there...then it sounded like *lots* of critters. Then everything went quiet – deathly quiet – but I still couldn't fall back asleep. So I thought I'd go down and get an early start on things, y'know? Then I stepped out for some fresh air." She pointed across the field at the trees. "When I came outside, the swamp fires were sprouting fierce, all over the place out there. You could see 'em flashing for miles back through the trees, it seemed like. Ain't seen 'em do that since I was a girl."

Since she was a girl...since before the children who'd long since come along, then grown up and scattered. She hadn't ridden him like she had in the dream since then, either. *Of course, even back then, she never ripped me open, pulled out my guts while we were still at it, nor bit my damn throat out as we finished.* He gazed with her, out into the echoing gloom of the swamp. Critters lived out there whose females did stuff like that to the males when mating. *But we ain't animals, not like that.*

He didn't know why that dream was still so strong in his mind. When he was younger, he used to have wild, vivid dreams all the time, some good, some bad, some just plain strange, but if he ever had them anymore, he rarely remembered. He stepped behind Ilda, wrapped his arms around her, and felt her snuggle up against him through the morning's chill. After all these years, holding her just like this in the chilly morning, it still made part of him feel wild and new, strong and feisty and ready for anything, like they weren't both such withered old sods. That was okay. Being withered old sods together was nice. It was comfy, knowing they'd survived everything else and could now just relax while running their quiet little business for weary travelers.

Remembering that dream, though, he now thought about getting her inside, upstairs, and back into bed, and for the first time in a couple of years at least, find out if there was juice left in their old loins yet.

Nah, here came that wagon, rumbling closer. By now, through the crooked, moss-draped trees, he could see the gleaming snouts of the sleashkills that drew it. "Aw, hell," said Hasell, "looks like time for me to get on inside and make myself presentable for our first company of the day."

"I suppose I should as well," said Ilda.

"Aw hell, you look fine," said Hasell, casting a smile over his shoulder at her as they went back inside. He even stopped at the door, held it for her, then slapped her lightly on her backside as she passed him.

Moments later, the wagon rumbled to a stop outside the front door. By then, they'd set about making breakfast. Hasell headed back outside, while Ilda stirred the soogi-noodles and fresh-harvested cluster of swamp-fish eggs on the stove.

He made it out onto the front stoop, then froze at the sight of the two men climbing down from the front of the wagon. The dust of a long, unbroken journey covered them, but he recognized their gleaming, narrow, purple-tinged faces and starkly tailored getup just fine…the black trousers and knee-high black boots, the dark gray shirts beneath the flowing black capes and studded leather vests, tailored to fit compact, cleanly muscled frames that moved sedately, almost ethereally, despite how they'd been sculpted for intimidation and violence. It had been years since Hasell had seen the like…except what the hell were Spirelight policemen doing, traveling so roughly, and on that shabby wagon, let alone this far south in this day and age?

Out of reflex, Hasell gave the old salute, as best he remembered. "Fine morning to you, gentlemen," he said, even while his palms grew clammy and the nerves buzzed tensely in his neck and limbs.

"And a fine greeting to you as well, sir," said the taller, older of the two, clearly the ranking officer. He already sounded pleased about something. "Do you run this establishment?"

"I do," said Hasell, nodding swiftly, trying to sound easy-going. "Have these past forty years, it must be by now."

"And before that?" said the Spirelight officer.

"Before I took over for Pa, I used to scout for guys like you. Empire boys that is. 'Fore the last of the Spirelights pulled back from this region. I for one was sad to see you go, if I'm to be honest. The rabble in the village weren't so bold, back when you boys ran the show, I can tell you that…the harbor town, I mean, back the way you just come."

Back by the cart, the younger officer chuckled under his breath, in a way Hasell didn't like.

"Yeah, we passed through it. Charming little village, but that's not why we're here." The older officer kept looking over the front of the building, at the sign that swung in the wind. "Anyway, that's very good to hear, Mister…"

"Hasell. The name's Hasell." He offered a handshake, which both officers ignored, except that the younger one maybe smirked more openly. Hasell straightened and tightened his spine, thinking of Ilda inside right now. Whatever was about to happen, he didn't know how much he could do, not the man he'd once been and all, but he sure as shit wasn't about to back down and let it roll over him.

"I appreciate that, Mister Hasell, your days of service that is," said the older officer, "as would the Spirah Empire, I'm sure. But I was inquiring about the history of your establishment here."

"Oh. My pa ran it before me, before my tracker days were done."

"And he also supported the local Imperial jurisdiction?"

Hasell's eyes lowered slightly, his boots shuffling in the dirt. "I'm…afraid not, no. He always resented you guys' throwing your weight around, as he put it, called me a young fool for trying to make my way in your service. Once y'all pulled out and I come back to tending bar here…well, the old man always *did* like to tell me *I told you so.*"

The older officer murmured curiously, then stepped away and took a long stroll up and down the road as it ran through the clearing, for a better look at the building. The place was an octagonal structure that lay perfectly at the center of the round clearing, with sharp arches jutting from each corner, with perfectly centered, oval-shaped windows of smoky glass, running between them like a chain of beads. Hasell stood planted like a tree while the officer assessed the scene. The younger one leaned against the wagon, eyeing Hasell unreadably. Hasell tried not to gulp too visibly.

Finally, the older officer came back and said, "I'm impressed, good sir. For a place so remote from the Empire's eye, your structure stands in perfect accordance with the Sacred Geometry of our mandates. You must have spared no expense in renovations, after inheriting it from your father, I mean."

"Well, uh, yeah, I kept it up over the years, but...nope, it's looked like this since I was a kid, when my pa run it, and his before him, and so forth, for as far back as I could tell you."

The officers exchanged looks, then smiled at Hasell. Even the younger one suddenly looked outright pleasant. "That's very curious, Mister Hasell," said the older officer. "Just all this splendid architecture you have here, I mean. Might we have a look around inside?"

"Well...the place won't be open for business for an hour yet...but...uh...Yeah, yeah, come right on in. The wife's fixing breakfast as we speak. We'll be happy to warm you up with a cup of chicory if you like, too."

"That sounds delightful, sir."

Both Spirelight officers started to follow Hasell inside, then the older one turned and checked his underling. "Not you, Arcon. Not yet. Go take a walk around the edges of that field out there. Report back to me with your findings. You know what to look for."

The younger officer – Arcon, apparently – made a slight nod, then walked off silently, striding across the clumpy grass through the morning fog. Hasell led the older officer into the spacious, dimly lit front room, just as Ilda came out of the back with two plates in hand. Steaming chicory had already been set at one of the tables, so that's where Hasell led the officer.

Hasell met his wife's eyes swiftly and said, "It's okay, honey. This man's just a weary traveling emissary from Trescha. Be a dear and fetch a third cup and plate, would you?"

Ilda set what she carried down at the table. The sudden appearance of the big, steely, uniformed man didn't seem to rattle her at all. That was strange. In the old days, Ilda had called Hasell a damn fool for working for Spirelights, worse than Pa had. For some damn reason, though, she'd still agreed to marry him, and Pa hadn't disowned him for being a tracker for glowsticks. In the years since, Hasell had come to realize that they'd both been right, that they were all better off without the fuckin' glowsticks around, telling everyone what to do. Now here they were to pull him back in, along with Ilda.

You assholes, just get lost and leave us be. We've made a good life for ourselves here that never needed you in the first place. He couldn't just blurt that out, though. If he did, he'd be dead, and so would Ilda. Shit, he hoped the officers didn't notice the gleaming sweat breaking out all over him.

Ilda beamed pleasantly as she set down the food and drink. "No trouble at all, Officer…"

"Just Keston, if you will, ma'am, thank you," said the officer.

"No trouble at all, Keston," she said before leaving the room breezily.

Hasell sat down stiffly across from Keston, who already sat comfortably, leaning back in his chair, one leg draped over the other, like they were a pair of drunken louts in a tavern, all pretense of militant formality forgotten.

Keston sipped his chicory. "Mmmmmm…I can already taste how one could grow comfortable living out here, in this marshland."

"Thanks, Mister…sorry…sir."

"No need for such formality, Mister Hasell." Keston savored another sip. "Roots harvested locally, I take it?"

"That's right."

Ilda came back with her own plate and cup. She sat down next to her husband and said, "I hope you don't mind our humble accommodations, Keston. We're not used to such fancy visitors out here."

"It's okay, honey," Hasell muttered. "These emissaries from Trescha are just conducting a routine inspection."

"Oh?" she said. "I didn't know Trescha's forces were returning to this region."

"Trescha's forces?" said Officer Keston. "Oh no, ma'am. I didn't mean to give the impression we were here on official business from Trescha."

Ilda leaned forward curiously. "Then...the Empire *doesn't* plan to stretch back out into these parts?"

Keston took another deep gulp of chicory. "No, I don't think so. Then again, you would have to ask Trescha's new Priest King about that. Last I checked, she's just as ignorant of our presence out here as we are of...well, whatever her inner workings might be. Had you heard Trescha has a new Priest King?"

"I'd heard something like that," said Ilda.

Hasell frowned and leaned forward. "So, Mister Keston. If you two officers –"

"My brother and I," Keston corrected him.

"Right. So if you and your brother ain't here on official Trescha business, just what –"

A dull smack sounded. Hasell's head lashed to the side. He slid out of his chair, crashed to the floor, and lay there motionless a tiny red stream trickling from his temple, where a short, black-feathered bolt had lodged itself.

Keston stood up and faced the doorway as his brother walked in and strode towards the table. "That took you a shorter time than I'd expected. I hope you were as thorough as I told you to be."

"Oh, I was thorough, all right. Just look at it." Arcon's eyes were wide as he came forward. One hand lowered his Imperial-issue bolt-caster to his side. His other hand stretched out, holding a wet gob of soil, through which writhed worms, millipedes and smaller squirmy bugs. Some of them crawled out of the muck onto his hand and arm, leaving little wet, brown trails on his skin and sleeve. "Smell it. The land here is rich and ripe as he told us it would be."

Keston leaned forward, inhaled the stench, and sighed, satisfied. "Ah, yes. Just look at the space in here, too, would you?"

"Yes, I've noticed. It's perfect!" Arcon drifted off around the room, circling it from one end to the other, sprinkling the moldering soil over the boards as he went. He shook the last of it from his hand as he returned to his brother's side. They both turned back to the old woman.

She sat silently, staring up at them. Her eyes weren't afraid. "Is it true?" she said in the voice of a much younger gal. "Is the god of the swamp coming home?"

"Sooner than you know, ma'am," said Keston. "Sooner than even we suspected."

A serene smile spread across her face. "And this land will drink up our blood, Hasell's and mine, so the god will find us living in it anew, waiting faithfully?"

"I expect so, ma'am." Keston nodded sideways.

Arcon reloaded his bolt-caster and shot the old woman right between the eyes.

ONE

"Oh, so you're Tia of the Nagga Mountains, huh?" The guy leaned sideways along the bar, leered, and pressed up against her.

"Slow down there, boy." Tia's hand pressed his broad, leather-tough chest, hard enough so he'd know she was stronger than she looked. "Yeah, that's me."

She took a slurp of local brew, then set the drinking jack aside to adjust herself within the tight lace-up leather top she'd bought yesterday. Fuck this garment! How did the so-called civilized gals breathe in these things? There went five red gems and a crystal chain she'd never get back...unless of course she ever caught that same swine of a merchant in a caravan raid.

"As in, *Tia and Ketz?*"

Ohforfucksake, even this far west..."That's right, honey."

At first, she'd thought this guy might be fuckable after a couple of rounds. Her travel-pouch was full of enough infertility roots from Silisha, the blend-lady back home. She'd chewed one this morning with breakfast, which had consisted of some berries and flank-strips cut from a member of the pack of hill-jackals that had tried to make a meal of her and her brother last night. That critter's loss, their full bellies.

This big boy's hatchet-face was ugly, though in a raw, masculine way that she found sort of sexy. She liked how his long, dark hair hung to his shoulders in tight braids, over a vest and leggings made from the strangely colored pelts of beasts she didn't recognize, such as dwelt further north, she guessed. She liked his swagger and his scarred, sunburnt, rangy arms, his deep chest, and raspy voice. At the same time, he looked familiar somehow, in a way that set off warning bells. So did his three buddies with the same deep aqua-swirl skin-shade as him. They stood over in the corner, taking turns throwing tiny knives at the wall. How'd they smuggle those in? The doorman had made Tia and Ketz hand over their weapons before entering.

Most of the folks in here were weary, stringy old farmers who looked like they'd never held a weapon in their life. The doorman slouched in his chair by the front door, looking half asleep, pretending not to notice the rowdy toughs. Everyone else was too scared to say anything. This guy and his buddies were Schomites, like Tia, like most folks in this region, but they were even less local than her and Ketz. Some kind of northerners, maybe Wallutions. Tia didn't hold that against them, yet. So, why the rotten feeling in her gut?

She kept on her fake smile. "Say, what's your name again, honey?"

"I'm Doveede." He stood up straight. His smile no longer matched his eyes. "So where's that famous brother of yours?"

"Man, I got no idea," she lied. "Hard to keep track of the little bastard sometimes."

Last time she'd checked, Ketz was still off in that corner nook, making out with some drunk tavern slut. When Tia had made the mistake of checking on them, she'd worried their public antics would get her and Ketz thrown out of the tavern. Whenever girls took a liking to Ketz in public, he had a way of forgetting he wasn't back home in the Nagga Mountains, where silly ideas like *public decency* were less the norm. None of the sad losers in here had seemed to care or notice, though…just like they pretended not to notice whatever was about to happen between Tia and Doveede.

The air crackled. The back of Tia's neck bristled as Doveede signaled over his shoulder. One of his buddies spotted it, left his tiny knife sticking to the wall, and slapped the other two across the shoulders. They sauntered over, swinging their arms and necks in that clownish way that moronic thugs always think looks intimidating, and stood behind Doveede. They peered maliciously over his shoulders at Tia with dull, hooded eyes. They'd left their knives sticking to the wall, as though they were confident they wouldn't need weapons. That was always a bad sign. One of them chewed on something with his mouth open. He gazed at her lazily without blinking.

"You know somethin', *Tia of the Nagga Mountains?*" said Doveede. "I ain't fucked a war hero in a while. I think maybe we'll go someplace and I'll fuck you. My boys here, maybe they gonna fuck you too. Shit, girl, whenever we catch that scumbag brother of yours, we might just fuck him. Hell, maybe we'll knock out all those pretty, sharp, white teeth of his, before we make him suck our dicks. Yours too, maybe. How 'bout that?" His tone stayed quiet and pleasant, which was the most chilling part.

Tia kept her cool, outwardly at least, even though her insides felt like a stirred-up hornet's nest. She stood up from her stool and held Doveede's gaze. Her purple eyes crackled. "Now why would some nice boys like you wanna do such an unkind thing to a pretty little gal like me?"

"Rothollow," said Doveede. The last of the pleasant act bled from his voice. "Still confused?"

"Actually, yeah." Sure, she remembered Rothollow. By now, it had been enough months that she'd almost gotten the stench of the Island of Skulls out of her nose. "What about it?"

"That's where you and your punkass brother killed *my* brother."

"Wait, hang on. This dead brother of yours. Was he one of them cultists, or one of those out-of-town guards they'd paid twice what they were worth to look out for their stupidass infernal ritual? You don't strike me as the pious type. Was your brother?"

Doveede's face twisted into a feral mask of hatred. "*Bitch, look at me!* I look like one of those moldy-skinned Rothollow degenerates? What you think? *Damn right, he was on the guard*, 'til you cut him in half."

"Well, he sucked at his job."

"You believe this little skank?" said the guy chewing with his mouth open. He talked funny like part of his jaw didn't work right. That might be because of whatever he was chewing on. Somehow, Tia didn't think so. He edged around to her right, so he stood almost behind her. "Talks mighty calm for someone about to get fucked and gutted, don't she?"

"Yeah, well," said Tia, voice still steady, "all this lizardshit's been amusin', but boys, seriously, go fuck yourselves. I ain't got time for it."

She started off across the tavern, towards the nook where Ketz lounged with his tavern slut. She couldn't see either of them from here. At any other time, that would be a good thing.

Doveede shouted, "Bitch, get your ass back here, I ain't through with you!"

He grabbed her arm and jerked her backwards, just like she'd expected. She stumbled and spun, letting the momentum carry her as her feet shifted. Her hips twisted while her free palm-edge shot up. It crashed into Doveede's face, right as she stepped past him. His jaw crunched, popped, and bent funny. So did his neck. He spun like a top, then hit the floor on his side. Tooth-chips drooled out of his mouth, through the spreading pool of blood, like little half-rotted boats on a lake. His tongue lolled out, his eyes stared glassily, and his head hung at an odd angle. Two ends of fractured spine pressed the skin of his neck outward, like a tent. A little tip of bone-shard jutted through the flesh, with a red trickle streaming from it. Damn. Tia hadn't thought she'd hit him that hard.

At the far end of the bar, some aging local gal jerked to her feet. She stared and shouted, "*Oh sweet lands, what did you just do?*" then doubled over and puked her guts out.

The moment unfroze. The guy who'd been chewing with

his mouth open shouted, *"You fuckin' bitch, you just killed Doveede!"* That's when all three of them rushed her.

They were all stupid and reckless with shock and anger, but there were still three of them and one of her, with a few drinks in her, while she wasn't armed. Her lashing palm-edge caught one of them in the throat, collapsing his trachea so he stumbled backwards, gagging and clutching his neck. He coughed up blood all over his dirty shirt, before sinking to the floor. In the same motion, Tia's shoulders swung so her other fist cracked another guy in the ribs. That's when the guy who'd tried to flank her jumped on his opening. He darted past her and yanked her backwards by the hair. Her feet slipped and slid beneath her, leaving her off balance. While he dragged her backwards, the other guy lunged in and slugged her in the gut. His fist wasn't small or soft, either. The air went out of her, so she doubled forward. Her temples throbbed and she almost puked. Next thing she knew, her cheek smashed against a tabletop.

~

Meanwhile, over in his nook, Ketz's sharp-tipped ears perked up. He recognized the slams, grunts, and rapid shuffling of someone getting into a scrape. When he twisted up and around for a look, the tavern girl pressed his shoulders back against the bench. She straddled him and ran her palms up and down under his shirt. She pushed up his shirt and kissed her way down his chest and stomach, her long, silky dark hair lashing back and forth against his skin.

For a moment, Ketz was happy to let her distract him. Then someone cried out, and he said, "Ah, shit."

Instinctively, he reached for the long knife that wasn't on his belt where it usually was. He shoved the girl away and sprang to his feet. She fell off his lap, hit the little table as she went down, and floundered around on the dirty floor.

"Hey, what the fuck?" she shouted. "You crazy sonofabitch, I thought you were nice!"

"Sorry," Ketz muttered.

He rammed his way out of the nook, looked across the bar, and saw two guys on the floor with blood splattered all around them. They both looked like they were from that pack of renegade Wallutions he'd spotted earlier. One of them had fallen funny and now lay still. The other one squirmed around, gagging and clutching at his throat. The other two were still standing. One of them kept trying to look tough, but he hunched slightly and clutched his side. His cheeks puffed when he breathed, like he had a broken rib or two. The other guy had Tia bent over a table.

A chill swam through Ketz's blood. It had been a long time since he'd seen anyone get the drop on his sister like that. The tavern girl came up behind him and yelled in his ear, then she saw all the blood, shrieked, and ducked back into the nook.

The guy with some busted ribs spotted Ketz. "Aw, there's our boy!"

The man lunged forward. Ketz put up his fists and made like he was gonna throw some punches, then kicked the guy in the knee instead. The knee imploded with a wet, ripping crunch. The Wallution howled, fell over, then lay writhing around on his back. His trembling fingers tried to clutch his ruined knee and winced back, so he shrieked louder.

As Ketz stalked forward, the Wallution who'd pinned Tia looked up and blurted, "What the –"

That's when his grip loosened while distracted. Tia twisted, heaved, and stomped on his foot. He yowled, let go, and stumbled backwards. When he saw the twins closing in on him, he righted himself, threw up his dukes, and spat, "Stay away from me, you cunts!" He looked around frantically for his companions, none of whom looked like they were in the mood for more…especially not the one who'd fallen funny, with the busted neck. The last Wallution crouched lower and bared his teeth. "*I said back off!*"

The twins didn't back off, but they exchanged cautious glances. It was a different animal they faced, now that he no longer had his buddies backing him up. He'd been dangerous before, along with the rest of them, but he'd been so smug and sure, his confidence bolstered by numbers. Assholes like him were never as sharp as they thought they were, with that advantage. Now that he was cornered and on his own, rather than deflate like a coward, he frothed and buzzed with crazy eyes, shifting jerkily from left to right. There was no telling what a guy like that might do next.

"*Hey*," barked a rough old voice. "That's enough of that, everyone!"

The doorman had finally unglued his ass and stepped forward. Seemed like he'd taken his good, sweet time, even though in reality, the whole tussle had lasted less than a minute. His burly arms bore his own battle scars, but that had been long ago. In the years since, he'd gone slow and sodden, too relaxed, looking out for the local regulars of this watering hole, which sat well off the main trade-routes where more bandits and cutthroat mercenaries roamed at will. His job didn't keep him in shape for this kind of shit. Still, he'd gotten himself together enough to project his old, confident heir of authority over the whole scene.

The last Wallution turned to the doorman and stabbed his finger sideways at the twins. "Mister, you see what this little bitch just did to my friends?" Brown drool ran down his chin from whatever he'd been chewing on, which by now he'd either swallowed or spat out. He still talked funny. "Her and her…her…brother there? She started it, man! Look, just…"

Okay, so maybe the last Wallution was a coward after all. While he distracted himself by pleading with the doorman, Ketz made ready to spring on him and finish him off. Tia reached to the side and gripped her brother's shoulder, making sure he didn't do anything stupid just yet.

Meanwhile, another gentleman walked through the front door and strode calmly past the doorman. This guy was older than the doorman, but he'd never let himself slow down or soften up. Beneath the wide brim of his black hat, there shone a chiseled, narrow, craggy face, shaded in milk-white and lily-pad green, with deep-set, dangerously sane pale blue eyes. His long, black coat hung open, fanning out wide behind him, showing off a big curved knife on his belt.

"Oh hey, Marshal," said the doorman. "Look, sorry you had to see this, but trust me, nothin' here's out of hand. I got it all under –"

"You're a rotten liar, Topen," said the marshal, with what might be condescending affection. "What's going on here?" His voice was as rough as his face, with a curious accent that sure didn't sound like that of a local marshal. His every word rolled out like thick, sweet syrup, in the manner of an outsider who's learned to speak the local language and dialect better than most of the locals. The doorman hunched up and skulked backwards, happy to hand the matter over to someone else.

The man in the long black coat walked calmly towards the ensuing standoff. He fixed his gaze on the last Wallution. "That'll be quite enough out of you, young man."

"Fuck off, you old bastard! You want some too? Come get it!"

In answer, the older man stepped in. His long fingers shot out and snatched the guy by the hair, quicker than the eye could follow, like the talon of some bird of prey. He yanked the punk backwards, spun him around, and dragged him up nose to nose. "Answer me one question, son. Don't play with me, now, here? A simple *yes* or *no* will do. Is your name Doveede?"

"Uh…uh…no?"

"You've been traveling with Doveede, though, haven't you, boy? Take care, I know a liar when one speaks to me. Do you speak honesty, boy? I speak it fluently."

"Nu…nu…no, man, I ain't Doveede. Don't believe me? Look over there." The guy cocked his head sideways, as far as the iron grip let him. "See that mess over there? *That's* Doveede, man. Doveede's dead." His shaky finger pointed at the corpse with the broken neck, which had by now started voiding its bowels so it stunk up the whole room.

"That is unfortunate," said the marshal, "for both of us."

With a swift, graceful motion, the marshal cupped the back of the Wallution's head and brushed a palm across his cheek. The kid's neck let off an ear-splitting *pop*. He sagged limp. The marshal flung the corpse aside like a bag of wet, moldy rags.

"*What in the everlovin' hell, Marshal?*" exclaimed the wide-eyed doorman. "I...I...thought you was supposed to keep things...things...not so..."

The marshal turned, caught the doorman's eyes, and silenced him with an icy smile. He made a *tisking* sound with his teeth and waved a finger back and forth. "There now, Topen. That is exactly what I'm doing." He added pityingly, "I hate to say it, but better than you appear to have done today."

Tia and Ketz glanced at each other, then back at the marshal, trying to take in this strange new turn of events. Next to them, the guy with the collapsed windpipe kept thrashing and gurgling where he lay, nearly gone. Off behind them, the one with the busted knee flailed and rolled from side to side on his back, squealing louder and louder. The marshal walked over and launched a sharp kick into the latter's skull. The Wallution fell over, twitched a few times, then shit his pants with a loud fart, so the whole room went twice as noxious. All the other patrons, who'd already done their best to get out of the way, curled up further into themselves against the smell.

The marshal looked around at everyone and said, "Okay, I'll ask nicely once." He pointed at Doveede's corpse. "Who killed this sorry excuse for a Wallution here?"

The lady at the end of the bar – the one who'd puked earlier – lifted her head from hiding. She stabbed a shaky finger at Tia. "It was her! I saw the whole thing, Marshal! Her and the rest of those...those *foreign kids*. They was just talkin', then they started arguin', then she...she just went crazy on those poor boys! It was awful!"

"That will do, ma'am," said the marshal. She kept blubbering and stammering, so he repeated, "*That will do.*" The old lady finally shut up. The marshal walked over to Tia. "Is that true, young lady?"

Tia looked the man over. He was armed and she wasn't, plus she was still shaky, but she wasn't off her guard this time. "Damn right I did," she said. "Him and his buddies wanted to drag me off and gang-rape me. Why don't you go ask some of these *nice people* about that, *huh?* Wanna make somethin' of it?"

"Yes ma'am, I very much do."

Ketz slipped silently up to the marshal's side. "Keep your hands off my sister, asshole."

The marshal smirked. "You can relax, young man. I have no desire to touch either of you. The two of you, I gather, are the famous Tia and Ketz of the Nagga Mountains."

"What's it to you?" said Tia.

"You're both younger than I imagined." The marshal sniffed. "And, I will point out, drunker. That young man you just killed, I've been pursuing him for some time."

"You're welcome," said Tia.

The marshal chuckled and shook his head. "I think you misunderstand, miss."

"Enlighten me," said Tia.

"I intend to, though I'd hoped to do so somewhere a bit more private."

"You see what just happened to those assholes who last took a notion to get indecent with me?" said Tia.

"I did," said the marshal, "and that has a good deal to do with the business I want to discuss with you…both of you." He stuck two fingers in his mouth and made a shrieking whistle that brought all heads in the tavern up sharp, including the barkeep who finally peeked from behind the counter. The marshal met the barkeep's eyes and said, "Stili, be a dear, take a look at that ledger you've got down there with you, and clean out a room where these two kids and I might have a private conversation, where we won't be disturbed."

The barkeep nodded sharply, pulled out the ledger, said "Yes, Marshal," and hurried off.

"Now," the marshal continued, "we can do this the easy way, or we can do this the hard way. The choice is yours, kids."

Before Ketz could open his big mouth, Tia said, "Fine. Let's do this the easy way."

TWO

Tia and Ketz sat side by side, in two flimsy wooden chairs, at a long dirty, wobbly, rectangular table in one of the tavern's upstairs rooms. They both felt clammy and woozy, despite the open window that let in the sweltering summer mid-afternoon air. It had been a nice enough day up to all this lizardshit.

The marshal peered across the table at Tia. "You're shivering, young lady. Is it chilly in here? I cannot tell." His eyes dropped to the scarlet leather corset she wore. "I beg your pardon, but my senses are often dull to air temperatures. Should I light a fire in yonder hearth?"

Neither of the twins answered. An impressive bruise was already rising on one side of Tia's face, from when she'd gotten it slammed against the table downstairs.

The man had kept his coat on, but removed his hat, showing off his more narrowly pointed ears and gleaming bald, white-and-green head...the skin of one of those deep-southern Schomites, from the Dragon Coasts. The twins, in their day, had only met one other Dragon Coast Schomite. They still knew the reputation of the breed; wily, cruel, ambitiously cunning, and most of all, fucking crazy.

"So while we're gettin' all friendly and such, maybe you can tell us who the fuck you are?" said Ketz.

Their host folded his hands behind his head. "You can call me Minquo."

Tia and Ketz went pale. They looked at each other, then back at the man. "Lizardshit," said Tia.

Ketz peered at Minquo. "Well, damn. So you're actually real, huh?"

Tia rolled her eyes. "You'll have to excuse my brother,

Mister. He's got a *man-to-man* hard-on for your reputation."

"I don't," said Ketz. "I really, really don't. Matter of fact, Mister Minquo, if half your reputation's true, then I hate your fuckin' guts. She ain't all wrong, though. We can't help but admire you…assumin' you are who you say you are."

Tia almost said *Speak for yourself, brother*, except that wasn't wrong either.

"Very interesting," said Minquo. "Well then, I'll bite. What *reputation* have you two young bucks heard about me?"

"You're a bounty hunter," said Ketz. "You take any job, wherever in Deschemb you find yourself, and you always bring in your prey."

"Until today," Minquo pointed out. "Because sweet Tia here managed to murder my *prey*, right as I was closing in on him, which brings us to our –"

"You're a *Schomite* bounty hunter," said Tia, "one who takes jobs from Spirelights, huntin' other Schomites."

"We got a word for that," Ketz chimed in.

"You are correct so far, my young friends," said Minquo. "But I do hope you let me continue. For all our sakes. You see, the price on Doveede's head specified that I bring him home *alive*. As such, you two have cost me a *very* heavy payday, from a very wealthy, very important Wallution family."

"There are wealthy, important Wallution families?" said Ketz.

"Shut up, Ketz," said Tia. "I'm still missin' the part where that's our problem, Mister."

"It just so happens, there's another *problem* I've been puzzling over. Now, what do you know, here's the famous Tia and Ketz, dropped right into my lap. Having just witnessed your clumsy display downstairs, a less perceptive fellow than myself might suspect I've been lied to about your reputations. But we three, we know better, don't we? I was once young myself."

"Look," said Ketz, "we *know* the glowsticks must have a bounty on us bigger than my swingin' dick. If you think we're gonna betray our own people back home, you can…"

Tia said, "Ketz, for once, just shut up and listen to the man, will you?"

Minquo chuckled. "I have no interest in turning either of you over to any of the Spirelight authorities. For one thing, their nearest outpost is a long journey east, longer than I care to endure either of your company, trussed up or no. I had, however, hoped to collect the bounty on young Doveede, from his own family, by bringing him home alive…both him *and* his brother."

"Hang on a second," said Tia. "If you are who you say you are, and you've been spendin' all this time chasin' that asshole, what the hell you doin' with folks 'round here callin' you the village marshal?"

"Because I tracked his trail, predicted his trajectory, and arrived in this little township, such as it is, roughly a week ago. The marshal made trouble for me, so I killed him and appropriated his job title, which has, as you can see, proven convenient. None of the good local people found it in themselves to object." Minquo shrugged and went on, "The far-northern Schomites, despite what you seem to have heard, have built a more civilized, cozy, prosperous way of life for themselves. Those two brothers, though…" He sighed and shook his head. "It seems they grew up hearing all the wild tales of life down in this region. Boys being boys, they struck out from home – along with some of their friends, the last of whom I believe you met – to answer the call of wild adventure. As they discovered, it was far different than the tale-leaves made it look or sound. Finding themselves lost and desperate and penniless, they enlisted as mercenaries for the Spirelights, which finished the job of hardening them into creatures as brutal and savage as anyone born to these lands."

"Not brutal or savage enough, I guess," said Ketz, grinning.

"Shut up, Ketz," said Tia.

"Either way," said Minquo, "they eventually deserted their

post, perhaps in a crisis of conscience for having betrayed their own kind. More likely, the realities of Spirelight military discipline disagreed with them. Who can say? The older brother, Doveede, made his way home. According to his family, he felt great shame for luring his impressionable younger brother onto the trail of ruin, so eventually he headed south again, to find him and bring him home. Meanwhile, his brother and some of their friends had struck out deep into the wilderness, where they made a career of other sundry sordid work. The younger one fell in with that abominable business in Rothollow, which ended when he met the two of you. His elder brother found out, learned the names of his younger sibling's murderers, and went in search of vengeance. Their family, meanwhile, had issued a hefty bounty to find both of them, to bring them home safe, with or without their cooperation."

"So cry me a river for a couple of dead Wallution assholes," said Tia. "What's this got to do with us?"

"Merely, it just so happens, that I've been on the lookout for both pairs of siblings," said Minquo, "them and you. The former proved significantly easier to track, though not by much. Once I picked up Doveede's trail in Rothollow, it wasn't hard to predict who he'd be looking for. All I had to do from there was place myself in your path and wait. I headed over here when one of my local informants told me of the scuffle in progress. I believe the rest requires no explanation. Do I make myself clear so far?"

"You said you didn't plan to sell us to the Spirelights," said Tia. "So what do you want with us?"

"When I heard you were out roaming the countryside, to the west of the Nagga Mountains, it occurred to me to present you with a proposition…for you to act as my agents, on a very special job. I'm prepared to grant you a generous sixty-forty split on the bounty. If you refuse this offer, rest assured, I will make no attempt to *personally* apprehend either of you. But keep in mind, I have connections everywhere, people high and low, who owe me favors. And I do mean, *everywhere*. I am privy to widespread networks of information, the workings of which your young, mountain-bred barbarian minds could not hope to comprehend. The long and the short, kids, is that if you walk away from this opportunity, your journey home to the Nagga Mountains, or wherever you wish to venture hence, will become a living hell, one which you will not survive."

Tia leaned over the table. She folded her arms beneath her breasts and glowered. "So if you're such a badass, what do you need our help for?"

"I have quarry that resides among people who know my face, personally, and they know not to trust me. While carrying on with the rest of my work, I've kept my eyes open for just the right accomplices, *not* so known to them, who might infiltrate that circle and act as my proxy. And now here sit the two of you before me – Tia and Ketz – with just the right reputation of your own."

Ketz said, "So who's this prey you're so eager to catch now, and who do we need to kill to get to them?"

"With a little luck, no one," said Minquo. "Tell me, have either of you heard of the Brendi family?"

"Who?" said the twins in unison.

"The Brendis," said Minquo. "A highly prominent Ghestru merchant family, one of the most affluent and influential still operating on this continent."

Tia huffed and slapped her knee. "Fuckin' meatskins! Figures. I can't stand fuckin' meatskins."

Ketz arched an eyebrow at her. "You fuck meatskins?"

"Shut up, Ketz."

Minquo smirked. "Three days from now, the Brendi family will be setting sail on a merchant vessel, the *Arlash*, from the river port town of Belcrasche. It's a two days' journey west of here, to where the Nagga River flows into the Great River. They sail from there, to the coastal port of Tatelle, where the Great River meets the Whispering Sea.

Their way takes them through one of the narrower, jungle-shrouded stretches of the river, one heavily infested with river pirates, but old Orcris Brendi, the family patriarch, prefers that route for its expedience. He will be personally overseeing the journey. He travels with his daughter, the young Hallucia. Lady Hallucia has…well…a reputation of her own in certain circles. I don't suspect you'll have heard of them, though many of them have agents among these river pirates. Let's just say, she's drawn herself the wrong sort of attention in these circles. Many of them either seek to abduct her or wish her dead, for reasons of their own."

"And you want us to abduct her first," said Ketz.

"That is correct, young man, but there's more nuance to this business than that."

"So spit it the fuck out, old man," said Tia.

"Once you reach Belcrasche, I need you to find your way to the harbor and enlist yourselves as part of Orcris Brendi's personal security detail for this journey. Over the course of the voyage, you're expected to gain his trust and work your way up through the ranks, until you are nothing less than the Lady Hallucia's personal bodyguards."

"Tall order," said Tia. "What makes you so sure this old meatskin patriarch's gonna take so kindly to us?"

"As we've established, your reputations precede you. Orcris Brendi, like all Ghestru of the wealthy immigrant merchant class, is a practical man as opposed to an ethical one. The likes of you should have little trouble getting yourselves hired onto his security detail. With a little luck, you won't even be the worst scum among his crew. As to your subsequent promotions…oh, don't worry, the opportunity will present itself, very quickly. That I can promise you. I already told you, I'm a well-connected man. You'll know what I mean at the appropriate moment. From there, I expect you to keep the Lady Hallucia in one piece and unmolested throughout the voyage. Once the *Arlash* docks in Tatelle, you're to abduct the Lady Hallucia, as discreetly as possible, and spirit her away to a place called the Spine-Rat. It's a humble roadside tavern, not so unlike this fine establishment, several miles out of town, along the main road to the northeast. The way is a rotted, swampy marsh, reputably as untrustworthy as, well, yourselves. I've no doubt you'll both weather it with gusto. It is of the utmost importance that you do not dally in this. The *Arlash* is scheduled to dock there at sundown, exactly one week after setting sail from Belcrasche. It is vital to the success of our mission that you arrive there, with your captive, before sunrise. The establishment will be kept open for your arrival, by special arrangement. You'll find me waiting there, and you will deliver the Lady Hallucia into my custody."

"So what's so special about this *Lady Hallucia*," said Ketz, "that she has so many folks chasin' her ass?"

"You'll figure that much out when you meet her face to face, I think."

"What *I'm* more curious about," said Tia, "is why *you're* so interested in this little fancy-pants meatskin bitch. I already got a feelin'…she's somethin' more to you than just another high-rollin' bounty, ain't she?"

"As ever, sweet Tia, you are an astute young lady. All of that, however, is my own business. Your business, children, is as I've already described. So tell me now – one chance; you won't get another – do we have a deal?"

Ketz turned it over in his head and said, "I don't know, what do you think, sis?"

Tia shrugged. "Honestly, man, I like it. A sixty-forty split, you say? Just how much does that forty percent get us?"

"Call it…more shiny jewels than either of you have seen in your lives, enough to buy a ship of your own, to see the whole of Deschemb if you like. Are we haggling terms, young lady?"

"Nah," said Tia. She stabbed a finger across the table at Minquo. "You *better* be on the level with us here, old man. If it turns out you dealt us dirty, I swear by these lands, I'm gonna cut your dick off, ram it up your ass, then stuff it down your throat, so you die chokin' to death on your own pecker while tastin' your own shit."

"Fair enough, young lady," said Minquo. He splayed a palm at the room. "These quarters are yours until sunrise tomorrow, and not a minute after. I have business of my own to attend to – such as retrieving your weapons and gear from this tavern's security staff and smoothing over any further unpleasant interest you might have stirred up among the locals. Word will get around, and as marshal of this township, they'll come crying to me for assurance that justice has been served. I do not expect to sleep tonight, myself. Nor do I expect you'll see me again before our next rendezvous, other than when I drop by to return your possessions. In the meantime, I suggest you both wash and rest up. You have a long journey ahead of you tomorrow, after all."

Ketz said, "So if you're the actin' marshal here now, what are these folks supposed to do once you uproot and get back to your real work?"

"I imagine they'll think of something…maybe appoint old Topen downstairs to the position. By then, it won't be my problem…yours, even less so."

THREE

Belcrasche lay further westward than Tia or Ketz had ever ventured. Growing up, they'd heard weird stories of the lands on the other side of the Great River, of a place of phantoms and madness even stranger than the tales that came out of Valaka, where the Spirelights had reared their great, haunted city-state of Spiralla.

So far, these forests didn't feel or taste so different than those they'd known since birth, just…lower, more jagged, something stale about the air. For most of the way there, they kept to the high, piney hills between the Nagga River and the main trade road. The feuds between the Spirelight city-state of Trescha and the Schomite hill-tribes impacted the countryside less out this way, closer to the southwestern sea. Ironically, that's what had drawn Tia and Ketz in this direction, when they'd caught some respite and decided to venture from their native hills for a while.

As romanticized adventure-tales lured northern civilized kids like that prick Doveede southward, so the twins had thought this quieter countryside sounded like a nice place to kick back and relax for a while. Showed what they knew…or maybe they were just magnets for this kind of lizardshit, wherever they went. Or maybe the whims of the lands were just funny like that, on whatever trails you walked.

The harbor town was said to be a melting pot of peoples familiar and curious alike, predominately merchant and trader Ghestru families and their indentured serfs they'd brought from their homeland, for the past two or three generations. Word went, the town wasn't what it had been mere decades ago, before Imperial wars choked the globe. The more the outlying conflicts hindered land-bound trade, the faster the place dried up, limping on in uneasy peace. The merchants shelled out extra coin to keep up at least the image of their pristine, sparkly lifestyle, paying everyone else less and taxing them heavier. Lucky for them, it remained convenient for both the Schomites and Spirelights to leave Belcrasche alone as a sort of neutral territory.

Late afternoon, on the second day of their journey, Tia and Ketz stood on a ridge of smooth, crystalline rock. The trees spread, so they could look out across the smooth, thickly wooded flatlands to the southwest, all the way to where the two mighty rivers met. Belcrasche lay nestled in the crook of the shoulder of the two rivers, with its swaying arches and spires stabbing the sky.

The twins descended the hillside, hopping, clawing and crawling their way along the sharp, jutting rocks like lizards. Even so, a lot more cascading shale and loose dirt sprinkled out beneath their feet and handholds than they were used to, which made for trickier, slower going. The hillside finally became a soggy, patchy incline. They darted and skipped across a small creek, over the clusters of rocks.

Not far from there, they found the road again and crouched in a ditch behind some thick bushes. There they sat still and waited for a while. It was cooler here than the rest of the countryside, thanks to the proximity of the Great River, but the bugs sure bit nastier, so the twins had a harder time slapping them away while staying quiet. Gilded merchant caravans and lone wagons often rolled by, in and out of the town ahead.

Watching these caravans, the twins' mouths watered instinctively at all that plunder within, ripe for the taking. Wouldn't be so hard to add to this job's take. Too bad they weren't in their native hills, nor were they here for a bandit raid. They needed to greet the town with friendly faces and sheathed weapons. At the same time, they'd have better luck with that from within, without having to deal with any border officials.

Before taking to the hills, they'd kept to the main road long enough to meet a few fellow weary roadside travelers coming from the opposite direction, whom they'd pried for recent gossip about Belcrasche. By all counts, a long wall bordered the town, with sentries standing watch at the city gates. Lucky for them, the place's dwindling economy had lately reduced the guards to a halfhearted skeleton crew. Still, it would be better to slip through the borders unseen. Those passing wagons were still their ticket to riches, just in a different way than usual.

They crouched deep in the ditch, waiting for the right one. This far southwest, the forest was brighter, with different shades of blooms than their own local turf. Their earthen, multi-shaded skin still blended with the dirt and rocks and foliage around them, as did their dull-hued garments…especially since Tia had ditched that stupid fucking constrictive black top, in favor of her usual tan leather sleeveless vest, along with her usual knee-length leather trousers, high-strapped sandals, the blade on her belt, and the light travel sack slung across her back. Ketz wore the same, except he'd stopped wearing the vest. Hence, when they sat perfectly still, they became all but invisible to any humanoid eyes.

The first three wagons were too heavily guarded for their purposes…not visibly, just the front coachmen and an armed rider or two on either side. They both knew how to spot where heavier defenses awaited unseen, or when some seemingly innocuous passenger moved with a hidden blade or caster beneath their clothes.

Sleashkills pulled most of the wagons – long-legged, long-necked reptilian steers with sullen yellow eyes, split talons, and powerful jaws of solid bare bone. Ketz winced at the sight and cracking sound of how the coachmen drove the creatures along so cruelly. Tia sensed his welling sentimentality and elbowed him sharply in the side. They were on a job.

Finally, a smaller, lonelier merchant wagon rolled along the dusty road, the cargo encased in a wooden frame covered in a thick leather tarp with frayed, flapping edges. It sagged from the tightly packed load within. The heavy wheels creaked by, less than two feet away from the twins' faces. Up front, there perched two tired mercenaries, decked out in treated leather and tarnished, rusty metal. They stood flanking a withered old merchant at the reins. Tia and Ketz had never seen such a trio, nor could they place their race. They had long, narrow, aquiline faces and smooth, sharp bone-structures like Spirelights, yet their skin was a strange swirl of brown and dull blue. That was all the detail the twins caught, before the wagon rolled by. At the back, two ends of tarp flapped loose.

Tia and Ketz waited 'til they were out of the right mercenary's line of sight, then sprang out of the ditch. They darted silently along behind the wagon 'til it rolled over a bump in the road. As the structure bounced and rattled, they sprang up onto the back, clinging by their fingernails to the wooden frame. They pulled back the tarp and helped each other inside. The tarp flapped down behind them, plunging them into darkness. They settled across from each other, squeezing themselves into the cramped, moldering space in the back, between the railing and the stacks of boxes.

The bumpy ride didn't bother them so much. Neither did sitting still for so long. What almost got unbearable, fast, was the air in there. What was so rotten and moldy, the wood of the wagon itself, the heavy boxes, or whatever was in them?

Through the flaps of tarp, they could see it getting darker outside.

After a while, someone shouted from up ahead. The wagon lurched to a sharp halt. Tia and Ketz drew up and braced themselves in their tight corners. A long, deathly silence followed.

"What's your business in Belcrasche?" someone asked in

the stern, bored tone of a city guardsman.

"Cargo for the merchant vessel *Arlash*," barked one of the mercenaries up front.

"Harbor-bound, huh. Well, let's see that ol' Seal of Approval. Come on, old-timer, I guess you know the routine."

"Oh, but of course, Officer," said a tired, crackly voice. "If you'll but give me a moment…"

Another stretch of silence followed, so profound that they could hear the old bastard rising with a groan and rustling through his robes. The old man would be digging out a token of assurance, with a recognized stamp procured wherever he'd struck out from, assuring his identity and his business at his destination.

The Arlash, one of the mercenaries had said…Tia and Ketz exchanged looks through the dim space. Popular boat, apparently, this one they'd been sent to find. They froze more rigidly than ever. More than once, they had to stifle sneezes against the fetid air.

Outside, the attendant guard shouted for a fellow officer. They spoke some muddled words that Tia and Ketz couldn't make out. The latter guard's boots tromped away from the wagon. A rusty, creaky metal door opened somewhere, scraping through mud.

After another pause, the old man said, "I do hope there's no trouble, Officer. You see, the journey has already faced some delays, and I daren't keep my client waiting any longer than necessary." What the hell was that accent? It sounded unnatural, foreign yet familiar, like some of the inflections were off…*someone faking an accent, almost pulling it off, just enough to hopefully fool some weary, overworked guards.*

"Nothing to worry about, I'm sure," said the guardsman. By his tone, it was impossible to tell if he'd noticed the fake accent. "Just a formality, sir. This shouldn't take long."

If there was one thing the twins could smell all the way from back there, through the stench of the cargo, it was that something was wrong. Very slowly, Ketz dislodged his right arm, which had been pressed between his side and the stack of crates. His hand crept steadily across his body, 'til his palm settled on the pommel of his blade in its scabbard. Tia's eyes had adjusted in the darkness, just enough to spot what he was doing. She wanted to tell him to hold off, but she didn't dare make a sound.

"If I may ask," sounded the old man's voice, "has this anything to do with some duress under which my client here labors? I would hate to be suspected of any –"

"Nothing but a formality, sir," the guardsman repeated, maintaining the professionally unreadable tone.

Tia and Ketz had snuck through enough tight checkpoints to know what that was code for: *I ain't buying your act, so you'd better hope you check out, or your ass is mine.*

"Just sit tight," the guardsman continued. "We'll have you on your way in no –"

Far off, the rusty metal door opened again. The other officer's boots sounded back through the mud, towards the wagon.

A moment later, the same voice said, graver this time, "Sir, we'll be needing you and your men to sit right where you are, while my man here has a look at your wares."

"By all means, good sir, go right ahead."

Well, this is just great, Tia figured. *One way or another, we're about to have to make a break for it. Assumin' we ain't just plain fucked.*

The second guard's boots tromped through the mud, around the side of the wagon. He yanked back the tarp. Tia and Ketz pressed themselves further back against the side walls, into the shadows. Their eyes widened on the man, who still didn't see them. They both stared in surprise from their hiding places. Beneath the black-and-silver bone-tough leather armor and helm of the Belcrasche policeman, he was a Schomite, like them…a softer, fairer-skinned inland breed, of whom they'd met a few in their young days, but his eyes hadn't quite lost all the primordial fire of the savage hills that had held back the imperialism of the Spirelight City-State of Trescha for so long.

Before he could take a good look within, let alone spot the twins, he got a face full of the noxious air. He coughed and turned away, his eyes watering. "*Aw, sweet fuck!*" He shouted around to the front, "Hey, what the hell are you guys hauling here, anyway?"

From up front, the head guardsman shouted, "Hey, what's going on back –" He let out a heaving grunt and said no more. A heavy, splashy thud followed.

"Easy, now, lad," came the old man's voice. "Remember, we need one of them alive."

The guardsman in the back drew upright at the commotion. Softer feet whispered around the other side of the wagon. The guardsman reached for the bolt-caster at his side. "Now what the –"

As he turned, his gaze went up into the wagon. He looked right into Tia's eyes. Before he could react, something slammed against his back with a loud crunch. His whole body arched and his eyes widened. The air heaved out of him in a low, moaning sigh. A long, tri-edged spike-blade burst out of his armored chest. He coughed and gurgled. Blood bubbled from his lips, trickling over his chin and neck in thickening splashes. He sank to his knees. The blade shrieked against the punctured metal of his armor as it jerked out of his body. He fell and landed face down. Behind him, there stood one of the old merchant's two mercenary retainers. Black droplets speckled the gleaming blade in the moonlight.

The retainer shouted towards the front, "Guess these Belcrasche men are slower on the uptake than we heard. Now to just –" He looked up into the wagon and spotted Tia. "*Hey, where'd you –?*"

That's when Ketz sprang from his hiding place. He caught the back rim of the wagon and launched himself into the air. He dove forward and slammed into the mercenary, so the man's knees buckled. They went to the ground together. The impact shook and winded the bigger man within all that heavy gear. This guy was no spring-bird, though, so he recovered his wits and reacted fast. The landing had winded Ketz, too, more than a little. Before he knew it, he found himself locked in a bone-straining grapple with a Gorlomong-muscled, scar-faced veteran. The segmented edges of the man's metal top pinched and scraped Ketz's bare chest and arms. The enemy was less limber in all that gear, which gave Ketz a moment's advantage, but only while grappling on the ground like this, with him on top. If this guy managed to get his legs under him, with the two of them locked together like this, Ketz would get twisted into all sorts of funny shapes before he knew it.

The man heaved upwards, teeth bared. Ketz slammed his own forehead right into the man's nose, shattering it at the bridge and spraying blood all over both of them. No matter how good a fighter you were up against, everyone had a plan 'til you broke their nose.

While the man blinked and gasped, Ketz seized the moment. He dropped his own blade, twisted the man's knife-wrist in both fists, then let his own weight sink on the pommel. The spiked tip jammed beneath the mercenary's gorget. The man tensed up, gasped and heaved. Ketz jerked the blade sideways, scraping the edge of the gorget, ripping the throat all the way open. A sheet of blood washed over Ketz's fists, across the chest plating in a glimmering sheen, and into the mud, where it mingled with that of the fallen guardsman next to them.

From up front, the other mercenary called, "Krek? What the hell are you doing back there?"

The fight had lasted only a few seconds but had felt like hours. Ketz disentangled himself from the corpse, his chest burning. When he rose, a head-rush hit him. He looked around and spotted Tia climbing silently out of the wagon. They listened to the front and nodded to each other. She slipped around the side of the wagon from which the dead mercenary had come.

"Both of you, keep it down," shouted the old man. He spoke with a different accent now, one that sounded more at home in his mouth. "You want to draw more of the town watch down on us? Remember, we need to be through the town gates, before –"

Ketz retrieved his blade from the mud. He sheathed it, then pried the caster and bolt the guard had been reaching for, out of the dead man's still twitching fingers. He nocked the shaft, drew it back along the slide, then he stepped out pointing it at the remaining mercenary. The armored man had jumped down from the coach. By now, he had the remaining guardsman twisted up with an arm behind his back, straining it to the breaking point. The guardsman's air was choked off, so he couldn't sound the alarm.

"That's it, assholes," Ketz shouted. "Playtime's over. You, ugly, let the officer go and step away with your hands up."

The mercenary glared. "What the hell are you, where'd you come from, and what do you think you're doing?"

The old man peeked out from the front of his wagon. "Oh, for pity's sake, man, it's just some filthy little forest beast! Look at him with that pea-shooter. He doesn't even know how to properly operate it."

That was true. What Ketz now held was the new bastardized model of the Spirelight International Police bolt-caster, a spring-and-pulley-operated single-shot projectile weapon. The original design was such that only the trained hands and genetically just-so muscle-structure of a Spirelight Agent could operate one effectively. Lately, though, ever more inland subjugated and allied merchant races had commissioned their own rough facsimile designs. They'd distributed them to their personal and municipal security. These models weren't as accurate or quick to reload, but still powerful enough for the bolts to punch through most any armor at close range. Ketz had only practiced with one a few times. Now that he held it loaded and pointed, it felt simple enough.

While Ketz distracted everyone, Tia snuck around and jumped up on the other side of the wagon. She caught the prune-like merchant from behind, pressed her blade to his throat, walked him to the edge of the coach, and snarled, "*This* filthy little forest beast knows how to use *this* weapon, you old coot. Tell your man there to let the guardsman go."

"Don't listen to this filth," rasped the old man. "We can still —"

As the mercenary was distracted by the sudden ambush, the guardsman seized the moment and twisted free. He spun and kicked his captor in the gut. The boot sole thudded against the plating, but still landed hard enough to send the mercenary staggering backwards, lurching and sliding frantically for balance.

The guardsman crouched, retrieving his own long, curved blade from the ground. By the time he rose, the mercenary had already recovered. They squared off, poised for a fair fight. As they circled each other, Ketz stalked towards them. He took keen aim with the caster. He wanted to shoot the mercenary, but the men kept moving, in and out of each other's path. Ketz waited, aimed as wide of the guardsman as possible, and let fly. A meaty *thunk* sounded, followed by an agonized, hopeless sigh.

Ketz blinked and realized where the short quarrel had found its mark. *Shit,* he mused, *these things are even less accurate than I thought. Who bothers with these pieces of junk, anyway?*

"*Are you fuckin' crazy?*" Tia screamed at him, while the merchant convulsed in death spasms in her arms. The bolt stuck out of the old man's neck on both sides. "*You almost stapled my damn arm to this bastard's neck!*"

"What you bitchin' about?" Ketz shouted back. "We're down to just one asshole now. You gonna help, or what?" He charged in, ripping his blade back out.

As soon as he closed the distance, though, he saw that the mercenary had whipped out a second blade. Ketz and the guardsman both clashed with the man at once. The mercenary's twin blades licked and flashed, smacking back both opponents. Even after Tia leaped down and joined them, the guy was no easy pickings. He knew how to fight with two swords at once, one blade always doing one thing while the other did something else. His footwork blurred about beneath him, sending up dust-devils into everyone's faces. Out of that dust came darting, razor-edged glimmers that Ketz barely avoided. His own darting feet kicked up more dust, out of which flashed closer razor swipes and thrusts. No sooner did the man drive Ketz into a retreat, but his left blade lashed about in a powerful chop that sliced across the guardsman's chest, cleaving the chest plate then ripping free in time to bash aside both the guardsman's and Tia's blades. In the same motion, he went into a deep sideways lunge, his right blade jabbing for Tia's belly.

She sucked in her abdomen tight, which was the only thing that kept her guts inside her in that moment. That's when Ketz spotted the opening and swooped in low. His blade went beneath the mercenary's lower left side, sank deep, and pierced a kidney. The man reared up like a wounded snake. Dark blood spilled from beneath his armor in rivulets, painting one side of his ass. When he tried to lift his arms, both of his hands fluttered open. His blades clattered at his feet. He crumpled to the ground, convulsing through death-spasms.

The guardsman stumbled back and leaned against the side of the wagon, catching his breath. "I don't know where you two came from, but...thank you. Can't believe, just those sneaky three managed to..." He looked up through the moonlight. "Hey. You two are Schomites."

"Good, you noticed," said Tia. "So are you."

"I am. So's...Oh, shit, Pehnsh, where'd..." He started towards the back of the wagon.

Ketz caught him by the collar. "You don't wanna look back there, man. It ain't pretty."

The guardsman shrugged Ketz off. "This ain't my first

damn week in uniform, kid. That's a man down back there, and he's —"

"Dead is what he is," said Tia. "And you ain't." Her palm settled on his chest and drew back, wet with blood. "C'mon, sit down over here. We gotta get this chest plate off you, have a look at that wound."

The guardsman pushed her away, then paused and looked at her. He seemed to just now notice that one of his rescuers was a pretty girl. All at once, he seemed a little more open to reason. Still, he waved them back, then pressed his chest, winced and gasped. "It ain't deep…I don't think so, anyway. Hell, I'll live. Looks like you got a nasty cut of your own there, miss."

Tia lifted her forearm. A shallow slice streaked across it. Bloody streaks ran from it in crazy patterns. "Oh, this. Nah." She glared at Ketz. "Just *someone* ought'a learn how to aim a damn caster sometime."

"*Someone else here* can aim a caster, just fine," said a new voice, deep and hard.

Out of the front gates, all at once, had spilled four more uniformed patrolmen. Two of them had already crept around the opposite side of the carriage and stepped out. They trained their bolt-casters on the twins as they fanned out and converged inward, in a semicircle.

"*Shit*," Tia hissed.

"All right, hill-trash," the one in the lead shouted. This one was a Schomite, too, same local breed as the guardsmen. It was hard to tell about his companions in this light. He was a big man, too thick in the middle for his profession, but with big, hard arms, with the outlines of muscles showing through his sleeves. A long mustache hung over either side of his mouth, to the base of his jaw, like a long, soggy hairball stuck to his upper lip. He dressed much like the others, except the decorations on his chest and cap marked him as the town sheriff. "Now both of you, step away from the officer with your hands up."

"Ah shit," Tia muttered. She and Ketz obeyed.

"Water and lands, what a mess," said a patrolman who'd circled the carriage, as he pulled his boot from some bloody sludge. "What happened here?"

"We'll find out soon enough," said the sheriff. His beady, malicious eyes met Ketz's. His caster lowered slightly, in the direction of Ketz's crotch.

"There's a man down back there, behind the wagon," the guardsman shouted.

"Either of these two still breathing done it?" said the sheriff.

"*Ohforfucksake*," said Tia. She gestured at the guardsman. "We're the reason *he's* still breathin'!"

"Shut up and let the man talk." The sheriff addressed the guardsman, "What about 'em, Skids?"

"They're telling the truth, sir," said Skids. "This wagon here, we got a funny feeling about the merchant and his crew. Pehnsh and me decided to check 'em out. They didn't check out, sir." He huffed and rubbed his forehead. "Craziest thing. One minute, they were cooperating just fine, then next…everything went crazy." He indicated Tia and Ketz. "These two came out of nowhere. Saved my ass."

"Yeah, I heard the fracas," said the sheriff. "That's why I come running with these boys here." He got up in Skids's face. "Huh. So our city-gate guardsman needed a couple of hill-trash kids to come to his rescue. Ain't that something."

Skids looked worried, but he held his composure. "Sir, you don't understand. I deal with sketchy folk like them on that wagon every day. Never seen anything like what those armored bastards pulled. I thought I was dead, then these two kids…Sir, you should have seen it. They took out these devils like a couple of naturals. It was amazing!"

"*Came out of nowhere*, huh." The sheriff nodded. He sounded a little closer to civil, but not much. He stepped around one of the spreading pools, then spotted the dead merchant lying in it. He shoved the corpse with his boot. "*All three of 'em*, so I see. Yep, that's a fact. Hey, for someone who don't know what he's doing with a caster, that looks like a pretty clean shot to me." He stepped closer to Tia and Ketz. "So you two kids *just happened along*, huh, right as all this went down, *decided to jump in, play hero, out of the goodness of your hearts?*"

"That's us," said Ketz.

"Shut up, Ketz," said Tia.

"Lizardshit," said the sheriff. "C'mon, speak up." He looked Tia over, a little too slowly. "Ladies first."

"My brother and I've been on the road for days," said Tia. "We heard there was security work available here, on a merchant vessel sailin' on the morning tide tomorrow."

"More mercenaries, huh," said the sheriff. "Well, maybe you are and maybe you ain't." After a tense pause, without breaking eye contact, he gestured for his men to lower their weapons.

Ketz felt the mud welling and sinking around his boots. It had gone soggy from the blood of the surrounding corpses. "Guys…somethin' ain't right here."

He looked at his dirty hands and spotted a greasy dark smear on his fingertips, something that was neither blood nor mud. He looked around at the corpses, spotted the rounded ears of the nearest one, then abruptly crouched and darted over to it. Before anyone could stop him, he ran his hand across the face. His palm came up smeared brown and blue. Everyone around him gasped and peered closer. Part of the mercenary corpse's face now shone, gleaming purplish white, from beneath a coat of the greasepaint. While Ketz was at it, he took a swipe at the leathery old merchant's face, too. The same pale gleam showed through.

One of the patrolmen leaned in, gaping. "The hell?"

Ketz stood up. "These guys who just tried to kill your guys – *did* kill one of your guys – they're Spirelights, that's what."

The sheriff threw his head back. "*Aw, shit!* Great, just

what we need around here."

"Doesn't make sense," said one of the patrolmen. "We got a deal with the Spirelights. Thought their new Priest King was supposed to still be cool with shit like that. So why'd they try to sneak in like —"

The sheriff cocked his head sideways. "Shut your hole, Mashi. Damn right it doesn't make sense. We're gonna get to the bottom of it, though. Truss these two kids up. Get 'em to the barracks."

FOUR

The sheriff sauntered through the streets like he was leading his prisoners on a victory parade, reassuring anyone watching that he most assuredly owned the place, swinging his bulk around with gruff, stiff-lipped righteousness. Behind him, his patrolmen escorted Tia and Ketz through the narrow, winding streets 'til they reached the barracks. It was a plain, square, two-story sandstone building, set back in a shadowy alcove at the end of a long, unpaved street. The place looked several generations older than the taller, cleaner, fancier structures that surrounded it. Most of those newer buildings had been built in accordance with sacred Imperial architectural standards. The plain, utilitarian barracks hadn't.

The sheriff brought Tia and Ketz upstairs to the interrogation room and sat the twins down at a long table. The patrolmen knelt to shackle their ankles. They left their wrists shackled in front of them, to rest on the tabletop.

"Okay, boys, clear the room," said the sheriff. "I figure I can handle these two just fine." Once he and the twins were alone, he sat down across from them, almost civilly, like they'd come together at a friendly business meeting. "Okay, the sooner you two start being honest, the sooner this is all over and done with."

"We already told you," said Tia, "We're here lookin' for a job from Orcris Brendi."

"Right," said the sheriff. "Brendi. That's a Ghestru name, ain't it? So this gentleman, he know to expect you?"

"I ain't sayin' shit, except to Orcris Brendi." said Tia.

"Look, man," said Ketz. "I don't get what your problem is with us."

"Really?" The sheriff looked honestly surprised. "There's four dead people out by the town gate. One of 'em's a policeman. Those weapons we took off you sure had a lot of blood all over 'em." He looked them both over. "So do you, both of you, still." The way his eyes lingered on Tia, it wasn't the blood on her he was looking at.

"There's blood all over us and our weapons 'cause we killed the guys who killed one of yours," said Ketz. "A lot of this is my blood, too."

"Looks like my brother could use some medical attention," Tia noted.

The worst injuries Ketz noticed on himself were on his bare torso, where the mercenary's armor had pinched and scraped him while they grappled. That, and a lot of fresh bruises. "I don't need medical attention," he said. "I need to get out of here, clear of this nonsense – we both do – so we can get to work on time."

"I ain't sayin' shit else, except to Orcris Brendi," Tia repeated.

Ketz went on, "Three of those four corpses out there – *the ones who killed one of yours* – are Spirelights. They tried to ride into your town, painted up as Schomites. Ain't you thought about this? Looks to me like you got bigger problems than us."

"Damn right I do," said the sheriff. "You little hill-trash cunts are still my problems, though, and you're the ones I'm looking at right now. As a man of the law, I ain't fond of liars. Liars don't thrive in my charge. So if self-preservation is an instinct you possess, you'd best start speaking honest with me."

"We don't like liars either," said Ketz. "We've spoke nothin' *but* honest with you. Look, man, go talk to your guy you found us with. What'd you call him? Skids? We're the reason he ain't one of those corpses out there. Didn't he already tell you that?"

"Aw, son." The sheriff rose, splayed his hands on the

table and leaned in over them. "You can quit flicking that tale-leaf seed in the dirt right now. Whatever happened out there, Officer Skids is the one who bungled his duties to the point of gross incompetence. Far as I'm concerned, he's the reason his partner's dead. He's lucky he ain't in manacles downstairs right now getting corn-holed and beaten to death. So are you two, for that matter."

"Such a generous gentleman, you are," said Tia.

"Watch your mouth, girl," said the sheriff. "As to Officer Skids…hell, come sunrise, best work he's likely to find 'round here is that same security work on that barge the *Arlash*, the one you two claim you came here for…uh…I'm sorry, what'd you say that fancypants meatskin's name was again, young lady?"

"You know damn well," said Tia, "just like everyone in this water-rotted shithole town seems to know. Orcris Brendi."

"Do we, now?" The sheriff's eyes gleamed. "Do tell…having just gotten here and all, about *how we all seem to know* this gentleman's name, huh?"

Tia's face stayed blank. "I ain't sayin' shit else, except to Orcris Brendi."

"Ha! Now here's a gal who likes to focus, *one thought at a time*. I like that about you, Miss…What did you say your name was again? Hey, come to think of it, I ain't caught either of your names." His eyes gleamed thirstily.

"*We'll give our names* to our employer, Orcris Brendi," said Tia.

"*Your possible future employer*, you mean." The sheriff glanced at the one high corner window. "Looks to me like just a few hours 'til dawn out there. Might be, we got just that long to find out whether you two have any kind of a future at all. Right now, girly, you sure ain't doing yourself any favors." He looked to Ketz, and said jovially, like they were just a couple guys shooting the shit over drinks, "So how 'bout you, son? You got any more sense than the little lady here?"

"C'mon, man," said Ketz. "Look at us! We're a couple of Schomites tryin' to get by under Treschan occupation, just like you. We came to your town lookin' for work, and right as we reached the gates, we saw a couple of our countrymen, your guardsmen, gettin' attacked by that wrinkled old so-called merchant and his henchmen. We jumped in and did what we could, just like anyone ought'a do, right? Hey, the assholes we killed are the ones who turned out to be Spirelights, remember? So take it up with the Spirelights. Look, sorry it didn't go better. Sorry that one guy died, but –"

The sheriff's face changed. He loomed over them, teeth bared, eyes blazing venomously. "*One of us?* Oh, boy, don't you even start with me. Yeah, you're Schomites, but you *ain't* like me. Couple'a hill-dwelling vermin from the northeast, am I right? Think I don't know your kind on sight? Yeah, working this job, in this town, hearing the tales the travelers tell, from around the Schlogmire Ranges, all the murdering, thieving, raping, pillaging you savages get up to. Just hearing about it makes me wanna puke. It's just gotten worse since they swore in that new Priest Queen in Trescha – *Kalesha*, right?"

Ketz lifted a finger. "That's Priest *King*, mister."

"What did you just say, boy?"

"I said Priest King. That's Kalesha's title. The Spirelight royalty, they don't have boy-titles and girl-titles. So she's just called the Priest King, like the last one."

"Shut up, Ketz," said Tia.

The sheriff barked laughter. "What do you know, girly, we actually agree about something! That's right, boy, shut the fuck up. You think I give a spine-rat's dick what they call themselves? This *Priest Queen Kalesha*, folks call her the *nice one*. They say she's been *negotiating* with those savages, thinks she's gonna win some kind of *peaceful compromise*. If Kalesha wants better relations with Schomites, why ain't she asking those of us who ain't murderers, thieves and rapists, will you tell me that? *Naw, don't say anything.* I wasn't really asking either of you. If it was up to me, she'd send the Blades of Bathshire out into those hills, wipe out every last one of you. Scum like you bring nothing but shame to our people. Hell, you're the reason Schomites 'round here ain't trusted, can't get better employment than ugly police work like I'm doing now."

"Figure you'll prefer the other Spirelights," said Tia, "once they finally get around to stickin' their fingers far enough out this way, all up in your asshole...when your sons and daughters and anyone else you've ever loved are gettin' their heads chopped off in the town square, for any little perceived aggression against their shiny fuckin' cloistered gods...the ones who want these lands yet can't stand any of the real dirt of it on 'em."

The sheriff drew upright and stared. "Well look who's got something to say, all of a sudden! Listen, girly, the Spirelights and their alliances with the foreign business fancy-pants, *they're* the reason this town's managed to hang on, barely, after the mess scum like you've made of the countryside. Shit, I don't know if the Spirelights' *gods* are even real, but I –"

"*We* do," Tia hissed. "Those Gods are real, and they don't give a shit about you, except for food. We've met them. In Trescha. Hear that, cocksucker? That's right, *Trescha*. We were there, from start to finish. The gods ain't all we saw, neither. There's somethin' else comin', out of the lands of Deschemb herself. It's comin' to eat the gods and all who serve them. If you think punkass turncoat race-betrayin' sonsofbitches like you are gonna be spared, you're in for a –"

The sheriff leaned across the table and backhanded Tia hard across the face. He struck Ketz next. The twins both wobbled in their chairs, smarting from the blows but absorbing it well enough. Tia went right on grinning maniacally. A bloody trickle ran from the corner of her mouth. The sheriff stood there shaking, staring through trembling eyes. The man wasn't just rattled. He looked ready to shit his pants. Tia wasn't the only Schomite to speak such predictions since Trescha, and she wasn't the kind to indulge in things like prophetic hysteria. Yet something primordial had rumbled like thunder through her voice just then, like the rage of the lands themselves erupting on her words.

Whatever it was, the sheriff felt it, shaking him as surely as though the floor had just quaked beneath his feet. He looked at his hand, then at the two short, small-boned prisoners shackled across from him, like he couldn't quite believe what he'd just done.

"You know what?" the sheriff finally said. "I don't think I need to ask any more questions just now. High time I went and checked in with some of my boys out there, at that bloody mess by the gate. When I get back, we're gonna have us a very different conversation. You hear?" He turned, walked out, and slammed the door behind him.

Ketz said something Tia usually said to him: "Great fuckin' job. Got any more brilliant ideas?"

Tia didn't answer. They sat there in silence, contemplating their possibly very short futures.

After a while, the sheriff came back in, smiling. "Turns out, I've only got a few more questions for you two." He dropped Tia and Ketz's travel sacks side by side on the center of the table, between them. "You recognize these, I figure. My boys found one of 'em lying right in the back of that wagon out there. Found the other dropped in the mud and blood, right *behind* the wagon. Also, you keep saying you arrived on foot, just happened to come upon that scene of slaughter with the right timing. Yet looking around, my boys say they couldn't find any tracks that might'a been yours.

"Now, girly, you're so eager to talk to this Orcris Brendi...and what do you know, your pal Skids says that's exactly who that merchant claimed he was here to see. We had a look at those crates in that wagon, too...full of some weird dirt, all wet, smells like something out of a swamp, crawling with exotic fungus."

"*Exotic*, huh," said Tia. "Ain't that a fancy word for some dirtbag backwater sheriff like you."

The sheriff grinned. "It sure is, girly. So I sent a couple of our boys down to the harbor, to have a talk with Mister Brendi. Turns out Mister Brendi did in fact expect some cargo like that, for his shipment that sails on the morning tide. That fungus was wafting its own special dust, all over the back of those crates. Same dust that's still settled all over the two of you...same kind I got all over the back of my hand when I gave you the business an hour or so ago." He studied them grimly, then smiled. "You know what, I been thinking, and I don't reckon I gotta bother asking either of you or your names anymore, neither. Hey girly, what did you call your brother earlier? Ketz, right? I'll bet that'd make you...no, don't tell me...Tia?"

Tia's guts sank, as it set in how she'd fucked up. Shit. And this whole time, she'd thought Ketz was the dumb one. Her cheeks fluttered and heated as she kept her breathing under control.

The sheriff smiled, oddly mirthlessly, as though on some level, he didn't like this any more than they did. "Okay, it looks like we're all finally on the same tale-leaf together. So c'mon, maybe before this gets any worse for either of you, how about you tell me what's really going on here."

Before either of them could answer, a knock sounded at the door. The sheriff gritted his teeth and shouted, "What is it?"

A man poked his head in. "Sir? There's someone here, insisting on an audience with these two suspects."

"Well they can shove it up their – Wait a second, how the hell does any *visitor* know about *these two suspects*? What jackass has been –?"

"I swear I don't know, sir, but...she comes to claim custody of the prisoners...on behalf of her father, Orcris Brendi."

The Officer went pale as a sheet. "You...you're sure it's..."

"I know who she is, sir. All due respects, sir, maybe we don't want to keep her waiting."

"Right." The sheriff tried and failed to hide his shiver. "So what are you waiting for? Go on, send that weird little bitch up here."

Moments later, in walked a richly-clad Ghestru girl…for lack of a better word. All Ketz could think was, *What the hell is she?* His red-swirling brain drank in the sight of her and answered, *The most beautiful woman I've ever seen, that's what!*

She must have been at least two years younger than him, and shorter, with a bright-eyed fairness that seemed more girlish than womanly, at least 'til you spotted the sultry, confident shimmy of her hips and plump, outthrust tits as she strode into the room. That wasn't the most confusing thing about her, either. She had the blood-red skin of a Ghestru, yet wore the thin, silken temple-maiden dress of those people from one of the southern octospheres, who the Ghestru were still at war with last time Ketz had checked. He forgot those peoples' name at the moment. That likely had something to do with all the blood rushing out of his brains, into his loins. He flexed his legs beneath the table, getting semi-hard.

The girl wore Schomite jewelry, had done up her hair in clumping locks like some hanging plant, in the fashion of a Schomite blend-lady. Her slim, supple arms were tattooed in the symbols of many places, some of which Ketz knew, some of which he didn't. On her bare, smooth chest, right above her ample cleavage, there stood out the most arresting tattoo of all…some weird, circular, maze-like pattern that seemed almost to glow. Ketz strained to make out its contours. Her eyes glittered bright yellow. Ketz had never seen a Ghestru with yellow eyes. Hell, *no one* had eyes like that! Beneath the table, Tia elbowed him in the side.

The sheriff faced the woman and bowed slightly. "Lady Hallucia. What brings –"

"Cut the shit," she said in a crisp, cultured voice. She smiled at the twins. "Tia and Ketz of the Nagga Mountains, am I right?"

"That's right, miss," Ketz said. Tia elbowed him harder.

"I understand you have business with Daddy." Before they could answer, she continued, "Sheriff, unshackle their feet. Have them shown downstairs and handed over, into the custody of my personal escorts, so that I can see them to my father."

"Lady Hallucia," said the sheriff, "all due respects, these are wanted fugitives in my custody. You gotta consider –"

"I know who they are, Sheriff. Didn't you just here me say so? I also know all about the bounty on their heads, as I take it, so do you." She winked at him. "We understand each other, yes?"

"Yeah, but –"

"Clearly we don't, so allow me to speak more plainly. You want these two fugitives, as you call them. So do I. You want them for the hefty bounty the Spirah Empire has on their heads…I'm sure, as a public official, for nothing less noble than your little harbor town's local economy, isn't that right?"

"Now c'mon, Lady Hallucia, I'm just the sheriff of this town, you know that. And I take my job serious. Far as I'm concerned right now, these kids are just suspects. It's for the law to decide what's to be done with them, not –".

"Whatever you expect to be paid by the Spirelights," said Lady Hallucia, "I come prepared, on behalf of my family, to double that price…with an extra pearl and gem or two, of course, to keep this whole grievous misunderstanding private, that's to say, from your general population. Were any townsfolk to start whispering among themselves, about any half-formed hearsay…well, with all the comings and goings through your gates, it would be a shame if, say, Priest King Kalesha were to get any questionable ideas about how you run your judicial system in these parts, wouldn't it?

"I reckon it would," said the sheriff.

"Your wife and babes would agree," said Lady Hallucia. "I take it we understand each other?"

The sheriff lowered his eyes and turned his head to the side. "Yeah."

"What's that?"

"I said *yeah.*"

"But you didn't look me in the eyes. That won't do, Sheriff. One thing I've learned over the years by watching my father, is that you never accept a man's word as good if he can't look you in the eye while he says it."

The sheriff made himself look up and meet her eyes, just long enough to shout, "*Yeah, we understand each other!*" He barked savagely, waving his palm, as though to convince himself he was still running his own barracks, "Go on, get 'em out of here!"

Lady Hallucia smiled warmly. "My retainer is already upstairs with yours, settling the particulars over this generous sum. You'll of course have your detainees' personal items delivered to one of my retainers at the door. Feel free, as a public servant, to distribute the payment in this township's interest, however you see fit." She pointed at Tia and Ketz. "These two are my playthings now, not yours."

FIVE

The guards unshackled Tia and Ketz's ankles, escorted them downstairs, and handed them hastily over to the Lady Hallucia's two personal escorts. By now, Lady Hallucia awaited them patiently outside, under the bright moonlight, in the small, barren, rectangular courtyard in front of the barracks. Once they emerged, she smiled then turned and drifted off down the street. The retainers shoved Tia and Ketz so they started walking. Lady Hallucia led the way, out into the night, through the streets.

The retainers taking up the rear were a pair of tall, swarthy, silent, lowborn Ghestru boys. Even their fine black-and-scarlet uniforms couldn't mask their hollow-eyed, dispirited manner. Guys like that had it beaten into them since birth that life was a bleak, thankless chore and they'd best not go expecting anything better from it, beyond the honor and privilege of serving such beautiful highborn masters. By now, they may or may not have the brain-power left, with which to comprehend the political machinations that had transpired here tonight. Either way, they knew better than to ask questions.

So that was the job-position the twins were expected to usurp, huh? Tough act to follow. Lowborn Ghestru were known to be the most formidable retainers when serving high-born Ghestru, especially on this continent, just 'cause they were so thankful they hadn't been sold off to the Spirelights. Tia and Ketz had heard stories of what happened to Ghestru slaves who met such a fate. They'd witnessed a little of it, during the occupation of Trescha. They'd eaten a few meals there, where used-up Ghestru had probably been the main ingredient. Those meals had been tasty. Hey, now that they were here, if all else failed, at least they knew all these meatskin assholes were good eatin'.

To displace these two stalwart bastards, the twins would probably need to murder them in the dark, in the back, at the earliest opportunity. These bodyguards didn't look dull-witted, either. Ketz hated cold-blooded murder. Tia didn't. He wasn't above it when necessary, though.

Throughout the walk along the lonely street, the twins' eyes met sideways with their keen night vision, exchanging wordless conversation through quick glances, nods, and twitches, imperceptible to anyone who didn't share the lifelong bond of their sibling partnership.

For Tia and Ketz, it was almost a pity the siege of Trescha hadn't escalated into a full-scale war engulfing the whole countryside, as it almost had. With their combined ruthless cunning at its peak, with real military might at their wrists for once, they could have won such a war, all with their uniquely coded methods of communication, the private language shared only between twins. After pulling off something like that, they'd have been set for life, living it up fat and happy 'til the end, the finest wines flowing free, with pretty boys and girls tending to their every whim and desire...hell, about like how these highborn Ghestru jackasses lived, except that they'd have actually worked for it and earned it.

Instead, they'd gone on to live deep, in the name of their father Jergus, who'd died in the taking of the city-state. That was how Tia and Ketz's people mourned their most sorely missed dead; you lived for them *and* yourself, 'til you joined them. They'd have a lot to tell Pa when they met him again, like about how their little brother back home was growing up so strong and fast, and more excitedly, what he'd missed during the occupation, a post he'd helped win, which they'd helped hold, while it had lasted.

The Siege of Trescha...No matter where they went nowadays, people talked about it, usually with strong opinions that were always dumber than a bag of dried shit. One thing they all had right, though, which the twins could no longer deny: something of the history of all Deschemb had changed course on the night of the siege, and in the months that followed. No one knew where things were headed from there, and they were all nervous about it. It hadn't felt like *history in the making* to the twins, just some crazy shit they'd let themselves get talked into, by one of their old childhood combat-trainers-turned-outlaw, who'd shown up in their village in the company of a turncoat Spirelight ranking officer who'd wanted to stick it to his former master, with just the right dangerous inside knowledge to pull it off, with the help of the right ragtag pack of mountain-dwelling Schomite fighters.

It had been the craziest shit Tia and Ketz had gotten themselves mixed up in, at that point in their young lives, and it hadn't sunk in just how crazy 'til long after it was over. They hadn't been exactly innocent beforehand, either, having taken part in bandit raids and such since their early teenage years, yet somehow, everything before the siege now felt like the hazy recollections of a naïve childhood. Maybe it was because they'd still had a pa before the occupation. Now the lands never seemed to run out of ways to remind them.

While in Trescha, they'd actually met Priest King Kalesha, up close, more than once. In a way, you could say, under the orders of Captain Severen Gris, they'd been instrumental in her rise to power, and not just because the whole point of the siege had been to topple her predecessor. That was a fact they liked to keep to themselves. When they'd met the future Priest King, she'd still gone by some other, more common Spirelight name. The meeting had involved them taking her into custody, on the captain's orders, and not gently. Since then, to her credit, Kalesha had done a lot to try to undo her people's injustices, at least on this continent, but she was just one regional ruler within a vast rotten theocracy. More pressingly, if the twins ever met her again, she hopefully wouldn't recognize them.

A lot of good that did them now, in this shithole harbor town, under-fed, under-slept and unbathed, their britches all sweaty and itchy around their loins, with iron manacles chafing their wrists, in the charge of this pampered, haughty, weird-ass bitch they'd come to abduct. Whatever she was, Lady Hallucia was clearly no Priest King Kalesha. She probably looked at the twins and saw as much a pair of degenerates as they saw in her.

While she'd tormented the sheriff, she'd revealed one thing to them, unmistakably: the Schomites in this town feared the Ghestru merchant class, more than they feared the forces of Trescha. But of course, they would. In the early days of Priest King Kalesha's reign, she'd already managed to piss off the Spirelights' Ghestru allies, so by now, the only places on this continent where the Ghestru did business openly were shitty little western riverfront places like this. Since then, their business was the only thing keeping such communities afloat, so they were free to swarm in at their leisure and do as they liked.

Lady Hallucia stopped abruptly in her tracks, next to a dank, dark alleyway. Her escorts halted, jerking Tia and Ketz to a stop with them.

When Lady Hallucia turned towards the alleyway, one of the escorts said, "Mistress…are you sure this is…?"

Lady Hallucia lashed her dark, cascading locks about. Her eyes flashed over her shoulders at the twins. "You big strong men are paid to safeguard me, aren't you? So safeguard me." With that, she shimmied her way into the gloomy alleyway, 'til only her bright dress was visible, shimmering like a floating phantom. She must have spent her whole life carelessly wielding such authority, yet the haughty power-trip hadn't worn off.

Once everyone stood deep enough within the shadows, Lady Hallucia turned and faced them. "Boys, unshackle the two barbarians."

One of them said, "Mistress?"

"You heard me."

One of them stepped around and produced a key. He lifted first Ketz's, then Tia's wrists, and unlocked the manacles. The chains slipped away and clattered on the mossy cobblestones.

Lady Hallucia said to her bodyguards, "You retrieved their weapons from the jailers, yes?"

After another concerned glance, one of them said, "Uh…yes, Mistress?"

"Give them back their weapons."

The one who'd unlocked the twins looked them over. "You sure about that? They look pretty feral to me…less predictable than I like."

"I gave you an order." She smiled at the twins. "They won't hurt me. Why, they're as gentle as lambs. Isn't that right, *Tia and Ketz?*"

Tia met Lady Hallucia's gaze. "Right. You know our names. We already caught that, remember?"

One of the retainers said, "Hey, mind how you speak to the mistress."

"Don't mind him," said Lady Hallucia. "I did ask you a question, though."

"Nah, we won't hurt you," said Tia. "We came here to work for your pa."

"Good enough, for now, I suppose." Lady Hallucia nodded to her retainers.

The bodyguards shoved the belts that held the twins' blades roughly into their arms. Tia and Ketz both threaded the belts back around their waists, then drew the blades and thumbed the edges to make sure they were still good and sharp. That asshole sheriff might have slipped someone the order to blunt the edges with a rock or some shit. Apparently not, though.

To either side of them, the Ghestru retainers tensed up, their hands drifting towards their own weapons. Satisfied with the inspection, the twins sheathed the blades.

"Great, thanks," said Tia. "Now what the hell do you want with us?"

"The same thing you two want, am I right? I know of you…knew enough to find you and extract you from your prior predicament. Word had it, in my father's camp, that a pair of detainees kept saying they knew him…two Schomite barbarians of the northeastern hill-tribe people. My father dismissed all such inquiries. He's old and set in his prejudices, I fear. He claims he doesn't know any Schomites of the Nagga Mountains. But I…*ah*…I've listened to all those stories, as my father never bothers to. I hear everything he talks to his business partners about, as I sail around the world with him, even when he doesn't know how much I hear. I wish one day he'd properly credit me, his own daughter, for how I've orchestrated so many lucrative opportunities to fall into his lap, that he'd have otherwise missed…opportunities like the two of you, for instance"

"I'm sure your knowledge of lizardshit is limitless," said Tia. "So like I said, though, all we came to town lookin' for is enlistment in your pa's security force on the *Arlash*. Can you get us that audience with him, or not?"

"The last time I checked, neither of you are in any position to demand terms," said Lady Hallucia. "Oh, don't look at me like that. Of course I can. Once your brother puts his tongue back in his head and closes his mouth, that is. If dear Ketz wishes to put his tongue someplace more useful, he need only ask…after certain other arrangements have been seen to, of course." She winked at Ketz. "But let's be on about our business now, shall we, children?" With that, she led them out of the alleyway, back along the street, towards the harbor.

As they walked, Tia said, "So in short, you want us for what we came here to do."

"Maybe," said Lady Hallucia. Her eyes twinkled coyly. "Really, though, I've sailed all over the world with my father, and I've never met a pair of Schomite hill-tribe bandits before…let alone two living-legend outlaws like yourselves. So when I learned that such a pair were in the custody of the Belcrasche police…well, I just couldn't resist."

"Lucky us," said Tia.

"So how we measure up to the legends so far?" said Ketz.

Lady Hallucia lashed her luscious dark locks about her slim neck. She flashed her wild, glimmering yellow eyes at him. "Oh, that remains to be seen, my boy. I know my father, though. Once it's made clear to him, how you've already assisted his enterprises, he'll be far more pliable to reason."

"Wait…already?"

"Those impostors you tussled with at the gate. Thanks to you, my father has his cargo, without those who appropriated it having made it into our midst unawares."

"Wait," said Ketz, "so your pa actually did expect that wagon, with those stinky, moldering crates?"

"Of course."

"So…what about the real merchant who should have delivered them…?"

"Probably dead in a ditch somewhere, wherever those Spirelight impostors caught up with him. How should I know?"

"Figure you're right," Ketz muttered. "It's those impostors I'm still curious about, though."

"What about them? They're dead. You saw to that yourselves. Or did I hear wrong?"

Tia stepped up to Hallucia's side. She reached over and stroked the lady's chest. "Speakin' of Spirelights, that's a funny little tattoo you got there."

Hallucia squirmed and shivered from Tia's touch, but kept her cool. The two bodyguards tensed up. Their fingers drifted again towards their weapons. Hallucia waved them back.

Tia continued, "That's some Spirelight sacred art you got inked on you, ain't it?"

"Why, yes, Lady Tia. So it is." Lady Hallucia twisted her hips, smiled, stroked Tia's cheek, then returned the favor by giving one of Tia's tits a little squeeze. She said huskily, "So there, now we have that out of the way, don't we, sister?"

Tia shoved Lady Hallucia's hand away. "You wish. And we ain't sisters. Not even close."

SIX

Before long, they reached the harbor gates. A long, high stone wall spread before them. A guardsman drew up sharp at their approach, dressed much like Skids, the one they'd met at the town gate. Once he recognized the lady in the lead, he bid them all pass.

On the other side of the wall, the crowded stone harbor spread out in either direction. All the humanoid clutter made it impossible to tell how far it stretched, though it seemed like it might run for miles in both directions. Not since being cooped up within the city walls of Trescha had the twins' senses felt so bombarded, by a noisy, compressed concentration of sensations choking the air. Everything stank of panic, of things hauled from the water to flounder and die and rot in the baking sun. Looking around at all the sturdy, trudging laborers, bitterly accustomed to toil through this deathly stench, it felt like nothing less than a camp of war. None of these guys had any real fighting spirit left in them, though, let alone the thirst for any kind of victory…just stiff-lipped resignation. The closest thing they had left, to the hot blood for battle, was a smoldering hostility if you met their eyes.

Ahead, the first shimmers of dawn rippled across the Great River. From the edge of the pier, a wooden walkway spread a hundred feet or more out across the water. Workers already bustled on and off the dock, hauling cargo from wagons, loading it up the gangplanks of the great vessel that bobbed there. High above, its gilded banners flew high and loud and bright. Lady Hallucia led Tia and Ketz towards the vessel. It was a bigger boat than you expected to see on the river, by far the longest and sleekest vessel in the harbor. With all its sharp, jutting, immaculately carved angles, notched full of symbols that made sense only to the sculptors, the thing looked more like a luxury liner than a cargo ship. The highborn Ghestru merchant class didn't seem to know the difference.

The Ghestru merchant class, so far as Tia or Ketz knew, didn't even have any gods they felt compelled to glorify through such extravagance, just themselves for being a bunch of rich assholes. That, the twins took it, was the proud ship the *Arlash*.

Fuck, Tia mused, *why doesn't this pompous meatskin bastard just paint a sign on his barge, sayin' 'Come get me, river pirates!'*

Up one gangplank, laborers hauled heavy crates on brawny, straining shoulders, then through a square, shadowy hole into the cargo hold. The other, narrower, shinier plank led down from the main deck. A big crimson-skinned man bustled down the latter, accompanied by four spearmen. He wore a flowing black robe embroidered in many silvery exotic patterns. A great mane of silken, silver hair fell around his shoulders. Deep, wavy lines creased his drooping-jowled face. His sad, dark, watery eyes still flickered with the spark of hard-won wisdom, of a man who'd tasted many lands, many wines, many women…the spark of a man long gone, his spirit ground down beneath the drudgery of the mercantile responsibilities his ambition had piled on him…what his kind called *success*. The only joy such a man had left in life was his love for his wild, wayward child. His face lit up at the sight of her.

"Darling," he bellowed, bounding across the dock, his robes billowing about him like storm clouds. Workers stopped in their tracks, lowered their eyes, and set their heavy loads down, until he passed them by, then they resumed. "Where did you go? Where did you stray so late? Haven't you learned by now, these foreign ports are not the civilized dens of leisure of our homelands? Do you not know by now how we must –?"

"Oh, you know me, Daddy," said Lady Hallucia, stopping and standing proudly before him as he closed the distance. "I can't help myself sometimes. Besides, you know, I have my loyal defenders with me." She splayed her palms to either side.

He frowned. "Of course. Yes. So I see. But these other two…" His dark, watery eyes flickered to Tia and Ketz. To their mild surprise, he addressed them directly: "I don't know either of you."

"These are my two new friends, Daddy," she said with a silvery giggle. "They're also my gifts to you…two legendary warriors to be our guide through this strange old continent, on our journey to Tatelle. Tia and Ketz, meet my father, the illustrious Orcris Brendi. Daddy, meet Tia and Ketz. They've come seeking security work on our journey."

The twins exchanged a quick glance, their eyebrows twitching pointedly at each other: *Damn, these wankers actually talk like that!*

Orcris Brendi looked the twins over warily. "Darling, I don't know…I mean, I can see that they're already armed, and with all the disturbing talk going about…are you sure it was wise, to associate with such…well…"

"Hill-trash beasts?" said Tia.

Orcris Brendi frowned at her. "Yes."

"Oh, Daddy…" Lady Hallucia tickled his chin. "Let's step away and have a word in private, shall we?" She walked off, back towards the gangplank. Her father followed her as though led on a leash.

Tia whispered to Ketz, "This family is fuckin' weird."

While their hosts talked things over, Ketz's eyes scanned the harbor. Among Orcris Brendi's milling crew, he'd spotted a familiar face, from not so long ago. At first, he hardly recognized the man, all dirty, clad in such humbler rags. The man bore the musculature of someone who'd learned to move fast while wearing heavy gear – broad, powerful shoulders, a little bloated in the gut, with bulging, tree-trunk legs.

"Skids?" Ketz shouted.

The burly man's blackened eyes jerked towards him, confused and resentful at first, then he lit up with recognition. "Ketz?" the man rasped wearily. "That you?"

"'Course it's me, motherfucker." Ketz swaggered over, caught Skids's wrist and shook it, then yanked him forward into a hard embrace. They didn't really know each other at all, but they'd stood side by side, in a moment where it had counted. "Man, you won't believe the night my sister and me just had!"

"Try me," said Skids. "I mean, hell, just take a look."

"Aw, man…"

"Yeah. I ain't a policeman anymore. That mess at the gate, turns out, I'm the most convenient asshole the sheriff could find to pin it on. Someone needed to take the fall, right? Anyway, look at me now, a crewman on this fancy new voyage."

"Hey, you too?" said Ketz. "Man, that's great!"

"Guess I'm glad someone thinks so…Wait, you mean you're setting sail on that big, fancy chunk of flotsam too?"

"Looks that way," said Ketz. "Look, it's still gettin' all hashed out, but it seems like my sister and me, we're gettin' the job we came here lookin' for after all. Tia's right over there, if you wanna go say hi."

Skids lowered his eyes and shook his head. "Later. Sure we'll have all the time to catch up during the journey ahead, right?"

"Hey Ketz," Tia shouted, "get your ass back over here."

"I'll see you soon, man," Ketz said hurriedly. He darted back over to his sister's side.

Tia was already in talks with Orcris Brendi, who'd returned from his private conversation with his daughter. Lady Hallucia hung back, a few yards away. She lounged against a crate, laughing it up with the same bodyguards who'd escorted the three of them here. When Ketz glanced back, Skids had gotten back to hauling cargo.

Orcris Brendi now smiled warmly. He shook Ketz's hand. "Friends of my daughter are friends to me, young sir. I welcome you into my service. There's always work for good, strong workers on any ship. Security work, you say? Tell me, have either of you done much fighting?"

"You could say that," said Ketz.

Orcris Brendi bellowed laughter. "Yes, of course! Well enough."

The old man glanced off at his daughter, as though making sure she was out of earshot. His eyes narrowed on Ketz. "I will tell you directly, young man, as I've already told your sister, while you and my new handyman were over there prattling: I do not like shiftless, scrawny dirt-worshiper vagabond scum like the two of you. I *definitely* do not like the idea of enlisting such unsavory mercenaries on my security crew for an important voyage such as this. However, there are some matters on which I've learned to heed my daughter's instincts. Times such as these call for strange measures."

"That's fine," said Tia. "We don't like fancypants meatskin twats like yourself, neither. We still won't complain if you pay us decent. Don't get any funny ideas, though. I work to kill whoever fucks with you, your family, or your crew, not to suck your dick."

Orcis Brendi looked taken aback for a moment, then he smirked. "I would not dream of it, child. No, really, I wouldn't."

While Tia bantered with the old windbag, Ketz noticed Skids set down a crate he'd been hauling. Skids edged his way towards the Lady Hallucia and her bodyguards. As Hallucia shoved herself off the stack and ambled about, Skids quickened his pace. He reached into his britches as though to scratch his balls. His greasy hand came out holding a small, clay dagger. He did it so easily and quietly that no one but Ketz seemed to notice, even as he lifted it in an icepick grip over Lady Hallucia's back.

In that moment, Ketz didn't even think about it. He

darted over and shoved himself between them, his own long, glimmering blade leaping into his fist. He slid into a crouch while the edge lashed up. It struck Skids's forearm in a meaty, reverberating chop that cleaved flesh and bone. Skids howled as his hand flew away, along with his dagger. Lady Hallucia spun and cried out, as blood sprayed all over her face. She wiped frantically at it. Skids fell over on his back. He rolled around shrieking while his spritzing wrist painted the stones in pretty, red spatter patterns. By now, the bodyguards had ripped out their own weapons and leveled them on Ketz.

Ketz ignored them and caught Lady Hallucia by the shoulders. He growled in her face, "You okay?"

"No, I'm not," she panted, chest heaving, eyes wide. "What the hell!"

Orcris Brendi bounded forward, his robes whipping about him, shouting, "What madness is this? Guards, seize…"

Tia caught the old man by the collar and dragged him backwards. "Cork it, old man. Use your eyes. My brother just saved your daughter's life."

Orcris Brendi's own retainers poised and leveled their spears at Tia. She pivoted, faced them, and snarled. While Tia and the retainers stared each other down, the old merchant drifted towards the bloody scene, taking in what had just happened.

Ketz's nerves pounded. He crouched over Skids, who writhed around in a spreading scarlet lake, clutching his pruned wrist. "Skids, man, why'd you do that? *Why'd you just make me do that, man?*"

Skids' eyes grew glassy as he stared up at the brightening sky. The more blood he lost, the harder he fought for breath. "I…I…I'm sorry…so sorry…He…he…he made me do it…Told me if I didn't…he'd…he'd…My wife and kids, they'll be safe now, right? He won't hurt 'em now, 'cause I…I…did like he…"

"*Who?*" Ketz shouted. "Who put you up to this?"

"It was…was…" Skids sank too deep into shock to get

more words out. He stretched out flat, lay still, and stayed that way. The spurt from his wrist weakened to a pulsing cough, then turned to seep. More than one set of hands tightened on Ketz's shoulders and dragged him to his feet.

"We found the guy's hand," someone shouted. "There's a shiv still clutched in it."

"Looks like the barbarians are telling the truth," said someone else. "I been asking questions, finding out who saw what. Sounds like that dead bastard *definitely* meant to stab Lady Hallucia."

The hands let go of Ketz, so he stumbled dizzily. Someone slapped him across the back. "Good job, kid. You're a hero now."

Ketz caught his breath. He didn't feel like a hero. He felt like a busted wreck, standing over the bloody corpse of his new buddy, who he'd just killed.

"Ketz." That was his sister now. She stepped in front of him, grabbed and shook him. "*Ketz!*"

The next face Ketz saw was Orcris Brendi, his panting face red and swollen, even for a Ghestru. "Thank you, young man. You've officially won yourself a position."

"I thought we already did," Ketz heard himself say.

"…As my daughter's personal bodyguards on the journey that lies ahead."

"Thought your daughter already had herself some bodyguards."

"Yes, well…they've failed."

Orcris Brendi looked up and glared at his daughter's lowborn retainers. The men looked at each other, then stared at their boss. As his meaning sank in, they trembled and shook their heads imploringly. Orcris Brendi sighed, lowered his eyes, and turned away. Four of his own retainers circled the young failures, wrestled them onto their knees, then cut their throats. The two men collapsed in a quivering, spurting heap together. Their blood ran out fast across the stones, 'til it mingled with that of the failed assassin. The rising death stench barely made a ripple in the thick, rank harbor air.

"I'm loathe to enforce such rigid policies," said Orcris Brendi, not sounding so sad about it. He didn't seem joyous about it, either. He didn't look or sound like he really felt one way or another about it, other than mewling distress at him and his daughter being caught so close to such squalid grotesquery. It was like ordering the deaths of men who'd served him loyally stirred no more emotion than changing some old, smelly undergarments. He stepped between Tia and Ketz and placed a hand on either of their shoulders. "Business and family, I fear, have made a cruel man of me at times. There is no atrocity I would not order, no indignity I wouldn't tolerate, to keep my daughter safe. Her safety, for the duration of this voyage at least, is now in your hands, Tia and Ketz. I trust you shan't disappoint me."

SEVEN

Tia and Ketz followed Orcris Brendi and Lady Hallucia up the main gangplank, onto the deck of the *Arlash*. The merchant's spearmen marched close behind the twins, near enough to smell the body odor through those sweaty uniforms. All over the main deck, sailors busied themselves for the eminent launch.

Ketz took in the scene and lost his breath for a moment. He'd never been on a boat this big before. The mechanics of it all still eluded him. When he glanced to the right, he saw the gleaming, rippling expanse of the Great River, with the jagged, dark green gash of the distant shoreline. To stand on the deck of this mighty vessel, then to gaze out and see how the mightier body of water dwarfed even that…It was too much to take in just yet, so he pulled his mind back to matters at hand.

He turned to Lady Hallucia, smiled and said, "Right, then. So where do we start?"

Before she could answer, Orcris Brendi cleared his throat. Tia and Ketz both looked at him. He made a strange hand signal to his nearest spearman. The guy nodded, and marched off alone, to the gilded door beneath the poop deck, and vanished within. The remaining spearmen stepped in closer around Tia and Ketz.

"You'll now address such questions to me, young man," said Orcris Brendi.

Ketz blanched a little. And here, he'd gotten the idea that the strange girl had her pa wrapped around her little finger. He shot Lady Hallucia an incredulous look. Tia elbowed him in the side again.

"Fine, old man," said Ketz. "So what are our orders?"

"Your orders are quite simple. I thought you understood them plainly enough, or did I think better of you?"

"Sure, but –"

"My daughter will fill you in on the particulars. First, though, we must make you more presentable, as befits your station. All this…" He splayed his hands at what remained of their ragged garments. His face twisted like he'd just stepped in Gorlomong shit. "It won't do." He reached out and flicked a torn flap that hung from Tia's tattered vest. She snarled a little, but otherwise didn't move. If Orcris Brendi noticed, he didn't show it. Neither did the spearmen surrounding them, for once.

A moment later, the lone spearman reemerged from the door beneath the poop deck. He looked a little more stiff and awkward than before. He stepped to the side, stayed there against the wall, and left the door open. The twins' pointy ears twitched. Soft feet padded through the dark corridor within. No one else seemed to hear the faint sound. A moment later, out swarmed a cluster of shorter, softer, crimson-skinned bodies, a dozen or more. Though they were all Ghestru, none of them could have looked more out of place among the merchant's rougher servants. The fair creatures wore simple tops and trousers of pale silk, with loose, flowing sleeves. They favored simple, low-strapped sandals and heads shaved bald as newborn babes. Some of them had plump, round little tits budding beneath the silk, like twelve-year-old girls. Otherwise, it was impossible to tell which ones were male or female.

Lady Hallucia snuck between Tia and Ketz. She hunched, grinned, and whispered, "Now be nice, you two crazy kids. They just want to make you feel at home."

With that, Lady Hallucia stepped back. So did her pa. So did his spearmen. The little soft silk-clad creatures swarmed around Tia and Ketz like a school of hungry carnivorous fish, except they pressed with soft little hands instead of sharp teeth.

If this had happened a few minutes ago, back on the docks after Skids' death, Ketz would probably have whipped out his blade in alarm and hacked all these little freaks limb from limb without even thinking about it. By now, his blood had cooled, leaving him in a state of bleary bewilderment. He let them herd him along, through the doorway and down a broad staircase of flame-hardened wood, into a long, candlelit corridor. He looked around and spotted Tia, her head and shoulders bobbing above the swarm of soft, silk-clad bodies. They struggled to keep sight of each other amidst the hurried bustle. It felt like they'd been abducted and carried away by a hoard of shiny, sweet-smelling blood-red pixies, who giggled, poked and fawned over them like exotic new pets.

Midway through the corridor, the servants guided Tia and Ketz in opposite directions, off down two shorter, more dimly lit hallways. Ketz lost sight of Tia. The servants ushered him into a large, clean room, where they stripped off the last of his rags and plunged him into a vat of clear, heated water. They scrubbed off all the blood and mud that caked him. Some of them gasped in horror at his many neglected scrapes and gashes. They spoke in a low, broken form of the southern Ghestru tongue, of which Ketz knew only a little to begin with. All he could figure was that they were marveling that he hadn't died of infection. His rugged mountain upbringing had blessed him with a hardy immune system beyond their comprehension.

He had to admit, the hot water felt good. All those tiny scarlet hands on his body were a little weird at first, but honestly, that felt nice too. These simple creatures were obviously no threat, despite their overwhelming numbers and chatter, so Ketz relaxed in the tub and just let it happen. When he stepped out of the tub, they toweled him off and bandaged his wounds.

"*Ow*, careful," he said to one of them as it bandaged a cut on his thigh.

The creature on its knees froze, shrank back, and stared up at him with wide, pleading eyes. When he shifted, it flinched, like it expected him to strike it. Its companions drew to a pause and stared up at him.

"No, it's okay," he said, softly as possible.

He couldn't tell if they understood, but they finally got back to work on him. They no longer chattered so much among themselves, he noticed. Once they finished, they all unceremoniously scurried out of the room, vanishing like a swarm of red, silk-clad rats.

The sudden, silent solitude left Ketz more bewildered than ever. He stood there alone, damp and naked. Finally, he got a good look at the rest of his quarters. In the opposite corner from the tub, there waited a long, soft narrow bed. Across it, someone had set out a white shirt, scarlet vest, black belt, black trousers, silken stockings and undergarments, and black leather boots and gloves. He recognized it as the same uniform Lady Hallucia's previous bodyguards had worn. Next to this, there lay a three-foot sword with a leather-bound grip, a golden pommel and crosspiece, in a deep black, jewel-studded scabbard of hardened leather. Ketz picked up and examined the sword first. When he drew it, the metal shimmered pale blue, straight and thin.

Ketz looked around for the remnants of his old clothes, including his belt with his old blade on it. He couldn't find them anywhere. One of those weird little servants must have taken it all away while they undressed him. It bothered him, that he'd let himself get that distracted. He wasn't sleepy, and the hot bath had refreshed him, but he still felt sore and loopy.

He looked closer at his new sword. He'd seen Ghestru blades before. His own village's warriors largely armed themselves from an armory accumulated from caravan raids over the years. He'd partaken in such raids since he was thirteen, had been leading them by fifteen, and he'd never seen or wielded anything quite like this. When he thumbed the edge, yeah, it was sharp enough, though it was hammered thinner than any combat blade he'd wielded. When he flicked the flat, it hummed and vibrated. He slid into an en-garde stance, darted back and forth across the floorboards through his old footwork exercises, slashing and stabbing the air. Yeah, this was supple and well-weighted, but would it deflect a powerful chop from a heavier weapon?

For now, Ketz sheathed the sword, set it aside, then put on his elegant new uniform. He hadn't worn a uniform since Trescha. These duds fit surprisingly comfortably, even the boots. He paced the floor 'til they felt almost natural on his feet, then he buckled the new sword to his side.

He stepped out into the long, empty hallway. No sounds reached him down here except for the faint bustle of the crewmen above. He looked up and down the corridor, felt the steady rocking of the great structure around him on the water. On his way to his room, he'd had little time or presence of mind to take in his bearings. At one end, the corridor cut off to the right. He walked that way, rounded the bend, and found the staircase that led up onto the deck. When he opened the door, the bright light of high morning scorched his eyes. He blinked, stepped out, and looked around.

Off the side of the ship, he still saw the dirty, bustling harbor. Over the wall, there loomed the dirtier, sleepier rooftops of Belcrasche. With all the urgency everyone had made so much of, Ketz would have expected the ship to have disembarked by now. He didn't like that it hadn't. He'd barely met the town, yet the lingering sight of it already filled him with gloomy dread. He looked around at the deck. Crewmen and other servants went about their chores. Fewer of them gave him a second glance than before, probably because he was now dressed like one of them.

A small, spry shape leaned against the railing and gazed off at the harbor. Ketz walked towards his sister. She didn't seem to notice him at first. She now wore a uniform and sword that matched his.

Ketz stepped up next to Tia and said, "You too, huh?"

She scowled at him. "You mean we both got stripped and scrubbed down by a bunch of meatskin pixies? Yeah."

Ketz looked around. "Keep your voice down if you're gonna talk like that. We're on a ship run by Ghestru now."

"Is that where we are? I'm so glad you're here to keep track of that kinda shit."

"Look, I'm just sayin', they wouldn't like hearin' you call 'em *meatskins*."

"Yeah, all these *meatskins* can clean my ass with their fancy highborn tongues."

"Thought you said they weren't your type."

"Shut up, Ketz. Anyhow, the boss hired us to fight and keep his weirdass spoiled brat daughter in one piece, not to talk pretty."

"Yeah, speakin' of which, where the hell is our new charge?"

"Below deck, safe in her room, sleepin' off whatever local drugs she was on when she came to get us. A couple of those spearmen are watchin' her door. Our *services are not presently required*. Yeah, that's what she told me. So did her pa."

When Tia turned to Ketz, he noticed that her shirt and vest were unbuttoned halfway down, hanging partway open. It didn't leave much of her tits to the imagination. When the other men on deck walked by, they tried and failed to pretend not to look. Some of them, the lust in their eyes wasn't so decent.

Ketz knew his sister could handle herself. Hell, she was the better fighter of the two of them, if he was being honest with himself, and he wasn't one to scare easy. He still prickled whenever he noticed men eyeing her with the kind of lustful ambitions that didn't necessarily require a woman's mutual interest. The further they ventured from home, the more unfamiliar their company, the more he found himself fighting the impulse to gut any man who looked at her the wrong way.

Tia obviously spotted his thoughts, so she looked herself over and said, "Yeah, I know. Fuck it, though, this uniform's uncomfortable otherwise."

Ketz stretched, flexed, looked himself over in the new duds, and strutted back and forth. "Oh yeah? I was just thinkin' how it feels pretty nice. It's kinda amazing how they got my size just right, even the boots."

"Yeah, well, you don't have tits." She glanced around. "I don't think these Ghestru are used to women as warriors."

Ketz smirked. "Guess you'll learn 'em a thing or two, soon as we run into any trouble."

"Damn right." She stretched her arms, shook her head so her dirty red hair lashed about vibrantly in the morning sun. Her shirt and vest fell wider open, giving everyone on deck more of a free show.

Ketz gazed off at the harbor with troubled eyes.

Tia punched his shoulder. "Hey. Lighten up. We've made it. Everything's finally goin' smooth. We got this."

"We do, huh?" He frowned and spoke quieter. "C'mon, ain't you spotted it? None of this shit's right, and you know it."

"The fuck you talkin' about?"

"You already forgotten what happened with Skids?" He flung his palm out at the harbor.

Far out, near the wall, he still spotted the bloodstains that hadn't been washed away yet. The corpses had all been carted away by now. Dockworkers milled about their business with bloodshot, downcast eyes, ignoring the grisly lingering evidence.

Tia watched Ketz. Her eyes softened, in a way that was rare for her. "That wasn't easy for you, I know," she said. "It wasn't your fault, either."

"It was easy like it always is, 'til afterwards." He leaned close and whispered, "Did you hear what Skids said while he died? About someone puttin' him up to it?"

"I caught a little, but not much. It mostly sounded like a lot of delirious jabberin'."

"Yeah," said Ketz. "Like, about someone threatenin' to do

somethin' to his family if he ain't done what he did."

Tia's face sobered. "I didn't catch that part." She considered it. "Well, fuck!"

"Look, sis, I think we might'a just stepped into a bigger pile of shit here than we realized."

"Maybe. We've stepped in bigger piles of shit, though."

"Sure, but I don't like it when we're this deep into it, with this much of the whole mess we can't see yet."

"So we keep our eyes peeled, like always," she said. "Quit actin' paranoid. You get *me* paranoid when you do that. I hate it when you pull that shit!"

"Take it up with whatever I'm smellin' that's makin' me paranoid."

"Look, you're fadin'. I can tell. It's gotten your nerves all twisted up, and it's backed up into your brain. You've been through a lot."

"You been through all of it with me."

"Yeah, but hell, I feel fine. I'm good for a while yet. Go downstairs and get a few hours' sleep. I'll keep an eye on shit, hold it down for now."

Ketz's pride made him want to refute her, but his sore, sagging limbs told him she had a point. He needed to keep his wits sharp. "Okay," he said. "Thanks, sis."

"You owe me one," she said. "Remember that."

Ketz cast one more suspicious glance around, at all the lusty-eyed crewmen. "Yeah, well, you watch yourself out here, huh?"

Tia smirked and sputtered. "*Go get some sleep*, you asshole!" She slapped his shoulder. "You're the bestest brother ever, okay? Hell, sometimes I worry that you're *too* good, like we'd'a all been better off if you'd stayed at home as the blend-lady's apprentice."

Ketz ambled away. He reminded himself that Tia wasn't trying to cut his balls off when she said shit like that. In her way, he knew, she meant it as a compliment. Hell, sometimes he agreed with her, wished he'd taken a different trail. He thought about that asshole Doveede, what Minquo had told him about how that guy ended up the way he did. The guy's little brother had followed him into the madness, then stayed in it, long enough to get himself killed. Would Tia commit herself to such a cruel, heedless mission of vengeance on Ketz's behalf, if he met an end like that? He already knew the answer, he realized. Of course she would!

He went back below deck. The downstairs corridor spread silently before him. He reached his door and stepped inside. As soon as he closed it behind him, he sensed another presence in here with him. His hand drifted instinctively to his new sword as he crouched and pivoted. His lips drew back in a murderous snarl. Next to the door, a small figure pressed herself against the wall.

Ketz's fist tightened on the sword-grip. He glared into the shadows. "What the hell you doin' in here?"

Lady Hallucia stepped out of the shadows. "Looks to me like you're touching the wrong sword, boy." She'd taken off all her extravagant jewelry. Her dark hair hung free about her smooth, gleaming red shoulders. Her bright yellow eyes glittered in the gloom.

"Thought you were supposed to be in your own room," said Ketz.

Lady Hallucia cocked her head back and arched an eyebrow. "Oh, what's this, *are you telling me what to do?*"

Ketz looked her over. He knew it was a bad idea, but he still said, "Why, you want me to?"

She pointed at the bed. "Let's make something clear, boy, right now. You get me over there, you can make me do whatever you like. Use your imagination. Whenever we're not in that bed, though, remember that you're my daddy's bitch. When he's not around, that makes you *my* bitch. Does that sound suitable to you, boy?"

Ketz stared incredulously. No, he realized, she wasn't kidding. He wasn't imagining this, either. He grinned, stepped forward, close enough to taste her hot breath, and put his arms around her waist. "Sounds good to me, girl." He reached up and slid the straps from her shoulders. The scant, silken dress dropped to the floor around her feet, so she stood there naked as a bald cat. "I gotta say, I'm surprised, but I ain't complainin'." The sight and smell of her, her arousal, wafted all over him. He nibbled on her neck, ran his hands slowly up and down her smooth back, squeezed her cute little ass, then reached up and pinched one of her nipples. "I gotta ask, though…"

"I told you," she said, "I never met a barbarian bandit Schomite of the Nagga Mountains before." She chewed on his neck. "I've never *fucked* one before, either."

"Come to think of it," he purred in her ear, "I've never fucked a Ghestru gal before. Let's fix that."

He lifted her, carried her to the bed, threw her down on her back across the mattress. She drew backwards, pressed herself against the headboard, drew up one knee, and pouted at him as though playacting the blushing captive maiden. He sprang onto the bed, pulled her out flat by her ankles, and loomed up over her. He snatched her wrists, pulled her hands above her head, and pinned her there savagely. His lips and nostrils trailed her slowly up and down, lightly kissing and tasting her belly and breasts, listening as she responded with rising shudders, then he pulled himself forward and his mouth plunged down on hers. He let go of one of her wrists, so he could play with her between the legs. His fingers grew slick.

After the last few days, Ketz almost hadn't realized how much he needed a good fuck. Come to think of it, the last time the opportunity arose, he and that tavern girl hadn't been allowed to finish. His palms glided up and down Hallucia's sides. He turned her over and pulled her up onto her hands and knees. She cried out sharply as he entered her. She cried and squealed louder and more frantically, the harder he rode her.

An adrenaline boner, after a night and morning of combat and other dangers, was the best kind. It didn't hurt that Lady Hallucia was hot, exotic, fragrant, tight, and soaking wet. She writhed and screamed and clenched, clawing and biting at the sheets, in a way that told him he'd done his job right.

Right as he started to come, he remembered, *Oh, right, I took this job to abduct this bitch, to hand her over to that bastard Minquo. Damnit, Ketz, what are you doing?*

Afterwards, she slumped forward and sprawled on her stomach, quivering and panting. "Oh. Damn. Wow. Yeah. That was nice. *Holy shit!*"

He worked himself the rest of the way out of the new uniform, then collapsed next to her and stroked her cheek. "Good to know."

They cuddled for a while. Finally, he felt himself getting aroused again, so he rolled her onto her back, felt her up slowly and delicately, kissed her, reached down, and slipped his cock back inside her.

"Oh," she said, "hey now, hello there!"

This time, he made love to her slow and sweet and gentle. It was fun and friendly. Once they finished, they giggled and tickled each other like children at play, then fell asleep.

EIGHT

Ketz drifted through soft, rolling ephemera. He felt as one with living liquid light, something that spilled from the cosmic firmament into the great labyrinthine patterns of a world below. There, it flowed into a strange network of grooves and contours and channels. This place felt weirdly familiar, but not to him as he was now. He wasn't whole while in this state. Neither were the spaces he flowed through and filled out. His wasn't the only soul that lived in the liquid light, either. The other souls sang to him, and he sang as one with them.

Such bliss was all any of them knew, 'til he flowed further outward. The liquid light grew thin. The other singers sounded further away, from him and each other. Their voices still echoed all around him, though. He started to notice other things that filled this world. At first, it had all seemed like a series of hollow shapes and channels. Now it bubbled and churned with texture and growth, with the smells and tastes of life, even as its soil drank up the alien nourishment he brought. So that's where his singular essence settled. Here, the native life tasted ever juicier, wild and succulent.

Meanwhile, his brethren spirits kept singing, from wherever they'd landed. One by one, they swirled into their own individual pools. As they took root in their new homes, they sang louder and freer than ever. Some of the native terrestrial spirits had awoken to their presence. The nearer these primitive beings of crude meat and bone drew to the light, the more they livened to the song, danced to it.

Finally, they joined in the singing…the same great, glorious song he'd always sung, along with the rest of the eternal spirits with whom he'd shared the journey through the stars, to this world. The native creatures' dancing, in turn, invigorated the spirits with a new thirsty fire. The spirits fed them a louder song, stoking their tantalized awareness, so it became a need that became devotion, sprouting higher towards worship.

Not all of his brethren found such terrestrial spirits to sing with them, to bring their songs alive for this world. Those who did sensed their brethren wanting from afar, so they said to their native acolytes, *Rise up strong as our song fills you. Go forth across this globe. Spread it to all ears, especially those where our brethren dwell, where none yet accept their songs.*

In his own bubbling, churning haven, his own strange transformation had begun. He sang a different song now…*his own song.* He liked the sound of it better than the old collective one. By whatever quirk or anomaly, his little corner of this globe didn't line up with the great, glowing symmetrical network of channels that united the others. As their ethereal network broadened and brightened, they sought to draw him back into their collective mind. By now, though, he much preferred this singular state of being he'd embraced.

As he still heard their song, though, so they heard his. They disapproved of his breaking from them, and they were coming for him. They couldn't reach him here on their own, but they'd armed their acolytes with the right knowledge and tools, marrying the ancient powers of the ephemeral realms with the crude weapons and sciences of this world. Hence, they carved out new channels, so he might one day flow back in as one with them…but they'd not yet seen what he'd evolved into, on his own. Rather than dissolve, he would leak his own new essence back into them, staining them forever. Let *his new song* ring out loud through this world, 'til it reshaped itself to *his* rhythm.

While they spread their bright wings and flourished, his power boiled up slowly, pressurized within this swampy cauldron.

He wasn't alone out here, though. Oh no. As their singing had stirred the fleshly acolytes to their service, other beings stirred within *his* lands…beings not quite fleshly though not quite ephemeral…spirits like himself and his kind, except these had been here for far longer, half-slumbering within the lands, waiting for him to call them forth. So he called to them. The lands roiled and shook, and his own acolytes danced obscenely to the vibrations…his vibrations. He felt the tortured convulsions of their flesh as though it was his own…and he liked it…so he stoked it ever higher within them, compelling them to thrash against each other in ever madder, crueler dances. He liked living within their cruel, tortured nerves, so he stoked the vigor with which they forced the slamming, crushing stimulation upon each other…

…The *Arlash* bobbed and coasted beneath him. Through the slatted windows, the full light of a high sun spilled in, along with the fresh smell of the river rushing by. The weightless, luminous sensation still rippled through him, then faded. He tried drowsily to hang onto it. Before he knew it, though, he couldn't remember what it had felt like. He was just a young Schomite man, with the body and nervous system of such. He wasn't…just what the hell sort of being *had* he been in the dream?

I touched a god. I danced with a god. I fucked a god. For a moment, I was a god.

A warm, naked body snuggled close to his, in a wide, soft, comfy bed, such as he wasn't used to sleeping in. Living rooted within a physical form like this wasn't so bad sometimes. He kissed the girl's cheek. She smelled and tasted sweet. Then he remembered where he was and who she was. He drew up, leaned on his elbow, and slapped his forehead. She stirred and nestled closer. He kissed her forehead.

She opened her eyes and stared up at him…black, deep-set eyes, like her pa's. As the mists of sleep cleared from them, they widened with alarm. She thrashed and squirmed out of his arms, then jerked away so fiercely that she toppled backwards and crashed on the floor. She scuttled backwards like a crab, then staggered to her feet. She panted and stared at him, petrified. Her slender, tattooed arms and hands scrambled to cover her breasts and crotch, like he was some intruder she'd just discovered.

Ketz sat up and splayed his palms. "Hey, hey, *hey!* What the fuck's with you all of a sudden?"

"Who are you? What are you doing in my quarters?"

She looked ready to scream to raise the alarm. He sprang from the bed, caught her, and clamped a hand over her mouth. She twisted weakly against him. Her teeth bit down hard on his palm. He drew a deep breath, so he wasn't the one to cry out.

Whatever was going on, he was now intensely aware of a few simple facts. Whatever this Ghestru rich-bitch had acted like earlier, she wasn't acting that way now. Her pa had hired him and his sister as the girl's bodyguards. If anyone else discovered them here like this, with her in this state, it wouldn't just be him who suffered. So would Tia. They'd probably both be put to death, and not swiftly like their predecessors.

"These are *my* quarters," he growled in Lady Hallucia's ear. "You snuck in and waited for me. I'm Ketz of the Nagga Mountains, remember?"

She tensed up against his grasp, more distressed than ever. At least she'd stopped biting his hand. Some kind of understanding filled her terror-stricken eyes. They weren't the same eyes he'd looked into earlier, at all. She reached up and tried to tug his palm from her mouth. Earlier, she'd felt so wild and strong in his embrace. Her protests now felt weak as those of a starved child.

He said, "If I take my hand away, are you gonna scream? Blink once for yes, twice for no. If you lie to me, yeah, you'll get me killed, but you'll get yourself killed too."

She took a few slow, deep breaths through her nose, then blinked twice. He withdrew his hand from her mouth. She didn't scream, so he let go of her. With a heavy shudder, she stumbled away, sank onto the bed, curled forward, and buried her face in her hands. The way she twisted around, writhed and contorted, naked on a bed, her bare ass pointed at him, still looked sexy as all hell, so he started getting aroused again. Clearly, she was feeling anything but sexy right now, so he felt bad about it, but there it was. He reached out gently.

She recoiled. "*Don't touch me!*"

He drew back. "Sorry, I just –"

"It's not your fault," she sobbed softly. "I should be used to shit like this by now. Just…bloody hell, *a Schomite bandit this time? Seriously?*"

"You said you'd never fucked one before, so you wanted me to fix that for you. So I…did. A lot."

She let out a long, pitiful moan and hugged herself tighter.

"Hey, look, if you're gonna –"

"I'm sorry! I guess you…seem nice enough." That had to be the sweetest thing he'd ever heard from someone whose neck he'd been ready to snap a moment ago. She went on, "I'm really, really sorry!" She spat it out fast, like she expected him to beat her if she didn't convince him quickly enough. When she looked at him again, he was still standing there watching, more irritated than anything by this point. "You can sit down if you like," she said. "Just…please, don't touch me."

"Okay." Ketz sat down on the bed. He spotted the sheet they'd cast aside earlier during all the excitement. He reached over, drew it up, and placed it carefully on her shoulders.

"Thanks." She tugged the sheet close around herself. After a frustratingly long silence, she said, "So. I guess you have some questions."

"You're tellin' me, you seriously don't remember, everything we just did in here? And I do mean *every* –"

"*Shut up! Stop that!* Do you really have to be so…so…?"

"Well, I didn't think we had a lot left to be bashful over between us, so –" She glared, so he threw his palms up again.

"Okay, fine!"

"I guess you're right," she said. "Hell, I can smell you all over me…I can still *feel* where you put your…" She squeezed her legs together tight. "What did you say your name was?"

"I'm Ketz." He peered at her. "Who are you?"

"I'm Lady Hallucia Brendi. Yes, that is *my* name. That…creature you…Look, there's no easy way to say this, so I'll just say it. You didn't have sex with me."

"Uh, I beg your pardon, Miss Hallucia, but we most assuredly –"

"You just had sex with one of the Spirelight gods."

"Okay…uh…what the fuck?"

She drew her legs up onto the bed and turned to face him. With a humiliated sigh, she let the sheet fall away from her breasts. She pointed at the tattoo above them. "See this? Recognize this symbol?"

He made himself focus on the tattoo. She had a lot of tattoos. They all looked good on her. This one was different, though; a whirlpool-like spiral, except the lines rippled, breaking in places into maze-like rifts. Bug-sized figures danced around the outer circle like tiny imps at a bonfire. The style did in fact remind him of carven symbols he'd seen all over Trescha during the occupation. He hadn't encountered this exact one before, though, he was sure.

"How much do you *know*, Ketz, about the Gods of the Spirah Pantheon? I know your people want to destroy them, but what do you –?"

"Destroy the gods? Nah. Girl, you've just watched all the wrong tale-leaves bloom. Sure, I know those gods are real, that the Spirelight Empire aims to reshape all these lands in their vision. And yeah, most Spirelights I've met are a bunch of assholes who can all suck my cock. Long as they remember to stay out of the Nagga Mountains, that's all I ever wanna know about 'em, and they don't have to die on my blade."

Hallucia gulped and stared at the floor. "I…just don't understand anymore. I thought I did, but I guess not. How can you…Why is there so much violence on these shores, in your hills…in your life, in *you?*"

"I might as well ask you, with all the travelin' you done, with your pa, all you've obviously seen, how do you not get it? Oh right, I guess *seen* it is all you've done, huh?"

"Maybe." She pulled the sheet back around herself and frowned. "I'll tell you this much, though. I understand more about the Spirelight gods than you do."

"I reckon you would, sharing a body with one and all. So how'd that happen?"

She kept looking him over, out of the corner of her eye. "Could you…maybe put some pants on? Sorry, it's just…maybe I'd feel more comfortable sitting here talking to you that way."

He shrugged, stood up, hunted around 'til he found his trousers, and slid back into them. He still felt a little sullen and crestfallen, like you will upon finding out things aren't as you'd thought, between you and a pretty girl who seemed to like you.

That's not what this was, he reminded himself. The one who'd *liked him* wasn't here right now. That was a good thing, assuming this girl was telling the truth. Even if she believed what she said, she might be crazy. She still had the sheet draped over her shoulders, but she'd forgotten to keep herself covered. That made it harder to concentrate. He looked at her eyes again. No, they definitely weren't the same eyes as earlier.

Ketz sat back down, a little further away from her. "Go on."

"Since I was a little girl, I've been on boats like this, traveling around with Daddy. You've met him, I suppose." She glanced at his trousers, at the other pieces of his uniform strewn about the bed and floor. "He hired you, it looks like. I bet it was that…that *thing* that lives in me. She manipulated him and you, into this arrangement, didn't she?"

"Not just me," said Ketz. "My sister, too. I mentioned her?"

"You mean…your family's been snared into this madness? Oh, Ketz, I'm so sorry."

"Forget it. My sister's another bandit like me, another fighter. We've both been hired by your pa, knowin' the risks. Just watch yourself whenever you meet her. She ain't as nice as me. Anyway, you were sayin'…"

She gulped. "In my travels with Daddy, I've come to know the ways of many people, many cultures and much lore, as I moved among them all. For Daddy, it's always been just business. He was educated back home. His family brought him his teachers in from all over the world, from all the cultures with whom he'd be expected to do business. Some of them, his family hired from the lands with whom we were already in business. Others had been taken prisoner during those nations' wars. They'd been sold to our family as slaves. Either way, Daddy studied hard under them. By the time he left home, he thought he knew all he had to know, about whatever cultures he dealt with. For me…I've been educated too, by various tutors, mostly slaves. I've always been more fascinated by what I see up close, though…all the other worlds, the histories, the ways of life…everything people live their lives as part of, that I never get to be.

"As I got older, while Daddy did business at various exotic ports, I was left to my own devices most of the time. So I went exploring. I talked to people, anyone who'd give me the time of day. I listened to their stories. I got to see how they lived their daily lives. I partied with the kids of Daddy's business associates. Those kids were all in the same situation I was, really, except most of them got to live their lives settled in one place, knew what it was to *have a home*. I'd spend weeks with them, 'til I felt like some of them were my own brothers and sisters…or what I guessed it must feel like, to have brothers and sisters…then I left with whatever gifts they bestowed on me, of clothing, jewelry, or just the songs and tales of their people they saw fit to share with me.

"Whenever my imagination got swept off into those

songs and tales, I'd imagine myself living some other, more exciting, exotic life like that. I tried to take along a little piece of it with me, as part of me, so maybe that part of me could live on as more than just Daddy's tag-along. Maybe you've picked up on that. The way I dress, how I wear my hair…even how I act. That wasn't all…that other one. Daddy, he's done a lot of business with your kind's enemies, the Spirelights. They're very friendly to Ghestru, at least the highborn ones like Daddy and me. They treat us almost like equals, at least when they do business with Daddy…or at least they used to, before their new Priest King took over. Everyone says she doesn't like the Ghestru people."

"None of 'em ever liked you," said Ketz.

"Excuse me?"

"Their kids who you took up with, sure, maybe they liked you okay, hadn't had it preached into 'em all the way yet. Their parents, though, the ones your pa did business with?" He shook his head. "Don't let 'em fool you. Maybe y'all are of a refined, cultivated enough stock, as they see it, so they'll break bread with you like that, but you ain't of their *sacred bloodlines*. You ain't *born with the kiss of the gods upon your foreheads*. At the end of the day, that means you ain't nothin' but livestock in their eyes. It's a convenient arrangement for 'em right now, to let your people think otherwise. The minute it ain't, they'll come after your people just like they come after mine."

She recoiled. Her face twisted in disgust. "That's some pretty ugly stuff to say! Maybe you're not so nice after all."

"It's ugly because it's true."

"I thought you said you didn't know much about Spirelights."

"Their gods, no. The Spirelights themselves, I know just fine. I got the scars to prove it, too." He splayed his arms. "Have a good, long look if you like."

She looked at the floor instead. "I'm all set with that, thank you."

"You're the one who knows so much about the

Spirelights' gods. Let's hear more about that."

"Like I said, I've adorned myself with the jewels and silks, with the art and lore of the gods of many lands. But it was only *that one* who ever captured my imagination…enough that I had the stupid idea to have this crest – the god's crest – permanently inked into my skin…*Trosola*, their renegade god."

"Wait, hold on. What's a *renegade god?*"

"Something bad."

"You mean, other than gods in general?"

She looked offended, then continued, "Yes. The Spirelights say, when the Gods of Light of the Spirah Pantheon first found their way into this world, they found the older, darker spirits already living here. The gods sought to drive them out, back to the Dark Lands from whence they came. Trosola saw another vision…to align themselves with the songs of the darkness, to carve out a new way, a wilder reality, born of a blasphemous union. Many modern Spirelight theologians say your kind, the Schomites, are the spawn of that unholy union, that you'll one day spawn their end of days, with *Trosola* leading the charge, to annihilate all their kind."

"Sounds like a happy ending to a fairy-tale," said Ketz. "I can tell you for sure, though, honey, us Schomites were here *long* before the Spirelights, or their gods."

"I'm just telling you what I've heard." She buried her face in her hands again. "I don't *want* to be the harbinger of anyone's destruction!"

"Yeah? So why do you have Trosola's symbol tattooed above your tits?"

"Because I was an inquisitive, rebellious kid, okay? The legend of Trosola…appealed to me. A being that was just along for the ride, going through the motions as one more of its kind…who found itself in new lands and decided to start afresh, to break the mold, to carve out its own destiny, beyond anything its own kind had ever allowed it to be. When we lived among Spirelights, I asked all around about those stories, of their gods…especially of Trosola. It turns out, within the bowels of their world, there are secret societies, outlawed sects, followers of Trosola, who feel the same way I did."

You mean like spoiled brats with too much time on your hands, Ketz almost staid. No, he realized, that was Tia talking. Maybe he'd spent too much time following her around. Either way, he shut his mouth and kept listening.

"One time, Daddy and I spent a month in Herngla, one of the great Spirelight city-states. That was before Priest King Kalesha convinced all her people not to do business with us anymore. Anyway, I'd never been treated to such a grand reception, and I can't imagine how any other could ever outdo it. They didn't just greet us at the harbor. They gave us a royal escort, on one of their great regal transport beasts. Once we reached the city-state, they even took us on a ride in one of those long flying boats of theirs, all the way up to one of the highest tiers of the city-state. I felt like a queen that day! While I was there, I got really close with a young man…the son of the businessman Daddy was trading with. While our parents haggled, he showed me around. He brought me to a place where he introduced me to his friends. They gave me sweet wine to drink. *You should have seen that place,* on one of the lower tiers…the third up, I think. It was just an abandoned market building, set back against the rise…but the way they'd made it their hideout, made it their own…"

"I told you, I was in Trescha. I saw plenty spots like that."

"Not like this one, I'll bet. If the city-state police had found them there…" She shuddered. "The walls were covered in sacred symbols, except altered. The way those symbols covered the wall, with the symbol of Trosola painted across the ceiling, holding court over all the rest…it was like they'd made it their own temple, better than the one at the crown of the city-state, which most of them were too lowborn to ever see anyway. My friend who brought me there, I told him about my fascinations with his people's lore. It turned out he was a member of one such secret sect…of the cult of Trosola. That place he'd brought me…that really was *her* temple.

"After we slept together, he gave me more wine to drink and asked me more about my interests. He couldn't stop staring at the symbol on the ceiling. He liked inking people up. He was good at his art. I asked him to ink the symbol of Trosola on me, and he said he could. He said the image would bring me luck, that Trosola would recognize me ever after as one of its own, would look out for me until the end of my days. He was handsome and smart, and the whole night was alive with unbridled excitement, and we were still in that wild, beautiful place that he and his friends used as a hideout, so I said yes. Just one more tattoo to take with me, right? He made me promise, though, to keep the tattoo covered until Daddy and I were gone from the city-state. He said if anyone there saw it, it could be bad for him and his friends. I knew something of how strict the Spirelights could be about their religion, I didn't want him to get into trouble, so I made sure I wore clothes that covered my chest for the rest of the visit.

"Daddy didn't see the tattoo 'til a week after we set sail. Or he was so busy that it took him that long to notice, even after I stopped keeping it covered. He frowned when he saw it, but what could he do? When people scold Daddy for how he's let me run wild, he just huffs and says, *I can manage my international business, or I can manage Hallucia. I cannot do both.*"

Ketz chuckled and edged a little closer to her. "I might just like the real you better than I expected."

"I'm sorry, Ketz, but...no. I'm not the wild girl I used to be...not when I'm *me*, not anymore. *She* kept all that for herself. As to this mark, I don't think Daddy even ever connected it in his mind with Spirelight blasphemy. Why would he? To him, it was just one more unsightly piece of body-art his headstrong daughter had decorated herself with, even after..." Her eyes watered and she pressed her fist to her mouth.

"What happened?" said Ketz.

"I guess it was a month after we set sail from Herngla, up along the coast. Daddy had another meeting, with another wealthy prospective Spirelight business partner. This time, we were to host a fancy dinner onboard, for the man and his entourage. By then, I was back to wearing dresses that showed off the tattoo in plain sight. I didn't even think about it much anymore…not when I was awake, at least. Not yet.

"The merchant came aboard. He and I didn't see each other up close until everyone was seated around Daddy's banquet table. I'd watched the guy a bit, and he'd seemed to be getting more and more nervous the longer he was onboard, especially once we were below deck, like he didn't like being on the water, or in the close space or something. Then when Daddy introduced me as his daughter, the man just stared. He went pale as a sheet, pale even for a Spirelight. Before I knew it, he sprang to his feet, pointing and screaming, accusing daddy of making his floating home a domain of devils. Then he turned, fell over his toppled chair, shambled across the room, and ran out. He ran up on deck and jumped overboard before anyone could stop him. No one found his body 'til a week later, washed up on a nearby shore. They say…by then, big worms from the bottom of the bay had crawled into him, were crawling in one way and out the other. I heard rumors that worms that big didn't live in those waters, or they weren't supposed to.

"Anyway, after he flipped out at dinner, no one was paying attention to me anymore. They were too busy trying to figure out what the hell just happened, even though he'd pointed right at me…at my chest." She touched the tattoo absently. "That's when I first heard her laughter in my head, like an icy whisper out of the shadows in the back of my mind. I'd been dreaming about her ever since leaving Herngla, but I never really remembered while I was awake…not until that moment. Then I remembered everything, as she remembered it. If I was already losing time in my waking life to her – hours, days – I hadn't noticed. She's made sure I notice ever since, though, just so I don't forget who's boss…what I've marked myself with…what lives within me now.

"Obviously, those other Spirelights he came onboard with hadn't seen the tattoo, but they must have recognized some of the crazy words he screamed…plus the way his body was found…because sure enough, at the next port we docked in, a detective from the Spirelight International Police was waiting, asking to come aboard for a look around. I made damn sure to wear something that hid the tattoo. That detective looked around, but he didn't seem to find anything suspicious. He only asked me a few questions, I could tell he didn't really suspect me of anything personally, but…he scared me all the same. Those Spirelight detectives have always given me the creeps, like they're made of ice. I got out of the room and went to hide 'til he was gone. It turned out, it didn't matter, because that's when Trosola…" She gulped. "He was the first. That detective. Well, by the time Trosola let me wake back up, he'd obviously seen the tattoo, but he never said a word about it, because he was more scared of me than I was of him, like petrified, worse than that businessman had been. I don't know what Trosola did to him in bed, but he looked at me like I'd shown him things he'd never imagined existed and wished he still didn't know about.

"I don't know what he said in his report, but long story short, we never heard from the Spirelight International Police after that. Daddy didn't do much further business with Spirelights, either, but I guess it didn't matter, because that wasn't so long before Ghestru-Spirelight trade relations started going to hell, on account of that new Priest King. I guess Trosola's my problem now, not theirs."

She went deathly quiet, so Ketz asked, "Who else knows?"

"What, I —"

"On this boat, this crew, the rest of these people we sail with. Who else knows?"

"None of them…I don't think. Daddy doesn't know…what it is…but…he must suspect something by now…but what can he do? Otherwise, at the end of the day, I

can only guess. I don't think any of the crew and her have…"
She shuddered. "No, I'm sure, that hasn't happened.
Whenever she takes someone to bed, she always makes sure I
wake up next to them…that I see what she's done. The thing
is, she never takes hold in front of anyone else. She only rises
out of me when I'm alone. Every time she does, it feels like
drowning. I never remember what happens, when she's…the
one in control. I don't know if she's privy to my memories,
but I guess she must be. She only talks to me in my dreams,
when she comes to taunt me about how I'm stuck with her,
how much she loves living within my flesh and bones, how
she means to milk it for all its worth 'til I'm used up. I can't
feel her or hear her now, but…Ketz, for all I know, she's
awake and listening to us talk!"

"If she is, we'll deal with it." Before he realized what he
was doing, he put an arm around her. Then he remembered
she'd asked him not to do that.

Before he drew away, though, she leaned her head on his
shoulder. "That's kind of you to say," she said. "Look, Ketz,
you do seem nice…"

"If you say so."

"No, believe me, you are. Like…I'm a little surprised
you're *her* type." She laughed bitterly. "You're even…kinda
cute, in the Schomite bandit sort of way. Please, though, from
now on, if she…if *Trosola* comes out again…don't take my
body again, please."

Truth be told, it was already straining his willpower not to
jump all over her now, holding her like this, their pungent
love-stink still fresh on each other, with her still naked except
for the sheet. "I won't," he said. "I promise."

"Thank you." She pressed her tear-streaked face against
his chest.

He stroked her arm. "Hang in there, girl. We'll figure out
a way to deal with this."

"There's no *dealing with it*. Ketz, please, for your own sake
and your sister's, just do the job Daddy hired you for, then get

yourselves as far away from me as possible. This is my damnation, not yours."

He looked down into her dark eyes. "Maybe I will and maybe I won't. I'll tell you this, though. Whatever you did to get this on yourself, how you've lasted this long without killin' yourself…that's some kinda guts, some kinda strength. I don't know how you got it, but I know guts and strength when I see 'em. I also know, as one of *my* people, that the Spirelight gods can be beaten. Those gods live in these lands, but they ain't *of* the land, and that's why they can't have it, why my people won't let 'em. This one, renegade or no, lives in your body, but it's still your body, still your soul that's the rightful inhabitant. You figured out how to let Trosola in? You can figure out how to take back control, make her get lost. Next time she comes to taunt you in your dreams, you can tell her Ketz of the Nagga Mountains said so."

Hallucia chuckled nervously. "I'll bet she'll just love that. I don't think she's used to men spurning her in that way, not after she's had them. Usually she's the one who does the spurning…or leaves me to see to it."

"Just try it," he said. "Build your strength up for it if you need to, but believe me, you can."

She pulled away, sat up straight, and dried her eyes. "I wish I could say you knew what you were talking about."

Ketz got up and hunted around 'til he found the rest of his uniform. He started putting it back on and arranging it neatly over himself. "Maybe I don't. Think about this, though. You say she only rises and takes hold of you when no one else is there. Maybe that's so no one pieces together what's goin' on. Or maybe, the only time she has the guts to come pull you down is when you're scared and alone. Sounds to me like a coward, just like the rest of her pantheon. I'll bet, if she found you waitin', not so timid and helpless, she wouldn't like it so much. I bet she wouldn't even have the first damn idea what to do." He buckled his sword back on. "Anyhow, you should get dressed. I'd better escort you back to your room.

Let me check the hallway first, make sure the coast is clear."

She got up and looked around for her dress. When she didn't spot it at first, her eyes widened with alarm. Ketz watched her, then remembered where she'd first discarded it. He cleared his throat, cocked his head, then pointed to where the garment lay. She scurried past him, stepped back into the dress, and to his mild disappointment, pulled it up over herself before letting the sheet fall off.

She frowned at him. "Are you…going to tell your sister about this?"

"You mean that we…well, that Trosola and me fucked? Yeah, I'm gonna have to. Like you say, she's in this deep as I am. If it makes you feel any better, I'm the one she'll never let hear the end of it. It's just how it is. Ain't a lot we can afford to keep from each other when we're on the job."

"Oh, but there's plenty you'll still keep from her, Ketz." Hallucia's voice and gaze darkened and deepened with icy fatalism. "Trosola's touched you already, and she's let you stay this long, alive and unmolested by the worldly powers you already fear, no less. I hope you get away before you find out what I mean, but I doubt it."

NINE

The corridor spread out emptily in either direction. Ketz moved swiftly and quietly, tugging Hallucia along, then paused to feel and listen to the rocking vessel around them. When he was sure they were unobserved, he nudged her into the lead. He sniffed the air for threats as they went. All he could smell right now was their love-stink all over each other, hers fragrant and spicy, his own musky and ripe from the trail –

Wait a second, that ain't right! I'd come straight from the bath when she – or that other one – ambushed me. I'm damn sure those little red pixies didn't leave an inch of me unscrubbed.

So what the hell was that rotten smell he kept catching on the air? It was faint, but impossible to ignore. Maybe it wasn't on either of them, but he couldn't shake the feeling that it had followed him from the trail. Either way, it was distracting him. For a moment, his head swam dizzily, like he'd just come up for air from some dark, suffocating place.

They reached her room, which was set back in a shorter hallway like his. Tia stood sentry there, as though she believed her charge waited safely within. Then she spotted Ketz and Hallucia hurrying along towards the short passage. Ketz spotted Tia, drew to a halt, and nodded to her.

Hallucia stepped behind Ketz, clutched his arm, drew up close against him, and whispered, "Is that your sister?"

"Yeah, that's her," Ketz whispered back. "Just play it cool."

"I'm standin' right here, and you know damn well I'm his sister," said Tia. "Play what cool?"

Ketz pried Hallucia's fingers gently from his arms. He met his sister's stern gaze. "Just give us a minute, will ya, sis? I'll explain then."

"You better," said Tia. "Okay, go ahead."

Ketz and Hallucia entered a room not unlike Ketz's, though more lavishly furnished, as befit a highborn lady. "Okay," he said, "this the right room?"

Hallucia looked around. "These are my quarters, yes."

"Good. So you got everything in here you're gonna need for a while?"

She nodded.

"Okay. Stay in here for now. Let me get out there and get back on the same bloom of the tale-leaf with my sister."

Out in the hallway, he took his place next to Tia, standing guard.

Tia kept her eyes forward. "So who's *fuckin' meatskins* now?"

"Piss off," said Ketz. He smirked and winked sideways. "Don't worry, sis, I'm still on the job."

"Right. *On it, under it, and any other position I don't wanna visualize*, you mean."

"Damn right." Ketz waited a moment, then listened to the great boat all around them. Once he was reasonably sure no one was around to eavesdrop, he stepped sideways, grabbed Tia's arm, and pulled her a short distance away from their post. He whispered, "We got shit to talk about."

She yanked her arm out of his grip. "Damn right, we do. Like keepin' that little meatskin princess alive long enough to deliver her ass to Minquo, so we can get paid and put all this lizardshit behind us."

"No, seriously, listen. There's more to it."

Tia snarled and put her face in her palm. "Shit. I knew it. When you gonna grow the fuck up?"

"Hey, c'mon now, that ain't fair."

"Oh really? Lemme guess, now that she's lettin' you plant your pecker in her, here comes the whole song and dance of *Oh, no, Tia, we can't abduct this poor girl! She's too special and wonderful. It would be wrooong!* Brother dear, I'm tellin' you right fuckin' now, *shove that shit up your ass, before you get us both killed!*"

She wasn't completely off, but he still said, "How 'bout *you* keep *your* voice down? To answer your question, no, it's somethin' else."

"Shit. That sounds even worse."

"It is."

"Of course. Okay, spit it out."

Ketz described how he'd gone to bed with one gal and woken up with another, how he'd fallen asleep gazing into one set of eyes, then woken up seeing a completely different person. From there, he told her Lady Hallucia's story, about the renegade Spirelight god Trosola that had seemingly fused itself with the girl, body and soul.

Tia kept her cool while she heard him out, then stood there thinking it over. No one came down here to intrude upon them, except a few of those weird little Ghestru slave-pixies, all of whom strode back and forth through the hallways, eyes fixed constantly forward, as though they wore blinders on either side of their eyes. The rest of the ship's hustle and bustle echoed down from the deck above.

Tia stood still, 'til she was sure she and her brother were properly alone. Then she backhanded Ketz across the face. "Damnit, Ketz, when you gonna learn, *don't stick your dick in demon-possessed!*"

"*Ow!*" That had been no light sisterly love-tap she'd landed on him. He took a second to absorb the blow. "Fuckin' bitch. God-possessed, in this case, actually."

"Whatever!"

He thumbed at the hallway leading back to Hallucia's room. "Look, god, demon, whatever you wanna call it, if our little charge in there has the damn thing livin' inside her, it's a safe bet it has somethin' to do with what Minquo wants with her."

"Of course it does," said Tia. "How's that our business?"

"This whole job so far, we've been gettin' jerked around, moved like pieces on a game-board. All of it...Our arrest,

Hallucia or Trosola or whoever showin' up just in time to bail us out…then that shit at the docks with Skids…Look, it don't take a damn genius to figure out it's Minquo behind it all."

"Obviously not, since you managed to put it together. I still don't get what you're bent out of shape about. It's the job. The asshole told us he'd be usin' his connections to pull some strings for us. Far as I can see, that's exactly what he's done."

"So are you cool with handin' a god over to a guy like Minquo?"

"I'm *cool* with puttin' as much space between us and Minquo and all these rich weirdos as soon as fuckin' possible, preferably with a big sack of coins to show for it, in whatever direction the lands spread clearest before us." She paused. "But no, you're right, sort of. I *ain't* so cool about bein' this up close and personal with a glowstick god, inhabitin' some meatskin girl's body or otherwise. I would say, let's just kill her and hopefully the god along with her, 'cept I'd kinda like for us to get off this damn boat alive."

Ketz thought about that. "Push come to shove, we could jump overboard, swim ashore."

"You been up top, had a look at that big ol' Great River since we shoved off? No, of course you ain't, 'cause you been too busy gettin' your dick wet."

"Yeah, yeah, yeah…"

"My point is, the river's big, and I don't like the idea of havin' to swim that far if I can help it. How good a swimmer are you?"

"Now that I think about it, not very," said Ketz. "So what now?"

"We ride this shit out, that's what," said Tia. "After that, it ain't our problem."

Before Ketz could answer, he and Tia both froze where they stood. Their sharp ears twitched. Far away, several sets of soft, tiny feet padded down some stairs. The twins raced back to the short hallway outside Lady Hallucia's door. They retook their places to either side of it. Five of those weird little

Ghestru slaves came around the corner and drifted down the hallway past them.

The first four of them drifted by, as though not noticing the guards. The one in the rear trudged to a stop next to them. Her companions walked on without her. The twins could tell this one was a *her* because of the nubs on her chest beneath the silk, which were a little plumper than average for the females among these creatures. She lifted her skinny arm and held out a small bag, made of the same silken material as her garments. All the while, her eyes stayed fixed forward, like she was scared to make eye contact.

"A gift on behalf of the servants of the true bloodline," said the girl, in a meek, blank, high-pitched voice, "in thanks of your services to our mistresses."

"I think you mean *mistress*, just the one," said Tia.

The servant girl kept her eyes forward, her arm outstretched, the silken bag dangling from her fingertips. "I know what I say, woman who kills people. *Please, accept the gift,* for I must deliver it into your hands, before I am let to return to my place of rest, to lie beside my love and my boopa." Her face still didn't move, but her outstretched arm trembled.

Ketz snatched the bag from her. "Okay, we got your *thank you* present. Much thanks right back at your boss. Okay. You can get along now, you hear? Go on, catch up with your little friends."

"Yes, sir. Of course, sir." With that, the little red girl scurried to catch up with the others.

"A lot of good that did us," said Tia. "Okay, let's see what the little bitch gifted us with. Well, c'mon, take a look."

Ketz drew a thin, silken string, so the bag sighed open like a blooming flower. He spread back the edges.

"Well, what is it?" said Tia.

"Ease off, will you? Looks like a lot of chopped-up dried fruit, with some nuts and such mixed in there." Ketz dipped his fingers in and scooped up something. He sniffed it, then tasted it, then munched on it. "Hey, this shit ain't half bad."

"What a humble gift from the *true bloodline*."

"I don't think it's from Brendi," said Ketz. "Maybe those little things just like showin' gratitude."

"You really think they got that much love for their *mistresses?*" Tia kept peering over Ketz's shoulder. "Hey, what's that?"

Ketz looked in and spotted a thin, yellowy scrap of folded parchment. He dipped his fingers in, pinched it out, and unfolded it.

"What do those markings mean?" said Tia.

"Hang on a second," said Ketz. The study of marks – of words set down in symbols – had been one of the things Silisha, the village blend-lady back home, had been teaching him recently. He wasn't what you'd call an expert. Little by little, the markings on the parchment started to make sense, sort of. "I think it says…more or less…*I know what she is. I know what you are.* Then…somethin' else, I ain't sure." He squinted. "It could mean a couple different things. I think that little critter reads and writes in her own language even worse than I do. Here at the bottom, I'm pretty sure this means, *In the servant's quarters, at…*"

"At?" said Tia. "*At* what?"

Ketz squinted closer. "It's…some kinda number symbol, for how the Ghestru keep track of what time it is."

"What time of day she want us to meet her?"

"I can't quite tell yet. Silisha schooled me more on their words than their numbers."

"Right then, so work on that."

"*What?*"

"I'm gonna take me a little nap," said Tia. She started off down the hall, towards her door. "It's time for your shift at her door, brother dear. Keep the little bitch subdued and safe however you like. See if you can figure out the rest of that message, huh?"

TEN

Ketz spent too many hours standing still, outside Lady Hallucia's room. He kept listening for movement within. All he heard was her slow, slumbering breathing…the breath of a normal, humanoid gal, enjoying some peaceful sleep while she could.

Little by little, he grew accustomed to the rocking of the *Arlash*, as it coasted down the middle of the river. The only means by which to tell the time was a small skylight, at the far end of the hallway. Night had fallen a while ago. He no longer smelled that weirdly familiar, faintly rancid earthy scent. *Maybe it* was *Hallucia after all*. Except her scent was still all over him, and it definitely didn't smell like that. In fact, it kept making him want to turn from his post and knock on her door. He kept hoping to hear her door opening behind him, to turn and find her inviting him into the room with her. Except if she did, would he see Lady Hallucia's eyes, or Trosola's? He kept imagining that scenario – either set of eyes – and caught himself getting stiff. He reminded himself of the promise he'd made to Hallucia. That didn't stop the sweet, savage daydreams about the other one.

A loud lurch echoed from within her room, like she was moving furniture around or something. He slipped down the short corridor and almost knocked…to see if she needed a hand with anything, honest. It had already gone deathly quiet within, though. He caught a faint ghost of that other smell on the air. When he sniffed harder, he couldn't find it anymore. If he could just figure out where it was coming from…

For now, he returned to his post, munched on more of those little fruit treats, and glanced with growing unease at the scrawled-on parchment.

Tia rounded the corner and came towards him. She looked refreshed, clean and spry. Her hair hung damply around her shoulders, so she must have taken advantage of the tub. Otherwise, she wore her Ghestru uniform pristinely. She'd even buttoned it up far enough so her tits weren't falling out.

"Any progress?" she said.

"I think so. Basically, the critter wants to talk, at the stroke of midnight, in the servant's quarters."

"Great," said Tia. "Got any idea where the *servant's quarters* are on this boat?"

"How should I know?" said Ketz. "I been standin' here all day."

Tia glanced off at the distant sunroof. "Looks pretty close to midnight to me."

"Yeah. There's more to it, though. You ain't gonna like it."

Before he could say more, soft little feet padded towards them. Around the corner, there came that same little Ghestru slave girl. She stopped in front of them, then just stood there, deathly still, like a statue.

"Well?" said Tia. When the creature didn't answer, she muttered, "Damn, those critters are creepy." If the creature took offense, it didn't show it. "Okay, so what now?" she said to Ketz.

Ketz looked around, listening for unseen interlopers. "I think she wants you to follow her," he whispered.

"Okay," said Tia, "so…Hang on, did you say she just wants *me* to follow her?"

"Yeah, that's the part I was gettin' to." He held up the parchment. "See these two marks near the bottom here? I'm pretty sure they mean *woman who kills people*."

"Nice to know I've made such a shiny impression," said Tia. "Can't figure how. Hell, you're the only one who's done any killin' since we got anywhere in sight of this damn boat, where they might'a seen."

"Like you said, these folks ain't used to female warriors." He nodded towards her sword. "I reckon she's figured out that ain't for choppin' vegetables."

"Fine, so why not the both of us?"

"One of us has to stand here and guard Lady Hallucia's door."

"Okay, so why me? You're the one who actually understands some of this lizardshit."

"Ask her yourself." Ketz indicated the little silk-clad creature, who still waited silently.

Tia crouched and said, "That true, you weird little bitch?"

The creature gave the slightest of nods, then turned and walked back in the direction from which she'd come.

"Huh," said Tia.

"I think she means for you to follow her," said Ketz.

"I still don't get it," said Tia.

"Me neither. Maybe we will once you hear what she has to say. That's kinda the idea of, y'know, gettin' information from folks."

"Yeah, yeah, yeah, piss off."

"Who knows, maybe she just feels more comfortable, confessin' to another woman."

"Right," said Tia. "To the *woman that kills people*."

With that, she hurried down the hall, caught up with the weird little messenger, and let it lead the way.

ELEVEN

The little creature led Tia down a much narrower hallway. The ceiling was lower, so she had to crouch to get through it. The shorter girl opened a wicker-lace doorway, beckoned Tia to follow, then vanished into the darkness within. Tia had to duck down even lower to fit through after her. Almost unconsciously, her hand drifted towards her sword as she entered the darkness. Her feet passed over looser, older, rougher boards. The stench of humanoid waste flooded up, from somewhere further below.

"Hurry, hurry," whispered her guide from somewhere ahead.

As Tia followed the voice, the floor went away beneath her front foot. She tumbled forward. Her hands flailed and caught a thin, splintery railing, then her feet settled onto a narrow set of stairs, so steep it was almost a ladder.

The servant girl reached the bottom, tore two chunks of fungus from the wall, and rubbed them together 'til they lit up incandescently. She then pressed the two chunks of glowing fungus to the walls so they stuck there, weakly illuminating the straw-strewn space of this lower, secret hold. Tia reached the floor and stepped out between two rows of thin, dirty mattresses. The creature led her to the back then huddled under a low-swooping arch, next to a row of five small, rectangular wooden boxes. She busied over something within, then turned and waited for Tia. Tia couldn't see what was in the boxes. The waves outside lapped heavily at the walls around them. Tia kept trying to figure how low they were, and where this was in relation to the rest of the ship's layout. She glanced back across the long room, to the stairway out of there, still half expecting an ambush.

"This is where we come to sleep," said the girl. "There is a small window of time, where no one is here but you and I."

"Fine," said Tia. "So talk fast."

"Quiet," the creature hissed. "Sleeping boopa." She thumbed over her shoulder at the rectangular boxes.

Tia peered at the boxes, then gasped as the meaning set in. "You mean they breed you critters on this boat, too? Figures. Fuckin' meatskins."

"You are a cruel bitch," said the little figure dispassionately.

"You're the one who keeps callin' me *woman who kills people*. What did you expect?"

"Mistress of the true bloodline is not a cruel bitch. Others are, but she is kind. She was not ever cruel, but she was not kind. Her misery, I think, has taught her how to be kind. Since the other mistress appeared. Other mistress is cruel. She is worse than you, woman who kills people, far, far worse. Did the mistress of the true bloodline tell you where she found the other one?"

"Not me personally. She told my brother. He filled me in on the long and the short of it. So what's —"

"Where?"

"What?"

"I said *where?* Where did our mistresses meet?"

At first Tia thought the thing was asking where she'd met Hallucia. But no, she wasn't one of this thing's *mistresses*, thank fuck. She wracked her brain, for all the details Ketz had told her. "In...some glowstick city-state, yeah? Right, the one called Herngla. Who cares, one glowstick stronghold is much like another, right?"

"You are wrong," said the jittery silk-clad shape. She sat forward, so more of the fungal glow fell across her face. Her eyes brewed livelier now, deep and haunted. "Did you know, that boy and his family died last week?"

"What boy? What family?"

"Ink boy. He...gave ink to the first mistress." The servant ran her palms up and down above her arms, then paused above her heart. "You...see? I mean...I am the mistress, and I show where the ink goes. You see what I show, so you see the mistress behind your eyes, so –"

"Right, I get it," said Tia. The servant's eyes narrowed at her disagreeably, so she spoke softer again. Apparently, the little thing didn't feel the need to be so timid or reserved, now that they were alone, especially this close to its young. "Yeah, I've seen her tattoos, most of 'em anyway. I reckon she has more. You'd have to ask my brother about that."

The servant's eyes narrowed. "Your brother...he has bred with the mistresses?"

"Shit, I hope not," said Tia. "But yeah, he fucked her...them...whatever. I guess so did...what did you call him, *Ink boy?*"

"Ink boy served the spectral mistress. She lived in his ink. Then he put the ink in the mistress of the true bloodline, so now that other lives in her."

Tia almost said, *I don't think that's quite how that works.* "You say Ink boy's dead. How do you know that?"

"I hear things. We all do, we of the small bloodline. They do not think we listen or understand, but we do. A messenger came and told the master of the true bloodline –"

"Orcris Brendi," said Tia.

The girl nodded. "He is the master of the true bloodline. That is what we call him. You may call him whatever you wish. I dare not. Not my place."

"I can think of plenty of things to call him," said Tia. "What's that about a messenger comin' to tell him those folks were dead?"

The servant nodded. "The messenger told him in private. He said that the master's boopa the mistress was not to hear of it."

"So he found out about what the son was up to with his daughter, so he had the kid and his friends killed," Tia muttered, mostly to herself.

"No, no," said the servant. "You must not think that of the master. He was greatly saddened. He had had much good trading with that family and had hoped to do so again. But now he will not, because he cannot trade with the dead. He was very worried afterwards, as well…very, very worried. Ever since, he has had the mistress watched far more closely. He hires the guards for her body, like he has hired you. But the other mistress, the spectral mistress, she is crafty."

"How do you figure that family died?" said Tia.

"Knives in the dark," said the girl. Her eyes rolled around, at whatever lay in the shadows that surrounded them.

"Whose knives?" said Tia.

"Not knives."

"Wait, but you just said –"

"Not knives. Knives in the dark. That is how we say it, of how they died."

"Fine, so whose *knives in the dark* killed 'em?"

"No one knows," said the servant, sounding less patient now, like she wasn't the one being a confusing bitch. "That is what knives in the dark means. I thought that was a thing the woman who kills people would know."

"No," said Tia, "if I'm gonna kill someone, I don't know so much about makin' a fancy secret out of it. I prefer to stab 'em face to face where I can see 'em…like if someone's supposed to be tellin' me about how I'm in danger, but instead they keep wastin' my time and givin' me lip."

If the servant understood the threat, she didn't show it. "All I know is what I hear the men up top talk of, of the latest business on these continents. I only know what I have heard. They say that Ink boy died the most horrible death, one no one can make any sense of, torn to pieces by claws, as though some wild beast had found its way into his chambers. Within the same week, everyone within his family was also found dead, with bolts through their necks…but their deaths were not half so bad as that of those…policemen?"

"Wait, what?"

"The policemen. The ones who worked in the same place to which that…seeking policeman returned."

"*Seeking policeman?*"

"From the same shiny-skinned people as Ink boy, with whom the master did his business. Another of the shiny-skinned people come on this boat, and he sensed the *other mistress* within the mistress of the true bloodline, sensed her throughout all this boat, so he go crazy and –"

"Right, right," said Tia. "The guy who went crazy and jumped overboard. I know about that."

"No, not him. The other one, who bred with the other mistress."

"Right, but you just said he also killed some people while he was here."

"No, not here. Back where he went to report his findings. Where the other policemen stay."

"To their barracks. Or headquarters. Or wherever the fuck."

The creature nodded swiftly. "Yes, yes. There, there. The shiny-skinned people tried to keep others from knowing of it, from talking of it, but it still became known, in whispers, in ports where this boat has docked. The men above say that policeman…he went back to that…*head-quarters*…and when others came in the morning, they found that he had killed all the other policemen there. He had not only killed them. He had…opened them up, taken out their insides, and decorated that building with them, arranged them so that they hung everywhere, with the blood smeared on the walls, arranged so it looked like the picture that is inked upon the chest of the mistress of the true bloodline. Others found him there among the dead and the art he had made. When they asked him what it meant, he laughed as he used broken glass to open his own neck. That is what is said. Ever since we hear that, here on this boat, we hear of stranger dangers, in whatever port wherein we dock. That policeman was not the last whom the other mistress has swayed over, to whom she calls. It draws ever closer to our first mistress…because our second mistress calls out to it. All is a game to the second mistress…all that is within this world."

"So why are you tellin' me all this?" said Tia.

The girl's little hands shot up and squeezed Tia's arm. "Because you and your brother are of the people they call Schomites, yes?"

Tia resisted the urge to yank her arm free. "Yeah, that's us."

"It is said, creatures like the *other mistress* fear you Schomites…that you are the *only* fleshly beings that she fears. The mistress of the true bloodline, she is kind to us, we of the small bloodline, kinder than any other of the true bloodline. But while that other one runs wild within her, I fear for myself. I fear for my boopa upon this boat. I think you and your brother might…drive the other mistress away, so that our true, kind mistress might fully be with us once more. I hope you do it before the others who seek her come for her…

"Within their ranks, there are those who have learned of what she carries. They know that one of their gods dwells among us. I think they learned it from Ink boy before he died by their torture. They suspect more of it because of what the crazy policeman painted on the walls. They do not let themselves make war on us for her directly, because of the…the…*diplomacy*, its…its…*mutual benefits*. But they know she is here. They are coming for her. So are others. You have already met their agents. Yes, I smell it on you both."

"Why are you more scared of them, than you are of me and my brother?" said Tia.

"Do not misunderstand me, woman who kills people. I am *very* scared of you. I am more afraid of your brother."

Tia drew back. "Wait, what, Ketz? Naw, girl, seriously, Ketz is the last person in the world someone like you should be scared of. He's nicer than me, mostly 'cause he's always too stupid to be as mean as he needs to be, in times like –"

"Oh, no, woman who kills people. He is far more frightening than you, because he has bred with her. He is now one of the pieces in her game. You must watch him closely, or he will help her to –"

A mewling cry rose from within one of the boxes behind the girl. The servant rose, hurried over, and lifted a squirming bundle, rocking it and trying to calm it. In the fungal glow, Tia glimpsed what almost looked like a humanoid baby, squirming within a glistening larval sack.

The servant girl frantically rocked the churning entity in her arms. "I will tell you more at other times, woman who kills people. For now, please go! Get out of here, before they find you! If they find you here, they will…will…" The little red creature broke down sobbing along with her child. *"Do not trust your brother any longer! He is no longer himself. Now that he has bred with her, he is a piece in the game she plays!"*

Tia hurried back through the dirty servants' quarters and up the stairs. She squeezed herself through the tiny door and went quickly back to where Ketz waited.

TWELVE

"…So his buddy looks down at the two of them and goes, *Sweet Lands, man, what the hell you doin'?* The young brave looks up and says, *She's my new love. We're to be wed.* His buddy says, *Man, she's four days dead!* The brave looks down at the lady he's been fucking and says, *I thought she was a Spirelight.*"

Ketz slammed his glass down on the table and nearly sprayed his drink out of his nose. He laughed uncontrollably, for a whole minute, before he could speak again.

Across from him, Hallucia giggled more quietly, then reached across the table and stroked his arm. "There now, boy, breath. *Breath!* Don't kill yourself over it. It's not *that* funny."

The two of them sat within her quarters for luncheon. Ketz had made sure to sit so he could see the door behind her, along with all but one of the windows in this cabin. He caught his breath, sipped his drink, pounded his chest with his fist, and let out another long, gusty laugh. "No, it is. It really is."

One of those short, pixie-like servants came in and silently collected their bare luncheon platters. Ketz took several deep breaths, settled down, then looked at the servant. She lingered and looked at him.

Hallucia giggled at Ketz, then noticed the servant lingering. "Is anything wrong, Brili?"

"No, mistress," said the servant. "Not a thing. I apologize if I have intruded."

Ketz looked closer and recognized the one Tia had gone off with three days earlier, for their little chat. *Brili.* So that was the girl's name. All those little short-bred Ghestru servants looked alike to him. He still felt bad about that, whenever he caught himself looking at people of the stranger races that way. Back home, Silisha the blend lady had warned him against doing that, paying so little heed to the folks you met so *they all look alike to me.*

Silisha was a Schomite of his own breed, but she'd traveled with many of the stranger races, since she was younger than he'd been when he first discovered the trail, before he was born. "Among any folk who's humanoid," she'd always taught him, "never forget that they're closer to what you are than the soil of any lands beneath your feet, you hear me? You forget that, you'll find, it's all too easy to treat them like nothin' more than the tools in your travel pouch. That's what the unkind folks out there always do. The higher up they're born, the worse they're like to be, and they're the ones who'll call you a savage. Don't be like them…except always remember that you *are* the same as them, at the bottom of it all, no less than you're just like me and I'm just like you. That's good to remember for two big reasons. You know what those reasons are?"

Younger Ketz had thought her words over. "Because…you forget that people are people, so you shouldn't treat 'em like tools, 'cause otherwise you turn into an asshole, and you oughtn't be an asshole, 'less they're an asshole to you first?"

She'd slapped him across the top of the head for that. "*Hey.* Watch your language in this sacred hut here, boy."

"But you said earlier not to worry over that, how words was just words, how it didn't mean a good fuckin' hell what we say, long as we say what we —"

Silisha had slapped him again. "I know what I said out there, when we was off in the woods. We're seated across from each other now, boy, in this sacred hut, between mistress and student. Your choice of words matters more in here."

"Why?" Ketz had asked.

"Because your mistress says so, that's why. If you can't discipline yourself enough to talk like your mistress tells you to talk, how's she supposed to trust you discipline yourself with whatever dangerous power she imparts upon you, here during our teachings?"

"Okay." Ketz had gotten the point, at the time, or thought he had.

"And it's *don't give a flamin' sack of shit*, not *don't give a good fuckin' hell*. If you gotta talk raunchy, talk raunchy right." She'd winked at him. "And even if folks are a…even if they're jerks to you first, that still ain't call to be jerks to them, unless they leave you no other choice."

Ketz guessed he'd never taken to that part as well as Silisha would have liked. "So…I'm sorry," he'd said, "I don't know what the second lesson is."

"A lot of the folks you'll meet out there, of the so-called stranger races and besides, they *will* look at you as somethin' other, as a thing they can use. And they will, if you let 'em. When they do that, though, you gotta be ready to spot it. 'Cause that's when they're gonna underestimate you, forget that you're playin' your own game, with your own mind, just like they are. You remember that, while they don't, when they're aimin' to hit you, that's how you're gonna hit them first, so they don't see it comin'."

Silisha was now far away, back at home in the Nagga Mountains. For a while, everyone had expected Ketz to stick closer to home as her pupil, before he'd followed his sister along the bandit's trail. What would Silisha say if she saw him now, seated here like this? He had no idea. He relaxed as best he could and looked back and forth at the two women in the cabin, one seated across from him, the other collecting his leavings. They were both of the same *stranger race*, and the highborn one treated the small-bred creature with the same kindness she showed Ketz. He'd watched the other highborn Ghestru, and the rest of the crew for that matter. They treated the small-bred creatures as little more than livestock, just livestock that knew how to speak the same tongue.

It's in her best interest to treat you kindly. She knows you're protecting her because you're gettin' paid for it, but you also know things about her that she doesn't want anyone else to find out. She's been brought up to look at you and see something lower than livestock, as vermin. The longer they sat here chatting, though, the easier it was to forget all that. *No, I ain't the vermin here*, he reminded himself. *I'm the predator closing in on the prey. That's the job I came here to do. She called me a barbarian when we first met…and she was right. Best remember that.*

The servant girl still peered at him uneasily. He reminded himself that the highborn Ghestru had intentionally bred their slaves from their lower classes, to produce these stunted, subservient mouse-like creatures…and in doing so, had let themselves grow all the more complacent, underestimating them. The servant now lifted the painted porcelain pitcher, found it still heavy, with a little less than half its original contents.

"Leave that, if you don't mind," said Ketz.

"Yes, yes," said Hallucia, "but have another on the ready before long. This one's evaporating all too swiftly." She topped off her crystal glass. "And fetch a glass for yourself if you like."

"Oh, Mistress," Brili murmured, "I…do not think the master would like to see that."

"Do you see him here watching us?" Hallucia winked at the girl.

Brili's eyes sparkled. Her mouth slowly twitched and stretched into a nervous smile, as though working its way free of a series of complicated knots. "Perhaps I will later, Mistress. There is still much for me to do. You forget that I am smaller than you, so the waking-dream water overwhelms my head faster."

Ketz lounged back in his chair, feigning stupid, civilized indolence, and said to the servant girl, "Say, uh, Brili, you ain't seen my sister, the mistress's other dirt-worshiper guard, while you been out and about, have you?"

"I have not, sir, save when noticing her here and there,

abroad from her room, at her own menial duties. It is not my place to pry into the business of the woman who kills people."

"Well, if you run across her, tell her to come see me when she gets the chance."

The servant girl walked out. Ketz gazed across the table at Hallucia. She smiled back at him. The longer Ketz spent in her company, the easier it grew to not to give a fuck. It had been a while since he'd felt this relaxed. He gazed into her deep, dark eyes…*not glowing yellow eyes*, he kept noticing.

No, you don't want *to see those eyes again, remember? They bring nothing but bad news.*

He still sometimes recalled the lust with which those glittery yellow eyes had looked at him, ignited within himself, so he searched her dark eyes for any trace of the same interest. He couldn't help it. The longer he was around her – *the real her* – the more he liked her. She wasn't stuck up like her pa, or like she'd seemed at first honestly. Twice or thrice, he swore he caught her looking back at him invitingly, but always when they were too surrounded by her kinsmen for him to try his luck.

"What were we just talking about?" said Hallucia.

"That yarn you just spun me about my own race," Ketz chuckled. "You're one sick, twisted little bitch, you know that?"

"Hey, *I* didn't make that joke up! I first heard that from someone back in…S'cria, I'm pretty sure?"

"S'cria…That's one of them big stretches of land over on your people's native continent, am I right?"

"Countries," said Hallucia. "I think you mean *countries*…when you talk about big stretches of land."

"Sure. Right."

"Anyway, yes, S'cria is a little island nation, off the lower coast of what people on your continent would pronounce as South Ghestruland." She shook her head. "Gods, I'm sorry. I don't even know if that's a Spirelight joke or a Schomite joke I just told! My bad impersonation of a Schomite accent must drive you crazy, too."

"Naw, it don't sound so bad, for an impression of a brain-damaged third-octosphere Lepod, anyhow. I'm gonna guess, though, whoever told you that joke never met an actual Schomite *or* Spirelight."

She frowned. "You know, there *are* Schomites who live in Ghestruland."

"No, actually, I didn't know that."

"In some of our countries, sure. The swirl of their skin doesn't look anything like yours, though. In some of the more rural Ghestruland nations, there are breeds of Schomite who've been settled there for so many generations, they've evolved and become interfertile with the native races."

"What's that word mean?" said Ketz.

Her dark eyes lingered on his. "It means there are Schomites and Ghestru who can have children between them. They've given birth to splendid, beautiful new hybrid races."

Ketz blanched and drew back. "Wait, hold on. What did you say a second ago about *interfertile?*"

She glowered and spoke quieter. "Relax, Ketz. No, I said *other* breeds of your race, breeds of which you certainly aren't one, trust me. *So no, when you fucked her, there's no chance of you having gotten me with child.* There, are you happy now?" She looked away and muttered, "I almost wish there was."

"Hey," he said softly, "what do you mean by that?" His hand slid across the table and settled on hers. He noticed his own heart pounding. Damnit.

She jerked her hand back. "Because if it turned out you'd gotten me pregnant – which you can't – once Daddy found out about that, he'd be obligated to cast me out on my own, across whatever shore we next landed on, along with you. A man of his stature, he couldn't get away with having a daughter who'd been knocked up with some dirt-worshiper's baby. But he's still my daddy. I know him. There's no way he'd see me put to death, the way his station demanded. He'd have no choice but to cast me out into the world, with no one to look after me but you and that asshole sister of yours. That way, maybe I could finally start my life over, with my own ideas, not in the box he's kept me in my whole life."

"Yeah," said Ketz, "you, me, my sister, and that little bastard or bitch we made between us, plus that glowstick god you still got inside you. Even if your pa let you go, he might not let me or Tia go. Anyhow, what kinda new *freedom of a life* you think you'd get out of that?"

"I don't know," she snapped, "because it's not going to happen! It's just the sort of thing I daydream about, when there's nothing else for me but daydreams. Same way that, no, I'm not gonna take you by the hand and invite you back into that bed over there so you can fuck this body except with me in it instead of her. So if you want us to be friends, quit looking at me like you think it's gonna happen! *And stop glancing at my bed like you're still getting ideas!*"

Ketz blinked. It was true, his gaze had drifted absently towards the bed when she'd first mentioned it. Now, though, he lingered on it for another reason. He'd spotted something that wasn't quite right. Just what that was, he didn't yet know. He sniffed the air, and his suspicions solidified. For now, he made himself look at Hallucia again.

"Okay, fine, fine!" He flung up his hands, then thought quickly about how to change the subject. "How many different kinds of Schomites have you ever met, anyway?"

"Promise you won't be offended by my answer?"

"I been *offended* by anything else you just said, you weird, twitchy bitch?"

"Fine. I just like to be respectful. That…other one doesn't, I know, but I do. The truth is, I think I've seen more breeds of Schomites than most Schomites even know exist. You know, in Valaka, there are even Schomites whose skin changes color, to match their surroundings."

"Huh? You mean so they look just like whatever people they're minglin' with?"

"No, I mean like whatever forest, mountain, field, or wherever they are, their skin actually changes color, to blend in with *that*, so they become practically invisible."

"Sure sounds handy," said Ketz. "I'd love to figure out how to do that."

She giggled. "I don't think it works that way, silly."

The cabin door opened and Tia stepped in. Ketz peered up at her over Lady Hallucia's shoulders. He hadn't even heard her approach.

"Reporting for duty," said Tia. She came up next to the table, picked up the pitcher, sniffed it, then peered at Ketz. "Are you drinkin' on the job?"

Ketz leaned back in his chair. "Sis, relax, will you? I'm just washin' down lunch, is all."

"Well, you're welcome to the rest of…whatever this is." She sniffed the pitcher again, made a face, and set it back down. "Anyhow, it's time for me to take over."

"Good to see you, Tia," said Lady Hallucia. "Just as I've been getting tired of all this male company."

"Good for you," said Tia. "We still ain't sisters."

"She ain't…the other one right now," said Ketz.

"I can tell that, dumbass," said Tia.

"Can we go up on deck, Tia?" said Lady Hallucia. "I've been cooped up inside enough for one day. I feel like looking at your gorgeous countryside and smelling the river air."

"In a minute," said Tia. "I need a private word with your other bodyguard here."

Ketz followed Tia out into the hallway, shut the door behind him, glanced and listened up and down the corridor to make sure they were alone, then said, "Y'know, you don't gotta talk mean to her."

"Better than you lettin' her talk to you like you're lettin' her jerk you around by the dick. That's how it sounds, from what Brili's been tellin' me."

"Who?"

"That girl I got an in with among the servants, no thanks

to you."

"Yeah, good to hear how well you two have been gettin' along. She tell you anything else useful, other than how she's been keepin' her nose up my ass, apparently?"

"Look, you leave her alone about that. Brili, I mean, her and her kids."

"She's got kids?" said Ketz. "I...didn't know that."

"No, you wouldn't, 'cause you've had your nose up the Lady Hallucia's ass this whole time. Me, when I ain't catchin' a few winks of sleep, I've been around those special short-bred servants they keep. Been watchin' and listenin' to 'em. They all fuck a lot, and they pop out kids a lot, and I mean *a lot*. You know how the meatskins are known for bearin' 'em so quick, like in just a couple months? Well, they've bred these servants to pop 'em out even quicker, like over one month, or even days sometimes. They've had to, 'cause a lot of 'em die young, while out here seein' to their master's whims. So they have to keep themselves in good supply. It's...gross, to have to watch how they all go about it. How they spawn and die. Hell, Brili showed me her *boopa*. Damn thing was like a sack of larva a couple days ago. Now it's already walkin' around on two feet. Thing's already callin' me *Auntie Tia*. You believe that lizardshit?"

"Aw, ain't that cute," said Ketz.

"Fuck you."

"No, seriously, what else you picked up on from 'em?"

Tia sighed. "Not as much as I'd like, but I been thinkin' about what Brili told me, about how there's bound to be Spirelight agents out on the hunt, who know about that girl and the god she's got on her back. Then I got to thinkin' about those ones ridin' in, in disguise, the ones we tangled with back in Belcrasche. You forgotten about that shit?"

"I wish I could," said Ketz. "I'm still wakin' up from bad dreams, where I still feel Skids' blood splattered all over me. I still keep worryin' about that wife and kids he mentioned before he died."

"Yeah, well, right now, I'm more worried about our problems, *like how that fucker Minquo might'a just dropped us into the middle of a damn civil war about to bust out between the Spirelights.*"

"I don't follow you, sis."

"So maybe quit thinkin' with your dick for a minute. Look, those glowsticks who tried to sneak into Belcrasche all painted up, tryin' to get to the *Arlash*, those weren't really outlaws. That's what they were supposed to look like, if they got taken alive, but they weren't. Now listen, Priest King Kalesha, she's real popular on this continent, but not everyone likes her."

"Yeah, I ain't forgotten about that asshole sheriff."

"Me neither. From what I hear, the Spirelights the rest of the world over have even worse things to say about her, especially most of the high-rankin' somebodies in their other Priest Kingdoms. They think she's a blasphemer, out to bring their whole race down…or just some uppity woman in charge, like that prick sheriff thought. But she's got plenty of her own powerful supporters among 'em, too, enough so she's lasted this long. If her enemies know about this renegade god, so do her and her friends. That makes us the two little dumbasses standin' guard between her and a whole multidimensional shit fight brewin' within their whole damn empire."

"Man," said Ketz, "and here I thought we'd finally gotten clear of all that politics lizardshit."

"So which side you think Minquo's on, huh, and what's his angle?"

Ketz considered the question, then glanced back at Lady Hallucia's door. "I don't know, but I got a hunch about where to start lookin'."

"Do tell."

"I ain't sayin' shit else 'til I got more to show for it. I also recall our Lady Hallucia in there sayin' she wants you to take her for a stroll around the deck, up top. I think you should do that. It'd be nice."

"Oh, it would, huh?"

Ketz leaned close to Tia's ear and whispered, "Yeah, 'cause I want a chance to poke around in her quarters without anyone watchin'."

"Yeah, I can do that," said Tia. "*Please* tell me this is about more than you gettin' a chance to sniff her undergarments."

"Nah," said Ketz, "I wasn't gonna do that 'til afterwards."

THIRTEEN

Ketz stood at his post 'til the ladies promenaded together out of the room, down the hallway and around the corner. He tried to get a look at Hallucia's eyes, to see if they were deep black or bright yellow. She didn't glance his way. Tia did, with a look that said, *I'm trusting your judgement right now, so don't fuck this up.*

I won't, sis, his eyes tried to tell her before she and Hallucia vanished around the corner.

He steeled himself, looked around to make sure no one else was coming, then ducked back into Lady Hallucia's room. He shut the door slowly and noiselessly, then walked to the back end of the bed. He squatted, slid his arms beneath the frame, and lifted it as quietly as possible. That noxious smell now tickled his nose thicker than ever.

He twisted the bed around. The back legs moaned against the floorboards, so he winced and drew up rigid. The hallway outside remained silent. That didn't mean none of the servants were out there, he reminded himself. Those weird little fuckers could move quieter than him and Tia on the open trail. He didn't like being stuck on a boat with critters who were better at stealth than him. For now, he slowly lowered the bed back to the floor and surveyed what he'd uncovered.

There was nothing under the bed but a long, rectangle-shaped sheet of wood set across the floor. That's what he'd thought he'd seen when he'd glanced sideways from the table. He pulled the board to the side. As he'd expected, it slid away loosely. Beneath it, he saw exactly what he'd expected to find, and yet...not.

"Trosola," he muttered, "what the fuck have you been up to, you weird bitch?"

The hole in the floor loomed blackly. The boards didn't look like they'd been sawed, but rather torn apart by infernal claws that had left the edges jagged and burnt black, yawning like sharp teeth. As he peered into the blackness, Ketz's next thought was, *You put your dick in the thing that did this. You fell asleep in its arms.* He lowered his ear cautiously to the hole. No sound came from it but faintly moaning wind. He willed his eyes to adjust to the blackness. Little by little, he made out the network of support beams. The source of the smell was down there somewhere, far below. Ketz eyed the inner structure 'til he made out the spots he could use as footholds. From there, he felt around the charred edges, 'til he found proper grips that wouldn't tear his palms to shreds with splinters.

He swung around and lowered himself slowly into the gaping maw. His boots settled on the nearest support beam. He let his eyes adjust further, then looked around 'til he spotted the next spot where he needed to jump. He let go, kicked off, and free-fell for a breathless instant, twisting midair like a cat, so his feet landed on two far apart parallel beams. It strained his groin-muscles a little, landing and planting his feet like that. The drop had been longer that it looked. 'Til now, he'd gotten used to the constant, steady bobbing of the ship around him. Now as he balanced here precariously, he felt more aware of it than ever. He swayed back and forth, then caught hold of some crisscrossing overhead beams and steadied himself. When he looked up, the light from Hallucia's bedroom already seemed impossibly far away. Some far fainter source of light shown from below.

He swung himself around so both his feet planted on the same beam. Then he hopped backwards, dropped, caught the next beam, and lowered himself 'til his feet found another perch, and so forth. His limbs already throbbed exhaustedly, like he'd been fighting for hours, trading blows with some bigger, stronger opponent.

The lower he climbed, the darker everything grew around him. The air stank down here, and not just with the smell he'd come looking for. He went deathly quiet and still, then let go with one hand and found his sword-grip. Nothing moved down here except him. Any dangers awaiting him, he suddenly sensed, weren't the kind he could use a sword on. An icy flash pulsed from the core of his being, threatening to turn into panic, so he wanted to scramble out of this. He looked up and saw that the last beam he'd let go of was far out of reach. Retreating wasn't an option, so he let the panic roll through his nerves 'til it settled into numbness.

Through the darkness, the faint light below had grown more distinct. So had the smell he was following...enough that he finally realized where he'd last encountered it. His heart hammered against his ribcage, strong enough that he struggled to hear his surroundings over it. Not too far down, he saw a lot of boxes stacked on top of each other, in front of the tiny round porthole windows.

Ketz realized where he was. This was the ship's cargo hold. He lowered himself from the last rung, dropped and landed on his feet, in front of a surprisingly humble arrangement of crates that had been set aside from the rest.

The utter silence of the cargo hold turned his blood to ice. Before, the silence had felt like his ally. Now it taunted him, closing in maliciously through the murk. His hand settled again on his sword. He wanted to draw the blade, to slash at the darkness 'til it opened like a meaty, pulsing wound, one that would bleed answers he understood. No, he realized, that's what this darkness down here wanted him to do, to lose his head and collapse beneath its weight.

He looked around 'til he could see the whole hold clearly. Part of him still *wished* some external threat would jump out at him, just so everything could be simple again.

What lay in front of him was the same stack of boxes he and Tia had first encountered in that wagon they'd hid in to get through the town gates, before everything went crazy. His palm nudged the edge of the nearest crate. It wasn't nailed shut. The lid slid away easily. He peered inside. All he saw was moldering soil. He pawed and dug through it, looking for something, anything other than...well, just a box of dirt. It was tightly packed around the sides, but the middle was loose, as though freshly churned. His palm brushed a tangled, barky vine. The vine moved. It slithered through the loose soil and coiled languidly around his searching forearm. Then it tightened and dragged his whole arm in deeper and deeper. Whenever he thrashed against it, it only tightened worse.

"Hey, now...what the fuck...*Hey, what the fuck?*"

His free hand darted for his sword. That's when the vine in the dirt yanked him so hard that his chest struck the rim of the crate. His jaw clenched and the cords in his neck bulged as he heaved backwards. The harder he fought, the more it tightened.

"Just relax, Ketz," whispered a soothing voice, from...just where the hell *was* it coming from? Behind him? The air all around him? Within the box? "Just let it happen, baby. You already know the alternative, don't you, my sweet boy? You find hell no matter where you go, don't you? All those other girls you find there afterwards, they'd *judge* you if you told them the whole truth, wouldn't they, about who you really are? I already know, Ketz, and I'll never judge you. You can be your true self forever...as long as you serve me."

The moldering aroma of the alien soil wafted up thicker than ever around him, as the rest of the world swam away. Other scents now steamed up through it, no longer stale, but bubbling and churning with wild, wicked life. Limber, impish phantoms pranced around him, through the haze behind his eyes. They looped their arms through his before spiriting him off into their ancient dance.

FOURTEEN

Trosola rising naked from within the fetid soil, with slimy roots and moldy dark clods clinging to her soft, tattooed skin. Trosola, her arms snaking around his neck and pulling him down 'til his whole body sank into it with her.

Was that how it happened? He seemed to remember it that way, but it was already so far away and long ago. Was that how he'd gotten here?

He no longer felt the boards of the *Arlash* beneath his feet, but rather the beaten soil of a winding road through an ancient swamp, churning with rot and bubbling, gibbering life. It snaked out at him from either side of the trail, caressing him with slick, velvety feelers that ignited his nerves with obscene sensations.

He liked it here. The sweat that bubbled from his pores seemed to taste the soupy humidity of the swamp as it tasted him. His feet were bare, which was good. So was the rest of him, he noticed. That was even better. Back home, Silisha had reminded him constantly of the healing power of bare skin on the bare lands.

Whenever you're at your lowest, whenever life feels most hopeless, like you've forgotten who you are and all the evil darkness won't let you remember, take off your shoes, go outside and press your hands and bare feet to the lands. Feel it flow up through you, feel it draw out of you all the evil darkness clogging you up, and you'll remember what you need to remember.

He'd been cooped up on that damn boat for less than a week, but it had felt so much longer, weighted down by highborn finery. Free of all that, he felt born anew, as this sweetly poison swamp absorbed him, let him absorb it, invigorating him with something even the forests of his mountain homeland had denied him. Silisha would probably call the sensations that ruled this swamp evil darkness, but whatever.

Some luminous glow cast beams of light that were sharp as blades, through the leaning trees and hanging moss, drawing him towards some unseen point ahead. The sweet, sultry voice that beckoned him didn't echo so much from the source as *from within the spilling light itself*, which seemed to echo more and more from deep within his own head, the further he walked. If he leapt at those beams of light, it seemed, he could bite into them, drink their glow like sweet sap-wine.

Throughout the nighttime swamp around him, flames of green and blue spouted from the marsh, around which creatures that may or may not have once been humanoid thrashed and splashed and capered, galvanized by the merciless ecstasy of the song that lived in the glow...*the song of Trosola.* They couldn't stop themselves from dancing, even when their muscles collapsed from exhaustion, any more than Ketz's rising, slavering thirst would let him stand still, as he stalked down the trail...

Some of the dancers crashed against each other so hard that their bodies split each other open like fists rupturing faces, so gleaming bones showed beneath the skin. They screamed like you'd expect people to do from such injuries, yet they couldn't stop dancing.

What's that noise he's making?

That voice echoed not from the glow ahead, but from somewhere in the darkness at his back. He snarled over his shoulder and hurried faster, or tried. The path seemed to have turned to deep mud, so his legs pumped harder to take each step.

It sounds like there's some beast inside him trying to get out. Oh by the stars, get back!

Ah, calm down. That's just how he gets when he's wakin' up. Step back and give him some air, will you? He's comin' around!

The first voice was male. The second was female. The glow receded through the branches. So did the swamp flames, plunging him back into the blackness behind his eyelids. His sore frame stretched out across a soft mattress. A softer hand stroked his face.

"Ketz? Ketz, wake up, please!"

That sounded like the voice he'd been following, except she wasn't singing anymore. Her voice no longer taunted him with heedless wantonness. He wished it would, except it already drew him back towards the more familiar physical realm, stirring up nobler impulses he'd forgotten to miss.

He opened his eyes and recognized Hallucia's quarters. She sat on the bed next to him. Orcris Brendi stared down at him severely. The last of the swampy, fragrant dream fled his senses, leaving nothing but cold, stark reality.

This was not good. Except Hallucia still had her clothes on, and so did he. The next shape he spotted staring down at him was Tia. She looked even more pissed off than Orcris Brendi. With growing confusion, he realized that Brendi didn't look pissed off at all.

Ketz bolted upright. His head swam so he nearly crashed backwards again. At least he saw that the bed had been moved back into its original position.

That hole in the floor's still there, though, right beneath me.

He still smelled what lay at the bottom of that hole, down in the cargo hold.

"Take it easy, brother," said Tia in a hard, unreadable voice. "Whoever that asshole was, he ain't onboard anymore."

"What the..."

Tia's right eye and left upper lip twitched in a just-so rhythm. No one else here would notice, but it told Ketz loud and clear, *Shut the fuck up. Let me do the talking.*

Ketz grimaced with one side of his face so she knew he got the message. He rubbed at his scalp. His hand was still dirty, he noticed. The smell of that weird soil no longer enticed him. In fact, he wanted very desperately to get some clean water and wash it off. He looked at Hallucia. Or was it Trosola seated on the bed with him now? She'd turned partly away, her face lowered so he couldn't get a good look at her eyes.

"You say this…*stowaway*, as you call him," said Orcris Brendi, "he was a Schomite, like the two of you?"

Stowaway? thought Ketz. *What stowaway?*

"I already told you, *no*, not like us," said Tia. "He had way bluer skin, like someone from the far north…a Wallution maybe."

"Indeed," said Orcris Brendi. "From what I understand, the Wallutions are not a warlike people…not like you hill-dwelling barbarians."

"Yeah, well, it takes all kinds wherever you go," said Tia. "Anyhow, I don't know that I'd call that coward *warlike*. I caught up in time to see him get in that lucky swing, got Ketz upside the head. Ketz *still* managed to whack him good in the arm before goin' down." She smiled at Ketz as though to say *That's my brother, always on his game 'til the end.* Ketz did his best to smile back as though in affirmation. "Then the asshole saw me comin' and he dove right through that porthole window. Way those waves looked when I stuck my head out, I don't think we'll be seein' that guy again."

"I should certainly hope not," said Orcris Brendi. "More so, however, I hope there aren't more stowaways like him skulking about this ship."

"If there are, Tia and I'll find 'em," Ketz shot in. "Don't worry about that." As soon as he said it, he glanced at Tia, expecting her to give him a dirty look for speaking up. Instead, she nodded in agreement. Her face gave nothing else away, in their private language or otherwise.

"That's not what worries me," said Orcris Brendi. "I'm more alarmed that after a threat presented itself to my daughter, you *both* ran off chasing it, rather than one of you remaining to guard her."

"Daddy, I already told you," Hallucia pleaded. "Tia had

me lock myself in my room, after making certain it was empty, before joining Ketz in the chase." Her voice indeed sounded like Hallucia's...not that other voice Ketz had first heard coming out of her mouth, the one that kept leading him around through the infernal dreamland into which she pulled him whenever he slept.

"Yeah," said Tia, "that's why I had to run to catch up with Ketz and that guy. I hadn't been held up lookin' to your daughter's safety, we might've taken him alive, been able to get some answers out of him, about why he was here and what he was up to."

Ketz felt his blood quicken. Tia was volunteering too many details to her made-up story, where no one had asked for them. Neither of the twins were investigators by trade, but they'd spent enough time working for Captain Gris to pick up a few tricks. One thing that had stuck with Ketz was how people got themselves caught lying under pressure. Now he worried that Tia was walking herself right into that trap. Orcris Brendi's stony expression did nothing to reassure him.

Orcris Brendi turned his eyes on Ketz. "Indeed. And do tell, how was this *cowardly amateur* able to so easily best a seasoned warrior like yourself?"

Ketz leaned forward, groaned, and rubbed at his scalp. That part wasn't an act. His head really did hurt like he'd been hit in it. "Man, I don't know. It was dark down there in the hold. I don't even remember closing with the guy, let alone when he managed to hit me."

"I do hope your injury's not too severe," said Orcris Brendi. "Perhaps it's rendered you unfit for your duties?" 'Til now, the old windbag had sounded merely suspicious. Now there was an unmistakable note of a threat in his voice.

Ketz held his gaze. "I'm fit enough." He noticed he wasn't wearing his sword. He looked around and spotted it leaning against the bed, still in its scabbard.

"The cargo hold..." Orcris Brendi rubbed thoughtfully at his chin. "I wonder why this miscreant of ours would run down there of all places?"

"I don't know," said Ketz. He stood up, grabbed his sword, and reattached it to his belt. "Maybe that's where he's been hidin' out. Maybe you ought'a have some of your men search the hold for any more like him."

"Are you presuming to give me orders, young man?"

"Just makin' a suggestion."

"Indeed. Did you not offer, only a moment ago, to do such honors yourself?"

"Man, my head was still all out of sorts, okay? Now I got my head together, and it's your daughter's safety I'm rememberin' now."

The old man's face softened. "Perhaps you're right. I shall have it done." He looked to Hallucia. "Tell me, my dear. Do you still feel safe, with these two responsible for your well-being?"

"I do, Daddy," she said. Suddenly her eyes met Ketz's, in a way that startled him. At least he now saw for sure that her eyes were her own. He felt a twinge of disappointment. Maybe more than a twinge. "I trust no one better, as a matter of fact."

"Very well, then." Orcris Brendi looked at the twins with his usual haughty imperialism, though now with a strange discomfort, like his next words put a nasty taste in his mouth. "Thank you, both of you. My…apologies for doubting your resolve."

"Don't mention it," said Tia. "We're used to assholes underestimatin' us."

"Yes, well…If you'll all excuse me, I have much to see to." He turned and walked out.

FIFTEEN

Ketz followed Orcris Brendi out of the room and caught up with him halfway down the hallway. "Hey, Mister Brendi, wait up."

Orcris Brendi turned sharply and stared. "Yes?"

Ketz wasn't sure what Ghestru master-servant etiquette he'd violated this time. "I guess your daughter told you all about how she came by my sister and me, at the police barracks and such."

Brendi nodded. "She did. So did my other informants."

"I guess you know about where and how we got ourselves arrested, by that wagon manned by those imposters transportin' a shipment to you."

"I am aware of that, yes. If I understand correctly, you yourselves had stowed away amongst the cargo when the altercation began."

"That's right. We didn't know at the time that was your cargo. We had our own reasons for wantin' to get into town unobserved."

The old man loomed in slightly over Ketz. "Be careful, young man. For now, you have earned my goodwill, and my trust. Do not think that either are irreproachable."

Maybe the old bastard would have liked it better if Ketz had faked intimidation. Ketz had no time for such games. "I figured, sir. That's why I'm bein' honest, so it can't be said otherwise."

"So say what you have to say."

"What's in those crates that were on that wagon? Who did you buy 'em from, and who are you sellin' 'em to?"

Orcris Brendi huffed indignantly. "I fail to see how any of

my business transactions are your concern."

"Call it a hunch. Call it my hill-beast instincts. My point is, whoever those imposters were, there's a good chance they had somethin' to do with whoever you hired me to protect your daughter from."

"Has there been some misunderstanding between us, young man? I don't recall hiring you to conduct a police investigation."

"*Excuse me, sir*, but whether you *saw fit to tell us* so or not, it's gotten pretty damn obvious you hired my sister and me to protect your daughter from more than just common troublemakers. So yeah, I'd say protectin' her absolutely entails *conductin' a police investigation.*"

"Your boldness continues to astound me, young Ketz. I confess I'd given you more credit for tact than that sharp-tongued sister of yours."

"Normally, you'd be right. The more shit I see not addin' up, though, with me stuck in the middle of it, the less time I feel like I have for…what was that word again?"

"Tact." Orcris Brendi folded his arms across his chest. "So you believe yourself qualified to conduct such an investigation, do you?"

"Mister, I've served with the smartest detective the Spirelight International Police ever saw as my commanding officer. It'd be a damn shame if I hadn't learned a thing or three about that line of work."

"You are full of surprises, I'll grant you that."

It was all Ketz could do not to roll his eyes. "So now we got that out of the way, I understand you've…had some disagreements that have made things awkward between you and Spirelights lately."

Orcris Brendi hissed, "Who told you that?"

"Who do you think?" Ketz cast an eye over his shoulder, back towards Hallucia's door.

"Careful, young Ketz. If you mean to say this information has come from my daughter, it would seem you've grown more familiar with her than I like."

"She's been spendin' half her wakin' hours with no one to talk to but me and those weird little miniature meatskins y'all breed as slaves. If she wants to talk at me about what's on her mind, it ain't my place to tell her to shut up."

"It's a relief to know that you remember your place, over that much at least. Take heed, though, I am *not* the decadent, oblivious, spoiled fool you take me for. Do not pretend that all of this is professional to you. I have seen that you care for my daughter, and she for you. I do not approve of it, and yet…if it fortifies your dedication to your duties, all the better. I still hope that this has not clouded your judgement regarding —"

"I get it," said Ketz. "You're not a complete moron. About those crates."

Orcris Brendi's eyes drifted reflectively. "I've been thinking on that. I would of course have to look at the logs to be sure, but…I believe the boxes of which you speak were commissioned for delivery by someone in Tatelle. What is it, young Ketz? You look suddenly flustered."

"I'm…just tryin' to remember where that is, sir," Ketz said without looking up.

"It's the next major port at which we're scheduled to dock, in less than three days' time." Orcris Brendi rubbed at his chin. "Now that you mention it, it *was* rather peculiar how that arrangement all came together. The petition came to me postmarked from some establishment in the province called…the Spine-Rat, promising me a lucrative sum for the procuration and delivery upon the agreed-upon date, of five boxes of…*Trosolin soil.* Now, that name…*Trosolin*, it's not a place I'm familiar with, and I thought I'd sailed to every land throughout the eight winds. And yet, when I put out the word of the request, I almost immediately received word from some wealthy, reclusive, apparently quite eccentric distributor known as…oh…what was the name? Oh, yes, *Ouqnim.* At least that was the name given by his representatives with whom I met.

Strange name, stranger than *Trosolin*, even. In any case, he offered to sell me the requested goods at a tenth of the price I'd been promised the prospective buyer. How could I refuse, when…"

As Orcris Brendi prattled on, Ketz repeated that name, *Ouqnim, Ouqnim, Ouqnim* over and over in his mind, 'til it hit him. "Shit," he exclaimed.

"What is it?" said Orcris Brendi.

"I don't know yet," Ketz lied, when in fact he'd just figured out that Ouqnim was Minquo said backwards. "Call it another hill-beast hunch or instinct. All I know is, I've grown up surrounded by the kind of magic your kind probably think is just superstition, but it's real as shit in our land. People get killed when they don't heed it. If I was you, I'd have your crew haul every last one of those boxes out of the hold and pitch 'em over the side."

"You would have me break my word to such a lucrative buyer, based on your *hunch*…on your *hill-beast superstitions?*"

Ketz nodded. "Based on my *concern for your daughter's safety*, yeah, that's exactly what I'm tellin' you to do."

Orcris Brendi studied Ketz loftily, then said, "No."

"What?"

"You heard me, young man. I'm not about to jeopardize my reputation as a businessman on your hunch. I shall look into this matter and provide whatever details may assist you. Beyond that, remember your place, and don't stick any of your beastly little appendages where they don't belong. Are we clear, young man?"

"Crystal clear, your Grace." Ketz drew himself upright in what he was pretty sure was a proper soldier's pose.

"If you must insist on pretending to address me with proper respect, please call me *your Excellency*, instead of *your Grace*. You're not serving under the…what your kind call the *glowsticks* anymore…*beast*." With that, Orcris Brendi turned, strode down the hall, turned the corner, and stomped up the stairs to the upper deck.

Ketz huffed, turned, and walked back towards Hallucia's room. Tia was already standing there, leaning against the crook of the hallway.

"How long have you been standin' there listenin'?" he said.

She folded her arms across her chest. "Long enough to know that you're no Captain Gris. What the hell have you gotten us into?"

"*Me?* What are you talkin' about?"

"Why don't you tell me what you were doin' down in that cargo hold?"

"I…remembered how those boxes smelled, in that wagon, I put that together with that secret hole Hallucia's got in her floor under her bed, so I…went and…"

"I'm more worried about you and that other *hole* she's got, the one you been pokin' around in, while you're *in* her bed."

"Hey, keep your voice down about that," Ketz hissed. "Besides, that's none of your business."

"*It's my business*, when you start talkin' to the boss like you're forgettin' why we're here."

"I ain't forgotten," Ketz growled. As he said it, though, he tasted the air of the swamp on his breath…the swamp from his dreams.

"Look," said Tia, "while I was takin' her for a walk, she got all weird, managed to slip away from me for a second, and next thing I know, she's lookin' at me with those strange, *other* eyes of hers. She grabbed me by the hand, dragged me along, told me she knew you were in trouble, that we had to go find you before it was too late."

"You're tellin' me Trosola appeared before you?" Ketz exclaimed breathlessly before he knew he was about to.

"I don't know," said Tia. "All I know is we found you in the hold, in front of that stack of boxes with one of the lids pried off, you sprawled out unconscious in front of it, with your trousers undone and your dick hangin' out."

Ketz grimaced. "I took my dick out?"

"Someone did," said Tia. "I'm the one who had to put it away for you. You owe me one for that. Anyhow, me and…Hallucia, or whatever the fuck her real name is…we had to haul your unconscious ass back up all those flights of stairs, to her room. We couldn't do that without anyone seein' us, so we had to make up that story right quick, about some intruder attackin' her, where you played the hero. I had to go back down there, too, break one of them porthole windows, just in case anyone really looks into it before we have a chance to get off this boat."

"I ain't interested in bein' the hero," said Ketz distantly. "Not in this world."

"In this world?" said Tia. "C'mon, Ketz, what's goin' on with you?"

Before he could answer, the crewmen's feet on the deck above started thundering back and forth frantically, all over the place.

Some watch-boy started banging on a bell, shouting "*All hands on deck, all hands on deck! We're under attack! River pirates ahoy!*"

SIXTEEN

Something big crashed into the side of the hull, like a giant, sucking gut-punch, with Tia and Ketz standing in the center of those guts. The world spun and tilted around them. They braced their legs, grabbed the walls and each other to stay on their feet. Overhead, howls of animalistic bloodlust erupted and echoed down through the bowels of the *Arlash*. So did the rushing tromp of fresh boots, the metallic shriek of blades ripping free of scabbards, of bodies crashing into each other.

Ketz's temples throbbed and his heart pounded. He glanced grimly at his sister, took a deep breath, and rasped, "We gotta get up there."

He drew his blade. The strange, thin, supple metal quivered and hummed from his fist. He started down the hallway, towards the stairs that led up to the deck.

Tia grabbed his shoulder. "No, we don't."

"What are you —"

"You heard the old man. Our job is to guard that little bitch in there, nothin' else." She cocked her head at the door. "We stay right down here, hold this hallway, and kill whatever comes down those stairs."

She stepped up next to him and drew her own blade out into a high guard. There was enough space between them in the hallway to make it work as a defensive position. Still, the big boat kept tilting and bobbing, so they had to constantly readjust their stance. Ketz slid forward into a low crouch. His blade bobbed thirstily in front of him. Howls of combat echoed down, of men throwing their lives away in panicked frenzy. With it came the fresh, hot scent of spilling blood. He shared a look with his sister as his senses sharpened for what came next. They fixed their eyes at the distant stairway with grim anticipation.

Before long, the first visitor came downstairs. Tia and Ketz braced to meet his attack, then recognized him as one of the security crew. He stumbled down the first few steps, his hands clamped over a dark red patch that spread from his stomach. Then he tripped, spilled forward, and came rolling and bouncing off the steps. A stream of spilt entrails slithered behind him, leaving a slimy dark smear in their wake. After him, there thundered down three pasty-skinned, sharp-toothed men. Their rotting-fish stench hit him before he could take in the full sight of them. That probably had something to do with the vests they wore, which were cut from scaly fish-hides...not treated like leather, more like they'd been ripped straight off some big water beast, then crudely cut and stitched like any old fabric, then thrown on just so, still dripping and reeking of blood and guts. Through those open vests, the men's ribs stood exposed on their bare chests, like the flesh had been cut and re-sown behind the excised bones. At first, Ketz thought their teeth were filed to points. As they drew closer, though, he realized, no, they grew that way naturally...or rather *un*naturally, so long and twisted, it was a wonder they could shut their mouths without shredding their own lips. All the ragged scarring on their lower faces said they couldn't, or hadn't always been able to, before their whole facial structures had elongated into sagging snouts, one more grotesque mutation to accompany the first. Moss and barnacles sprouted from their arms, chests and faces, along with crude jewelry carved from lands-knew-what, dangling from their skin on rusty fishhooks.

They bashed and crowded their way down the hall, towards Tia and Ketz. Their knotted fists brandished jagged, shimmering curved blades, carved from the scales of larger river beasts. Their pale eyes gleamed with mindless, desperate hunger, like every nerve of their self-mutilations sang alive and well throughout their tortured flesh, keeping them perpetually mad and ready for every fight like this.

The first one howled and rushed to meet the twins, his scale-blade swooping down in a powerful chop. When Tia blocked it, the heavy impact shivered down through her arm, but her blade didn't break. She braced her legs wider as the riverman's blade whistled and crashed in a blurry flurry. Ketz lunged low to skewer the bastard, but that weird, nasty blade was all over the place. It smacked Ketz's blade aside powerfully enough to pull painfully at his shoulder, then nearly took his head off as he swayed back, his feet shifting frantically. There wasn't much technique to the creature's wild chopping, just frenzied speed and relentlessness, more like he meant to barrel straight through the twins rather than fight them.

Ketz already felt like the guy was about to do just that. There wasn't a lot to do against this kind of opponent in this close space without whacking Tia with his sword on accident. He jumped back, sucking in his gut from a fuming swish that nearly opened him. As the powerful chop swung wide, he lunged in past it with a surge of rage, caught the slimy sword-wrist with one hand and drove his own sword through this thing's gut with the other, all the way to the hilt.

Ketz and the dying pirate crashed into each other, Ketz still twisting the wrist 'til the scale-blade slipped from the gnarled fingers and clattered next to him. The clammy texture of the thing's rancid flesh felt so weird to the touch that Ketz swore at first he was touching some new, weird kind of clothing material instead of skin. The freak creamed and frothed in his face, its rotting breath making his eyes water, then those sharp teeth chomped down on Ketz's shoulder, biting into his flesh through his uniform like tiny, rusty knives. With a howl, he shoved the thing back and felt his own flesh tear worse as the thing's thrashing jaw came free. He ripped his blade out of the thing and got a noxious pile of intestines all over his forearm. He rose and sidestepped the quivering corpse as it crashed at his feet, his edge shearing loose of the tangle of guts, just in time to jab the second attacker through the side of the neck. He struck with such force that the blade slid out the other side, punched into the wall and got stuck in it.

Tia dashed between them in a blinding blur. "Fuckin' die," she yelled thunderously as she rose and struck. Her lashing blade hit the last man so hard across the chest that his whole rib cage split in half diagonally. His top half slid off and splashed at his feet. What was left of his torso sprayed blood all over the walls and ceiling, before his legs crumpled.

The twins panted and looked at each other. It seemed like forever before their heads cleared and reality set in, that the fight had ended and they were both still in one piece. It didn't help that the river pirates stank even worse in death. Hell, just the stench of their clothes, never mind their spilt entrails, felt like a continuous, assaultive barrage. Sopping, scarlet rivulets streamed off them from head to toe. Ketz yanked his sword from the wall and out of the river pirate's neck. The body flopped in a heap with its companions. Gore dripped from the crosspiece over Ketz's hand.

"*Shiiiiit,*" he said. "Y'know, these Ghestru blades ain't half bad."

"Huh?" said Tia, then let out a short, mirthless chuckle. "Oh. Yeah. Looks like one of 'em got you, though. Twice," She pointed at his torn, streaming shoulder, then at a weeping gash on his left bicep.

He looked at the second wound. "Fuck." He clenched his fist and flexed the arm. "Okay, it still works. *Shit*, it hurts, though. You okay?"

"Yeah," she said, listening to the pounding army of the next wave of feet that neared the stairwell. "This next bunch ain't gonna be so easy, though."

Behind them, a door creaked open. They both spun to look, swords ready. Out stepped Lady Hallucia, proud as she pleased. She didn't even appear to notice the carnage, let alone the smell. The room behind her looked brighter somehow. So did she.

Tia brandished her blade, shaking fresh spatter all over the floor. "Girl, get back in there and stay put! My brother and me, it's us got our asses on the line, keepin' your perfumed-princess bitchass in one piece!"

The Ghestru girl grinned. Her eyes blazed pale yellow. "You're paid to keep the Lady Hallucia safe, yes," she said. "As you must surely have heard by now, sweet Tia, I'm not the Lady Hallucia."

With that, she darted between them, raced through the hallway, and up the stairs, into the approaching throng before it had a chance to show itself. In the next moment, all the howls of conquering bloodlust turned to shrieks of pain and terror. A river of gore spilled down the steps, filled with juicy clumps of sundered viscera.

"I take it back," said Tia, staring wide-eyed.

"About what?" said Ketz.

"Givin' you shit all this time, for gettin' up her skirts. Hell, *I'd* fuck her."

Ketz felt the floor turn and tilt, in a new way that didn't feel right. "I think we should get up top. I think those river pirates ruptured our hull, and this boat's sinkin'."

SEVENTEEN

Up top, Ketz couldn't put his boots anywhere without stepping in bloody, lumpy slosh. Deckhands strained and heaved, at the wheel, along the sides, and overhead in the riggings, to get the *Arlash* under control. Everyone looked like they were fighting to stay conscious, breathing air that tasted like it had turned to poison gas.

"What the fuck just happened?" said one crewman to another as Ketz walked past them in a daze.

"Got me," the man's companion huffed. "I thought we were dead!"

"Who cares?" groaned another, as he hauled a bucket of water before spilling it over the fire they were putting out. "These degenerate riverman assholes are all dead. We ain't." The guy's choked voice didn't match the bravado of his words.

Everyone looked as delirious as Ketz felt. Still, though, they pumped their tortured muscles through their duties. Ketz figured he'd best heed their example and keep on task. Something crashed to his left. He spun and reached for his sword. Two guys had been hauling something heavy between them across the deck. One of them had dropped his end and now puked his guts out all over his companion.

For his own part, Ketz hadn't exactly acclimated himself to the oppressive air, but he'd forced himself into a state where he could function in spite of it.

Plenty of the crew *were* dead. It was hard to count how many, thanks to how hacked to pieces some of them were. At least it was easy to tell them apart from the slain pirates, many of whom sported even uglier mutations and self-mutilations than the ones he and Tia had faced. Most of the latter hadn't been cut down, but rather *ripped* apart. At first, Ketz thought it was the full physically destructive power of Trosola unleashed, at which he stared in awe. Then he took in how more of the pirate corpses lay, and it became obvious that most them had turned on each other. Many of them lay practically in each other's arms – those whose limbs were still attached – like sleeping lovers.

When Ketz blinked his stinging eyes clear, visions of the devil-haunted swamp assailed him again, and the thought struck him, *That's what they pretty much are…lovers at the end, in the grip of Trosola's love, in her garden of death.*

He listened to more fragmented chatter. Apparently, none of the survivors had any notion of who or what had saved them. Thank this river for yielding up one small favor, if salvation was what you could call it.

Orcris Brendi shambled forward across the deck, hiking his robes high, putting his feet in as little of the mess as possible, like someone stepping across stones in a creek. His cheeks puffed and his eyes bulged. His retainers flanked him closely, making sure he didn't collapse, even though they weren't fairing much better. Ketz saw only three spearmen now, where there used to be four. He figured he'd already stepped in the missing guy, somewhere on the deck.

The captain stepped up to him, a compactly built man, holding himself stately as possible, nursing his own score of wounds. He wiped a gob of sweat from his forehead. "Your Excellency. The ship is secure. Still, we've –"

"I can see that, you idiot," spat Orcris Brendi, forcing the words out of what sounded like a thick, gummy throat. "Where is Hallucia? *Where is my daughter?* Damn you all, someone just tell me –"

Ketz stepped forward. "Your daughter's safe, sir. She's below deck in her cabin. My sister's got her."

That much was true. By the time he and Tia had gotten up top, the whole bloody shambles had quieted. They'd made their way through it, while everyone around them was still rattled to the point of catatonia. They'd found Lady Hallucia curled up and sobbing on the bloody deck amidst the carnage the god within her had ignited. Between the two of them, they'd gotten her below deck as quickly as possible. Everyone else had been either too dazed to notice or looking to the dead and dying, as well as their own wounds. The little lady had been such a mess, no one would have recognized her as their mistress at a glance. Mountain life had taught the twins to move swiftly, quietly, and elusively, keeping their sordid business all but invisible. This ship wasn't their native forest, so the collective aftershock of battle had to do.

"What happened?" Lady Hallucia had moaned as they hurried her into her room. "Did I…did she…I didn't hurt anyone, did I? Where's Daddy? I didn't hurt…"

"Shut up," said Tia. She grabbed the girl by both arms and jerked her face to face. "It's done. You're safe." As she looked the poor girl over, though, some gentler, nurturing instinct stirred in her. "Look, just take a few slow, deep breaths. Easy there, yeah…That's it, girl, you're in one piece. You're doin' fine."

Hallucia hugged herself. "Why…why am I so cold?"

"'Cause you're soaked in blood. Hold still, lemme see." Tia had turned the girl from side to side and prodded at her in a few places. "Okay, doesn't look like any of it's yours. Blood gets cold quick, once it's spilt. Ketz, go find some of those meatskin pixie servants, get 'em in here, have 'em fix this lady a hot bath." She muttered, "Hopefully they didn't all get 'emselves killed just now."

Ketz had hunted all over below deck but couldn't find a one of the weird little things. He already knew there were none up top, and he didn't see any dead ones throughout the hall. Finally, he'd found his way down the narrower, secluded hallway, where he found the little wicker doorway Tia had described. He opened it onto deep blackness, reached up to take a lantern from the wall, then crouched and extended the light in, before crawling through. Tia had told him about how bad it stank in here. She hadn't lied, he now discovered, though such a smell was now downright tolerable, compared to the stench wafting up from the carnage in the sun on the deck. Many shuffles and murmurs rose up to meet him, along with a few stifled children's cries. Ketz crawled all the way in and held the lamp out over the chamber below. There, he saw a sea of tightly packed bodies, their wide, horror-stricken eyes staring up to meet him.

"You can all relax," he called down to them. "Show's over. No one else is gonna try to kill you." All those petrified eyes kept staring, unblinking, like they didn't understand him or didn't believe him. He started down the stairs. The more he saw of these conditions, the more his stomach rolled painfully, from something other than physical disgust. No wonder these critters died so frequently. "Come on now, y'all, snap out of it. I need three of you." As he reached the bottom of the stairs, he thought of something. "Brili. One of you's called Brili. She anywhere down here? I need to talk to her."

A meek voice echoed from within the throng, "I am Brili."

A moment later, Tia's little friend pushed her way to the front of the crowd. She stood bravely between Ketz and the rest of them, as though defending them. Ketz couldn't decide if the sight was more pathetic or admirable.

Brili looked him up and down and said, "You say you have made us safe, yet you are so all of blood, with the look of killing on your face." She almost managed to keep her voice from trembling.

It was true, Ketz's blood still ran hot from the melee in the hallway. Hard to believe, it had happened only a few minutes ago. He still must look and sound like a maddened, hungry predator. He took a few slow breaths and spoke softer. "Brili, listen to me. Tia sent me to find you. Your mistress…the one of the true bloodline…needs your help."

"The mistress of the true bloodline? She is with your

sister, the woman who kills people?" Before Ketz could answer, she looked him over again. "Who have you and your sister been killing?"

"The bad folks who attacked us. Who else?"

Brili's face sank. If Ketz hadn't known better, he'd have sworn she looked disappointed. "When we heard the howls of the invaders, then the letting of blood, we all ran away, down here, to hide." She beckoned him closer, then whispered, "When I heard the fighting, I thought it might be…more of you Schomites, that you had after all deceived the master and led his ship into a…I think you call it an ambush? That it was all in your plan to capture the other mistress. If it was so, I had hoped…that your sister would see that my boopa and I were not harmed, because I have spoken only honest to her, and she has been kind to me, in her way."

These critters were born and raised to stay stupid, like proper Ghestru slaves. Now, though, Ketz saw that they weren't stupid, or at least Brili wasn't.

He stood up and smiled sadly. "Naw, sorry. I'm afraid we ain't badass enough to mastermind somethin' like that." *I can think of someone who is, though*, he thought.

She squinted up at him. "You…would have done such a thing, but only if there had been something wrong with your hindquarters?"

"Never mind," he said. "Grab three others and follow me. Your mistress awaits your service."

Brili and three other servants followed Ketz back through the hallway. She stepped up next to him and tugged on his sleeve. "Please. Do not tell the woman who kills people what I told you of her kindness to me. She told me…that if I told you, her brother, that she had shown me the softness within her heart, that she would…break my jaw so that she could bite my tongue from within my skull."

Ketz squeezed the little critter's hand. "Not a word, I promise."

She jerked her hand free and gasped. For a moment, he

wondered if he'd squeezed too hard. These little things seemed pretty frail, after all. When he glanced down at her, he saw more confusion in her eyes than anything.

Finally, she just said, "Thank you," then fell back behind him with the others.

When they reached Hallucia's room, Brili and the others bustled in past Ketz. When Ketz stepped in, he saw Tia exchange a brief look with Brili. Otherwise, she gave no sign that she could even tell the girl apart from the rest of the little red pixies.

Tia stood with Hallucia while the servants heated the water and filled the pearly-white tub. Once the bath was almost ready, Tia grabbed up Hallucia again, spun her about, and ripped the ruined dress off her in a series of violent wrenches. Hallucia whimpered and quivered, but otherwise stood impassively to the rough handling.

Tia wadded up the ruined garment, pulled Brili aside, and pressed it into her hands. "Burn this," she said. "Don't talk to anyone outside of this room about what you've seen here." She jerked the pixie closer. "Make sure your friends here know not to talk about it either, even down in those shitty quarters of yours. If word of this gets out and it comes back to bite me in the ass, I'll know whose fault it is. Got it?"

Brili nodded tremblingly. "I understand, woman who kills people."

One of the other servants noticed Ketz still standing in the room. It looked up in alarm, then back and forth between him and their naked mistress. It rushed up to him and tried pressing and shooing him from the room.

He pushed it away, growled, "Ah, fuck off," and stayed put.

The servant scurried back over and joined the others in helping Hallucia into the tub. They set to scrubbing the blood off her.

Tia turned to Ketz. "I'll stay here, see she's put to bed, keep watch after this. You get up top and make sure we're square with the boss."

So Ketz had left the room and gone back up on deck. Now that he stared down Orcris Brendi, along with the captain and the rest of the able-bodied fighting men, he wished he could have stayed below and given this task to Tia.

"She's untouched and alive, you say," panted Orcris Brendi. "Swear it to me!"

"I swear it to you, sir," said Ketz. "The disturbance shook her up, but she'll be fine."

Orcris Brendi raised an eyebrow. "*Will* be fine?"

"She didn't witness any bloodshed," said Ketz. "My sister and I made sure of that much. A few of those freaks off the river got below deck. They almost reached her door, but we dealt with 'em."

"I looked things over below deck, your Excellency," said the captain wearily. "Looks like he's telling the truth. I couldn't tell you exactly how many of 'em there were, the river pirates I mean. Not a lot of 'em are…in one piece."

Orcris Brendi grimaced and shook his head. "Very good, Captain."

The captain looked incredulously at Ketz. "Seriously, you and your sister did all that? Just the two of you down there?"

Ketz grinned. "That's right, man."

The captain laughed deliriously and slapped Ketz hard on the shoulder. "Well, damn! You little mountain-bred beasts must really be as savage as everyone says!"

"You got no idea." Ketz glanced around the fuming, blood-spattered deck. "Guess you meatskin fighters ain't half bad yourselves."

Orcris Brendi's eyes widened. "Now look here, young man, remember your place, so you don't address my people so —"

"Ah, the lad's just cheeky," said the captain. His face went deadly serious again. "I'm afraid we have bigger problems right now, your Excellency. We're taking on water. We need to dock and make repairs."

"*What?*"

"Those pirates, when they set on us, they rammed straight into the hull, with some…spike fixed to the front of their craft. They set it on fire, before they all swarmed off it, onto the deck. We managed to sink it before the flames caught the sails, but the damage to the hull was already done."

"How long will we be delayed, Captain?" said Orcris Brendi.

"All I know," said the captain, "is we need a chance to assess the damage. One thing's for sure, if we don't dock somewhere in the next two hours, we'll sink straight to the bottom of the river."

Orcris Brendi stared across the deck. "You've looked at our maps, I take it?"

"I have, your Excellency."

"Where's the nearest worthy port on our route?"

"The next place we can dock is the village of Petrune. It's about a mile downriver from our present position, across the eastern shoreline."

"Is it safe, for Ghestru?"

The captain sighed heavily. "Word goes, it's mostly Schomite fishermen, with some lowborn Spirelights. They say most of the latter are runaway convicts and other outcasts from their own people, settled in the easiest community they could reach that'll turn a blind eye to them. It's been that way for generations, enough for a lot of those runaways to mate with the locals and raise their hellish spawn with all that thievery and lawlessness still alive and well in their blood. Most of them who've grown up like that wind up taking to the woods along the shoreline, in their own little communities. A lot of those ones take to river piracy. A lot of *those*…" His face twisted as he glanced around the deck. "Well, they've sunk to their own whole new level of degeneracy, like…these guys." He kicked at a stray limp pirate arm. "The others like that, the ones not fallen so low…well, word goes, they're the law in those parts."

"I see." Orcris Brendi sneered. "So you're telling me that our only available safe haven is with the very vermin who've left us in this plight."

"No sir, the river pirates aren't welcome in the town…not openly, at least. Like I said, they're kin to most of the local law, and folks like that, they don't forget it."

"And those are the sort of local officials in whom you'd have us place our trust, no less!"

"I'm sorry, your Excellency, but we don't have a choice. In our present condition, we'll be lucky to reach their docks before we start to sink."

"Damn this barbarous continent." Orcris Brendi clenched his jaws. "Do it, Captain. Set us towards the shoreline."

EIGHTEEN

The sun sank through thickening clouds behind the shoreline as the *Arlash* coasted inland. A heavy mist spilled from the distant treeline, out across the water, which grew ever more ghostly still, the closer the ship drew towards land.

Ketz climbed to the poop deck, above the worst of the death stench. It had grown almost tolerable since they'd pitched the last of the corpses into the river. He went to the railing and inhaled the mist slowly through his nose. There was a strange fragrance to it, almost like fresh fruit, one Ketz wouldn't normally think to associate with mist. The captain approached him from behind. The man moved quietly, but Ketz still heard him.

"Help you with somethin', Captain?"

The captain stepped up beside him. "You look nervous, friend hill-beast."

"Who on this damn boat ain't right now?"

"Nervous over more than you've shared with your captain, I mean." There was a faint, dull slur to the man's voice...probably just the lingering shock.

Ketz looked over and tried to read the man. The guy might be getting at any number of suspicions. He was, technically, Ketz's commanding officer. Ketz wasn't one for *commanding officers*, or anything about what the Spirelights or Ghestru called *military discipline*. He'd learned how to play the part, though, while occupying Trescha. Might as well play it now, if it helped his cover. He hadn't been raised to be a liar or manipulator, like these highborn so-called civilized people, but he'd served under Captain Severen Gris long enough to learn a few such subtleties. His present captain might not be dumb, sure, but he was no Severen Gris.

"Just gettin' the scent of this mist," said Ketz.

"It's a misty evening," the captain agreed. "Perhaps it is her doing."

Ketz looked over sharply. "What did you just say?"

The captain blinked, then looked at Ketz as though noticing him for the first time. "I don't like sailing blind through this mist, that's all."

"No, that's not what you said."

Ketz expected the captain to check him for impertinence. Instead, the man gazed at him quizzically. "Isn't it? What did I say?"

"I didn't catch it clearly. That's why I asked."

"I…don't know."

Ketz kept trying to get a read on this guy, then he realized it wasn't the man himself that was confusing him. There was something else going on, floating in and out of the man's mind, from beyond himself. Ketz tried to sense whether or not it was affecting him, too. He wasn't sure. For now, he looked back out across the river. "Seems weird, don't you think? This much mist in these parts, this time of year."

"It's unusual, yes, but it does happen."

"You say a lot of these river pirates are descended from runaway Schomite outlaws," said Ketz. "What kind of Schomites?"

"What do you mean, what kind of Schomites?"

"There's lots of different kinds of us, dependin' on where we're from. Took you for a seafarin' man of the world. The ones who settled here, where did most of them migrate from?"

"How should I know? I make it my business to know as much as I can beforehand, about whatever waters I'm about to sail my crew into it. That doesn't make me an expert on whatever lands lie beyond the shores we pass. Does that have something to do with all this mist?"

"Maybe," said Ketz. He'd also bet his left nut, it hadn't

been the river pirates who'd conjured it. It hadn't been Trosola, either.

Over the past few years, Ketz had heard of bandits in the Schlogmire ranges using old Schomite magic, the likes of which his own people didn't talk about anymore…like conjuring up big clouds of mist where they shouldn't be naturally, to drop on their enemies, to cloud their minds before a battle, in preparation for a sneak-attack. Ketz had never seen such mist, but he'd smelled this kind of old magic before, and he smelled it now. He knew exactly what kind of Schomites still practiced it, too…those who came from the Dragon Coasts, the ones who'd been migrating out of the far southeast.

Out of the mists ahead, two small crafts glided across the rippling water. At the front of either craft stood two men. More men sat behind them. The captain started back across the poop deck, then down to rejoin Orcris Brendi. He gestured for Ketz to follow. Without speaking, the two men fell in naturally side by side as they approached the merchant. Orcris Brendi stood flanked by his spearmen.

"All fighting hands on ready," the captain barked in a booming voice. As the men flooded into position, he reached Orcris Brendi. "Your Excellency, two smaller vessels approaching off starboard. Not sure yet whether or not they're friendly. Perhaps you'd best go below, 'til we know –"

"Whoever comes for dealings with this vessel," said Orcris Brendi, "I will be there to look them in the eye, so that they know who is the true master here. I trust you to see to my safety, Captain, you and your fellow officers, and…" His eyes settled on Ketz. "Oughtn't this one be below deck, looking after my daughter?"

Before Ketz could answer, the captain said, "That other one's down there with her, your Excellency. This one's her first line of defense, up here. He knows this continent, sir. Having him on hand might be useful."

Orcris Brendi scowled, then said, "Very well."

They all moved towards the railing, with the captain in the lead. Once again, Ketz fell naturally in stride next to him.

As they reached the railing, the captain muttered sideways at Ketz, "You have younger eyes than me, hill-trash. How many guys do you see on those boats, other than those two up front rowing?"

Ketz put his palm to his brow. "Half a dozen each, looks like."

"They look like more pirates?"

"Not like those moldy, rotten, self-mutilatin' assholes with shit growin' all over 'em, no. They're so dirty, I can't tell which ones are beasts or glowsticks."

"*Beasts?*" The captain chuckled deliriously. "I thought only us and the Spirelights called your kind that."

"Sure, just not to our face. I don't mind hearin' you use that word, sir. You seem cool enough to me. Just don't let my sister hear you say it, rank or no."

The captain chuckled and clapped Ketz's shoulder. "I like you, friend hill-beast. We have a deal…just so long as you and your sister do your job."

"We will," said Ketz. "Yeah, the mistress is a good kid."

"She's more than that," the captain whispered.

"Huh?" said Ketz.

Before the captain could answer, a man who stood at the front of one of the crafts shouted, "Who goes there?"

"This is the *Arlash*," barked the captain, a note of stern pride in his voice. He sounded like himself again, for the moment. "Be you more pirates, or river patrolmen from the village of Petrune?"

"We look like pirates to you?" The man who spoke peered up at the captain. He didn't look happy about what he saw, then he spotted Ketz. "The *Arlash*, huh? Never heard of it. We ain't scheduled to take in any boat of this size in this harbor, neither."

"Who am I addressing?" shouted the captain.

"Me, that's who, the sheriff of the province of Petrune."

Orcris Brendi strode to the fore, raised his hands, and put on his best smiling businessman's face. "Gentlemen, please. If I may. I am master of this vessel, Orcris Brendi. In exchange for your township's hospitality, I am prepared to offer —"

"Shut the fuck up, you old windbag," the sheriff called back.

"Good sir, are you aware you are addressing —"

"I said shut the fuck up. I'll talk to the captain of this vessel, and none other."

"I'm captain here," shouted the captain. "Keep talking."

"Howdy, Captain." The sheriff saluted sharply. "What's your business here?"

"The old man's telling the truth. We're a merchant vessel, en route to Tatelle."

"We ain't a merchant port, sure as shit not for oily little meatskin merchants."

"I'm aware of that, Sheriff," said the captain. "Our boat here came under attack by river pirates. We seek shelter in your harbor to make repairs. Our master here, the illustrious Orcris Brendi, is prepared to pay your township a generous sum for granting us asylum."

Ketz caught the boatman's twitching smirk, so he shouted, "That *generous sum* includes extended interest, granted our safe passage from your shores upon departure, includin' mercenary assistance goin' further, against whatever local rivalries y'all might be dealin' with."

"Have you entirely forgotten yourself?" Orcris Brendi hissed in Ketz's ear. "What the hell do you think you're doing?"

"Savin' the lives of all you cocksuckers, that's what," Ketz hissed back. "Which at this point, I'm only doin' 'cause it means savin' my own ass while I'm at it. So if you got so much as two brain cells to rub together, you'd best back my play. Otherwise, anything we've got to bargain with, they'd just as soon swarm on board and take, by killin' us all, while we're weak and desperate."

Orcris Brendi paled, then turned and shouted out to the boatmen, "My young Schomite guide speaks the truth, friends."

A long silence followed. The man at the head of the little boat said, "These river pirates who attacked you. You and your crew kill 'em all?"

"Yes," said the captain. "Yes sir, we did. And, as you can see, if you look around up here, my men are prepared to kill more. I'm sure they'd rather not, though."

"We got no love in these parts for meatskin merchants," said the sheriff. "We like those damned river pirates who plague these waters even less, though. We keep 'em paid off to leave us alone, but not all of 'em always heed those instructions." He pointed at Orcris Brendi. "Hey, Mister Hotshot Merchant. You say this deal might involve extending us some aid, maybe some real military force against those river pirates…"

Orcris Brendi put on his best smile, and shouted, "I would be all too happy to negotiate such arrangements with you, good sir, once my crew has had time to rest, recuperate, and see to some repairs on our own vessel."

The sheriff grinned, then turned to the side and signaled to the other craft. "Row back. Get three more boats out this way. We'll guide this vessel the…*Arlash*…to a proper shore."

The second boat glided around in a semicircle then rowed away.

The captain leaned towards Ketz. "Does he sound trustworthy to you?"

"If he weren't, we'd know it by now," said Ketz. "Tell all your men to watch themselves once we go ashore, though. Any of ours start actin' up, swingin' their dicks around, theirs won't hesitate for a second to make things real ugly. It won't matter how big a payment the boss waves in their face. Remind the crew, our legs are all weary from ship-travel. Theirs ain't."

"I'm glad to have you aboard, friend Ketz," said the

captain. "Now go below. Those wounds of yours look like they need tending."

NINETEEN

Once he was below deck, Ketz didn't see anyone on the way to his room, except for a few servants. They all kept their eyes lowered as they passed, pretending to ignore him. He watched for Brili but didn't spot her among them. Two of them waited in his room, imploring to see if he needed anything.

"*Go on, git*," he snapped, shooing them out. "I'll draw and heat my own damn water."

As soon as they were gone, he felt like an asshole. Was he already acting like one of those highborn assholes, treating underlings like dirt, just because he could and he was in a bad mood and they were too weak and scared to complain? The sooner he and Tia got off this boat, the better.

Before he bathed, he hung his stained uniform up to dry by the window. Only three days into this job, and the fancy new ensemble was already tattered and splattered, almost unrecognizable. Oh well. The hot water turned red around him as he lay back in it, letting his sore muscles unknot. He cleaned his wounds as best he could. The one on his shoulder wasn't as bad as he'd feared, but it still looked nasty. When he climbed out, he let the air dry him. He dressed his wounds, found some fresh undergarments, trousers and a clean shirt, then let the jacket dry out some more before he put it back on.

By the time he left his room, the hallway floor had been swabbed. The smell of congealed blood still reeked heavily in the air.

He found Tia standing sentry outside Hallucia's room and started filling her in on what he'd witnessed up top.

"I know what's happenin' up top," she said, cutting him off. "The captain came down to inform me personally, while you were off makin' yourself pretty. Who you botherin' keepin' pretty for anyway, at a time like this, huh? There a *soiree* I don't know about?"

"Fuck off." He did his best not to let his eyes drift to Hallucia's door.

"She's fine," said Tia. "She's sleepin', last I looked in on her. Speakin' of meatskins who wanna suck your dick for some reason, sounds like you and that captain sure been gettin' along. Just his tone when he mentions you, sounds like he's damn near ready to promote you to First Mate. Word goes, he's in the market for one. My, ain't you turnin' out to be quite the proper meatskin socialite lately."

"Sure," said Ketz, "you could try it, if you weren't always remindin' yourself that you gotta be such a fuckin' bitch all the damn time."

"Yeah, well, if we ever get clear of this damn mess, you can whine at me all you like about what a cruel, cruel cunt I am." She leaned close and hissed in his ear, "That mist ain't goin' to your brain, is it?"

"I don't think so, but it's sure gettin' to the rest of the crew. I was about to tell you that, 'fore you started in on me. Smelled it all the way down here, huh?"

She rolled her eyes. "Of course. You ain't informed the captain?"

"Nah, just keepin' an eye on him over it...him and the rest. This could get real weird."

"It's weird havin' that kind of mist churnin' up in these parts at all. From what I hear about these river folks, they couldn't scrape up half the brains between 'em to pull a move like that out of their asses."

"I can think of someone who just maybe could, though," said Ketz. "Like, out of his magical Dragon Coastal ass."

"Why would he go and pull a stunt like that, though?" Tia snarled. "We got this shit handled!"

"You call this bloody mess *handled?*" said Ketz.

"No thanks to him...*if* that little hunch you're gettin' at is right."

"We manage to get ashore," Ketz whispered quietly, "you still in the mood to make a break for it?"

"If he's out there waitin' for us ashore, so are some of those people he knows everywhere. He'll have told them to keep an eye out for us, in case we try somethin' like that. Or you forgotten why we let him talk us into this in the first place?"

"No, I ain't," said Ketz. "I ain't forgotten what happened back in the harbor, either, so I can't tell myself it was all hot air. So what do you say we do, then?"

Tia drew up to attention at her corner of the door. "Sit tight and keep doin' our jobs, that's what. While we're stuck between him and that thing we...with our mistress we've been assigned to safeguard."

"I like that option even less."

"You would. Look, on this boat or on foot, how are we supposed to handle her, anyway, now that we've seen what she can do?"

"It's the Spirelight god Trosola who did all that," said Ketz. "Not her."

"Right. You said she says the god won't take her over unless no one's watchin'. So unless this goes otherwise, we gotta make sure to snatch her while she's Hallucia. After that, we make sure at least one of us keeps an eye on her 'til she ain't our problem anymore."

At the end of the little corridor behind them, the door creaked open. A sheepish young face poked out with a downcast gaze. It was startling how small and plain Hallucia looked, her once lustrous hair falling straight and damp around her shoulders, over a plain robe that went all the way to the floor.

"Ketz," she said in a tiny voice. "Can I talk to you in here alone for a second? *Please?*"

Tia rolled her eyes, then waved a hand, as though granting permission. "You watch yourself in there, got it?" she whispered as he passed.

Ketz stepped into the room. As soon as he closed the door, Lady Hallucia's posture shifted. She grinned up at him, with pale, blazing yellow eyes. "*Haha, got you!*"

She snaked her arms around his neck and kissed him hard on the mouth. Before he realized it, the taste of her lips was all there was. He pulled her close and kissed her back hungrily.

"Miss me?" she sighed in his ear, nibbling lightly at his neck, sending a sweet, shivery tickle through him.

"You know I have," he growled, gnawing on her neck.

"We're gonna run away from all this soon, aren't we," she sighed in his ear, her arms convulsing around his neck, "together."

"Yes," he heard himself say.

"…To lands where I'll be reborn to my true power…to where you'll be reborn with me…"

Once more, he smelled the sweet rot of the swamp, felt the fire of the cruel, ecstatic dance in his loins, saw it in her glittering eyes, along with the rest of her promises. When she tugged him towards the bed, though, he halted sharply. "No."

"What?"

"I said no." He thrust her backwards, but still clutched her shoulders fiercely. "Look," he panted, "it just ain't right. You…a god…whatever you are…possessin' this young lady's body."

"Oh, you mean *this* body?" She pulled the cord so her robe fell open. He looked her over. Then his hands were all over her, too. She closed her eyes and let her head fall back languidly. She smiled and sighed, leaning into his touch.

He made himself stop again, somehow. "No. Sorry. Look, you can tell I want you, and you want me, sure. But she don't."

"Who? Wait…*her?* Oh, you gotta be shitting me. Come on, to hell with her, baby. She's not here right now. We are. What's she gonna do?" She started undoing his trousers.

She had a point. Hallucia said she didn't remember what Trosola did, right? Ketz was a twitch away from dragging her to the bed, throwing her down, and getting back to business with her. Hell, part of him *liked* the idea of violating Hallucia a little more, letting her wake up still throbbing and sore from what she'd missed while he got Trosola off. After all this lizardshit with her haughty, decadent family business, he'd earned it, right? As he stared down into those mad bright eyes, though, he remembered the soft, dark, scared eyes that belonged there...the eyes of a frightened girl, not much younger than him in years, yet so much more of a child in many ways.

"Forget it," he said. "It'd be against her will. Sorry."

"*Against her will?*" Trosola pouted, "Aw, and I always heard you Nagga Mountain bandit boys were so into raping and pillaging."

"Not me. I've done plenty of fucked up shit, sure. One thing I ain't never done is fuck a woman against her say-so."

"In case you didn't notice, that wasn't exactly *against my say-so* before. So what are you waiting for? *Ravage me again, barbarian!*"

"It's against Hallucia's say-so," said Ketz. "She was there first, in this...this very nice body."

Trosola let out a sultry, silvery laugh. "Aw, aren't you so cute. *The noble savage.* So honorable...so hypocritical." Her lips rippled ferally, reminding him of what else that mouth of hers could do. Her face twisted with fury. "Don't you see, it's more than a fuck I'm offering you? You could ascend to godhood at my side, but your small mind can't even look past your silly little humanoid ideas of decency. You think *I* had a choice? I thought I had time to sleep, to dream and bide my time, against *them!*"

"Who?"

"My enemies. *Your* enemies. The Gods of Spirah!"

"I thought you were one of them."

"So did they, until I had better ideas than them...a clearer, truer vision of what could be. So they cast me out into my hell, so the best way I could find to get back into the game was through the body of this spoiled little meatskin whore. Hallucia's the one who summoned me into herself. I only answered her call because *somehow* she made it in proper ritualistic accord, her and that ink artist."

"Hell, the way you tell it, it's like she's the one who raped you body and soul, over and over, not the other way around."

"You've never been a god, Ketz. Not yet. You've tasted it, though, haven't you, sleeping next to her…next to *me*…feeling those dreams of power seep through your brain. Ah, yes, I see, you remember now, don't you? But you still don't know how these things work. You also don't know of the hours they spent, she and that ink artist, setting their trap for me. Did she tell you she didn't realize what she was doing, like me and that pathetic boy were the ones who lured her into a trap? She knew, every step of the way, when she had that old symbol – *my* old symbol, from the Pantheon, our link to your realm – inked into her flesh, binding me to her." Trosola grimaced, her eyes watery and pleading. "I don't like having to live stuck in a meat-suit like this…except when it's on my terms, not hers.

"So yeah, it feels good to fuck. I have easy access to all the herbal medicines to avoid nuisances like pregnancy…medicines learned from *your* people, am I right? Her father's attendant physicians can always easily cure me of any infections her body catches. I like how it feels when a rough, wild creature like you takes what he wants, seizes and dominates this body. What the hell is wrong with that? You've seen what else I can do. What do you think would happen to you if I didn't want it?" She ran her palms and fingertips up and down his torso, then took his hands and pressed his palms against her breasts. "*Mmmmmm*, yes, young and frisky, always so hot-blooded from life lived as it should be, on a blade's edge…Lady Hallucia obviously wants it too, at least physically, or *I* wouldn't be so soaking wet." She guided one of his hands down between her legs, to prove it.

The smell wafted up to Ketz, so he drove her up against the nearest wall, squeezing at her, chewing on her neck and tits...then he shoved himself back. "No. On behalf of the Lady Hallucia and myself, no."

"*Ugh!*" She twisted away and stormed back and forth in a heat of frustration. "On top of everything else, there you go, trying to see your own silly humanoid morality in me, her, or any of this. Trust me, you've not seen anything yet." She tugged him stronger towards the bed, reclining back onto it, her thighs opening. "Come on, baby, we're on a sinking ship. Wouldn't it be sexy to drown while fucking?"

"No, actually. Shit, girl, you even possessed a humanoid critter before? You ever drowned in a humanoid body? 'Cause I almost have a couple times, and I tell ya, it's the worst thing you'll ever go through – stuck underwater, caught under a rock in a swirlin' undertow, your lungs collapsin' as it sucks your whole being deeper an' deeper..."

"My, don't you know how to talk dirty," she said huskily.

Someone banged on the door. Ketz jumped a little, stepped away from Trosola, and said, "Who is it?"

The door opened. Tia stuck her head in. "We're about to dock. The captain just sent word down to me. His Excellency would like an audience with you." She glanced at Trosola, on the bed with her robe still open, though now with her shoulders slumped, her eyes downcast, once again doing her very best impression of Lady Hallucia. "Hope the timin' ain't too bad for you."

TWENTY

The sun had mostly set when Ketz stepped outside. Everything felt so quiet up here now. Now that they were closer to shore, rotting kelp mingled with the fragrance of the mist and the lingering gutted-fish stench. The mist hadn't dispersed, yet it was oddly easier to see through now that they were in the thick of it. Ketz still smelled its alien energy currents of ancient magic…and something else. Some idle, weary crewmen stood lined up along the railings, staring over the side. The captain strode up and down the deck behind them, occasionally pausing to peer over with them.

Ketz walked up next to the captain, looked down into the water, and immediately jolted, his hand moving towards his sword.

"Relax, friend hill-beast," said the captain, his voice still droning slightly. "Yeah, I thought the same thing when I saw them."

Ketz peered harder at the dark water. For a moment, he'd thought it was more river-pirates swimming up on the boat, determined to climb the sides and make a stronger fight of it this time. Instead, the water churned with a thickening cluster of large, sharp-scaled, coiling, writhing fish. They seemed to circle the ship in an organized, star-shaped formation.

"What are they all doin'?" said Ketz.

"Got me," said the captain. "They ain't sharks or anything like that…not most of them, anyway. They first all swarmed in while we were pitching the dead over the side. Free meal, right? You should have watched that feeding frenzy! I've never seen corpses turn to skeletons so fast. When the corpses sank, a lot of those fish dove under after them. I thought they'd all go away once there was nothing left to eat. Now they're just…hovering around us, *like they're waiting for her to truly reveal herself in all her glory.*"

"What did you just say?" Ketz hissed.

"I said they're all hovering around the boat like they expect us to throw them more food. What's with you, kid?"

"I guess I'm just battle-weary."

The captain chuckled mirthlessly. "Kid, you're not old enough to know what *battle-weary* means."

"Fair enough. Just…*what the fuck* are *those nastyass fish?*"

"You got me. One of the boys speared one, hauled it up, thought we might as well get some good local eatin' out of this mess. He threw it back pretty quick. I just saw the thing for a few seconds, and I swore for a second someone had cut one of those river-pirate faces off and stitched it to one of those fish, as a joke or something. But no, it's more like those degenerates intentionally deformed their own faces to look more like those monstrous fish. *Man, what kind of fucked up lands are we sailing through?*"

"I wish I knew anymore," said Ketz.

Off past the stern of the *Arlash*, there rose clumps of high, thick treetops puffing against the skyline, swaying against each other at odd angles. The trees around here all twisted skyward in lumpy corkscrew shapes, with thick, soggy-looking foliage of purple and orange weeping and fluttering in the dusk. Between the water and the tree line, there spread a rocky, debris-strewn beach, from which several campfire lights already bloomed and blazed.

Two of Orcris Brendi's retainers marched towards Ketz across the deck. One of them thumped the butt of his spear against the boards and said in a hard, unreadable tone, "His Excellency wants a word with you."

"So I hear," Ketz said. "Any idea what for?"

"That's his place to tell you, and yours not to keep him waiting."

Ketz stayed cool as he fell in between the men. They

marched him around and back up onto the poop deck. Orcris Brendi stood staring out, statuesque, across the sandy twilit beach. If he noticed all those strange fish, he gave no sign. He turned, spotted Ketz, and moved forward sharply. As more light fell across the old man's face, Ketz saw him grinning, tears streaming down his cheeks. At that same moment, Ketz noticed Trosola's naked scent, still fresh all over his clothes. No, Hallucia's scent, he reminded himself. That was one thing that definitely didn't change about her, no matter which one was awake.

Relax, he told himself. *These Ghestru don't have noses like you. The old windbag doesn't suspect a thing.*

Orcris Brendi grabbed one of Ketz's hands in both of his own, shook it furiously, then yanked Ketz into a big, warm embrace. "Thank you, my young friend. Thank you so much. Forgive my rudeness earlier. My family is ever indebted to yours."

'Til getting this close, Ketz hadn't realized how much sweaty, smelly blubber padded the big frame beneath those robes. He disentangled himself as quickly as possible. "Thanks. Hey, man, don't worry about it. You hire my sister and me for a job, we do it. That's what you get when you hire Nagga Mountain fighters, yes sir."

"So I am coming to understand. Tell me, young man, have you any children of your own, back home in your Nagga Mountains?"

"Uh, no, I don't think so."

"One day you will, and then you will remember this voyage, I think, and you will know what my heart and mind have felt of late. For now, though, I can't have you or your wonderful sister getting worn down from fatigue."

"I appreciate that," said Ketz. "Don't worry. We're holdin' up fine."

"Nevertheless, I've decided to grant you this evening's shore leave. I expect you back on board at your post by dawn. At said time, your sister will be granted some hours of sleep, followed by her own shore leave. She will be apprised of the arrangement."

"There gonna be enough time for all that?"

"According to my engineers, we're to be stranded here for three days at least."

"Three days?" Ketz had to hide the sudden rush of anxiety. "Yeah, sure, of course. Thank you, your Excellency."

"The captain has spoken with the sheriff of the nearby village. I'm told you should find the main drag less than half a mile's walk uphill from the beach." He pressed a jingling little pouch into Ketz's palm. "Consider this an advance on what you're owed for your services thus far. It ought to be more than enough to purchase yourself…a fine evening's amusement, and a few hours' rest in lodgings…more to your liking than your accommodations here. I'll remind you, I do expect you to return fit for duty."

"Of course, your Excellency. Thank you."

Ketz descended onto the long, narrow dock. As he trod the boards, he kept glancing down into the dark water to either side. Many of those big, weird, ugly fish stopped congregating around the ship, and instead darted and slithered, chasing him through the water, like he was the one they'd been interested all along.

"Fuck off," he hissed at them. They didn't fuck off.

He reached the end of the dock and stepped down onto the beach. He was a little relieved when all his fishy admirers didn't sprout legs and follow him. From there, he made his way across the sand, between the campfires. He felt dozens of eyes lingering on him. He found his way up onto the winding trail that led through the bushes. The lights of the beach fell away. Feeling the lands beneath his feet was a divine gift, reminding him of who he truly was.

The lights of a village met him through the trees ahead. He thumbed through the little bag of jewels Orcris Brendi had given him. He could use a drink, for sure, but more than that, he noticed how hungry he felt, specifically for something that *wasn't* Ghestru cooking.

The way uphill was neither steep nor that long, though the higher he climbed, the sorer his legs got. They felt wobbly, back on dry land for the first time in days. The village, once he reached it, looked like one muddy little street with a few shops, already slowing down for the night. There must be some houses nestled out of sight. At least the local tavern wasn't hard to find, it turned out.

A fine evening's amusement, and a few hours' rest in lodgings more to your liking than your accommodations here, the old windbag had said.

Yeah, Ketz got the message loud and clear. Bonding over future brats or no, the old man had been telling him, *Go find yourself a whore, get all your filthy hill-beast lust out of your system, and sleep it off in her bed before you return to continue guarding my daughter.* Maybe that wasn't such a bad idea.

Ketz stepped into the dim, smoky front room of the tavern. He smelled stew cooking somewhere. That was good. Most of the faces he saw were Schomite. Before he reached the bar, though, something drew his eyes to a rear corner table, where three men sat playing cards. The two with their backs to Ketz wore matching faded, dirty yellow tunics and tattered, stain-speckled trousers. The dealer sat with his back to the wall, facing the door…a Dragon Coast Schomite who hadn't removed his long, black coat.

The Dragon Coast man looked up and peered into Ketz's eyes across the long, gloomy, tallow-scented barroom. Ketz took a deep breath and approached. On his way, he had to shove aside a few stumbling drunkards. Two of them, larger men than himself by a size and a half, shifted and sneered with mean, rough, stupid eyes that said, *Got an attitude there, do you, you little runt?*

Ketz placed his palm casually on his sword pommel and glared up with eyes that said, *Yes, I do, and I'll fucking kill you.*

One of the men reached for his own blade, one of those scale-carved weapons like the pirates had carried. His companion looked closer at Ketz's feral, murderous eyes. He caught his buddy by the shoulder and guided him out of the way. Ketz shrugged and walked past them. He stopped before the table, behind the men in yellow tunics, and stared across at the dealer.

The older of the two players twisted around in his chair and peered up at Ketz with diseased, watery eyes. They were both paler than most of the locals, with bad teeth and deeply pocked skin. They didn't have any barnacles growing on them, or any other monstrous alterations of those freaks who'd attacked the *Arlash*, not that Ketz could see.

"You want dealt in on this game, boy," said one guy in a scarred, raspy voice, "or you just gonna stand there jerkin' off while you watch?"

The dealer smiled out of the shadows. He said calmly in his rough, oddly cultivated voice, "Oh, I don't believe he wishes to do either. Don't mind the whelp…unless he'd care to be dealt in for a hand?"

Ketz shrugged and sat down. "Hey, why not? What's the game?"

"Octospheres," said one of the guys in yellow tunics. "Got somethin' to throw in, fancypants, or this look like a charity party to you?"

Ketz had been called a lot of things in his day, but *fancypants* was new to him. He remembered the expensively woven uniform he still donned, worn and stained as it was. "Sure," he said. He reached into the pouch Orcris Brendi had given him and drew out a sparkling crystal blue chip. He tossed it into the pile at the center.

The men in yellow tunics grunted, shrugged, and returned their attention to the cards. The dealer dealt everyone their hands.

It turned out, the man who'd challenged Ketz won by a solid flush. "Well what do ya know, lads!" He grinned, pulled the pile of coins close, then plucked up Ketz's blue crystal. "My lucky night! Looks like fancypants here ain't so bad to have around after all." He cast one of the lesser coins back to the center of the table. "Any of you bitches man enough for more?"

The dealer grinned. "Not just yet, gentlemen. Let's all take a little breather, shall we? Go on now, both of you. I'd like a word with fancypants here."

The men rose and took their drinks off towards the bar, in unquestioning acquiescence to the dealer's natural aura of casual leadership.

"What the hell are you doing here?" said Ketz.

"The way young folks speak to their employers these days! What are the lands coming to?" Minquo shook his head, made a tisking sound through his teeth, then smiled. "Are you honestly surprised to see me?"

"You know damn well, I ain't," said Ketz. "You wouldn't'a hired us if you thought we wouldn't smell what was in that mist, would you?"

"You sound upset about it. I'd have thought you'd have the sense to say thank you."

"*Thank you?*"

"You're too wound up, I see. You need a drink." Minquo gazed off at the bar and lifted two fingers.

A moment later, the barmaid approached the table. She carried a brimming, frothing drinking jack in either hand. She was a ruddy, lowborn Ghestru, not unlike most of the ship's crew. She set the drinks down before Ketz and Minquo, then hurried away, back behind the bar. Ketz wished she'd stuck around to ask what else he'd like. No doubt she was a runaway slave, so his uniform probably made her nervous. That stew still smelled mighty appetizing. He and Minquo raised their drinking jacks and clashed them violently together, in the custom of rough men meeting for business over drinks, so foam splashed over into each other's tankards. They held eye contact while they drank. Once neither of them died from poison, they slammed their jacks down on the table, ready to talk business.

"What the hell are you doing here?" Ketz repeated.

"Protecting my investment," said Minquo. "As I said, you should thank me. The river pirates in these parts...they can be bought, just like any other scum, but...well, whenever they're not acting in one's employment, they remain unpredictable. We wouldn't have wanted them to take further interest in you and your new friends on the *Arlash*...acting on their own whims, before you made it safely into port, would we now? It wasn't just the cover the mist provided, either. These river folk are a stupid, low-sunken breed, but they're not so low that they can't smell old magic in the air, and know that they want no part of it."

"Right," said Ketz. "So I'll bet now you're gonna tell me that first pack of 'em was just *actin' on their own whims* when they sailed out and ripped the *Arlash* a new one."

"Now why would I tell you such a thing?" said Minquo. "You know, Ketz my boy, I'm very disappointed in you, both you and your sister...yet maybe not so much as I thought. After all, here you are, still alive. So is your sister, I suppose?"

"Last I checked. So when did you plan to tell us what you actually sent us to snatch?"

"Oh, you mean the girl? I figured you would form some understanding about that on your own time. You disappointed me well before that, though. Come now, Ketz. You couldn't even make it within the city gates before you got yourselves so spectacularly arrested. Now, I will credit you, when I coerced that poor watchman as my assassin – by several liaisons removed, naturally – against the Lady Hallucia to further test you, as well as facilitate your subsequent career advancement – "

"Yeah, no offense, asshole, but that shit was pretty obvious."

"So it's the more unfortunate that you made such an unsubtle mess of things. It's a miracle the harbor patrol didn't get wind of your identity and arrest you before the *Arlash* set sail. The incident was the talk of the whole neighborhood within minutes. After further consideration, I decided it was in my better interest to redirect my travel route, to follow your boat directly along the shoreline, and at the proper tactical spot, hire the right disruption, likely enough to damage your vessel before their thwarting…rendering this little town the likeliest place you'd dock for repairs. As to our present meeting…that, I confess, is pure happy chance. I truly hope you've enjoyed your shore leave."

"Can't say that was as smart a move as you think. With all that water the *Arlash* is takin' on, those boxes of infernal dirt you got in the cargo hold are probably fucked by now."

Minquo now looked genuinely surprised. "Oh? Well, that hardly matters now. They've had all the time they needed to serve their purpose."

"What *purpose* is that?"

Minquo frowned. "Really, Ketz. I'm beginning to think you've grown confused about your own *purpose* in all of this."

Ketz snarled low, his hand drifting over to his sword beneath the table. "So which side of the Spirelight Empire you workin' for? Priest King Kalesha or her enemies?"

Minquo chuckled, leaned back, and folded his hands behind his head. "Why would I do business with either *side*…when I can do business directly with one of the gods themselves? That *infernal dirt*, if you must know, is the soil of the homeland of a dejected god, placed in proximity to her so she may grow strong in advance, on her way home to those lands."

"Went through all that trouble to deliver a bunch of dirt delivered to…exactly where it came from in the first place." Ketz shook his head. "Cute."

Minquo grinned. "Yes, young man, now that you mention it, I suppose it is. Do tell, how is that *cute* feisty sister of yours, or that *cute* sacred vessel of the god, back on that boat?"

Ketz sprang to his feet, his chair crashing over behind him. In the same motion, his sword shrieked partway out of the scabbard. "You fuckin' maniac, you got no idea what you're askin' for with that little –"

"Oh, but I do." Minquo lifted his hand and wagged two fingers. "I already told you, young man, that's my business, not yours."

Ketz sensed movement to his left. He spun, whipped his blade the rest of the way out, and saw one of the bad-skinned, yellow-clad men bearing down on him, brandishing a gleaming dagger. Before he could chop the bastard in half, something crashed against the back of his skull. Sparks showered through his vision. He went down sideways. His jaw smashed against the edge of the table. One of his back teeth shattered, so a shock of agony flashed through his whole being. Next thing he knew, he lay sprawled on his side across the floor, with the two gamblers kicking him in the ribs and head.

"That's enough, boys," Minquo shouted from somewhere. "*I said that's enough!* Remember, we still have bigger work ahead of us tonight. Leave him behind as a distraction."

The men stopped kicking Ketz. He still lay there quivering, half-numb, half-agonized. It was all he could do to spit and cough tooth-shards out of his mouth, on a lake of bloody drool.

TWENTY-ONE

Ketz landed with a splash in the wet mud outside. When he rolled around in it, light blazed into his eyes from within the tavern. Little by little, he blinked his vision clear. His jaw ached. When he tongued where his shattered tooth used to be, flashing raw nerves stabbed down through his jaw.

I need to wake up, pull myself together. Tia and Trosola are still back there, on that boat.

Hallucia. I mean Hallucia.

He tongued the shattered tooth a couple more times, so the shocking bursts wracked him into wakefulness. He pushed himself up. His empty scabbard flapped against his hip. A few times, he almost made it to his knees, then he slipped and sprawled on his face again. Finally, he willed himself upright, onto one foot.

Three figures had emerged from within the tavern. They stared down at him from the porch. At first, he thought it was Minquo and his two gambling buddies.

No, the one in the middle was the pretty Ghestru barmaid from earlier. She held his glistening bare sword in both hands, one on the grip, the other on the blunt quarter of the blade near the hilt, with the tip pointed at the ground...not like someone who'd ever wielded a weapon, but gingerly, like she was cradling an infant...an infant with the sharp edges she was afraid to cut herself on. To her left and right, there stood a pair of burly local Schomite men. Ketz recognized them from somewhere. Oh right, he'd butted up against them earlier, on his way to Minquo's table. They didn't look any more sober now. Most likely, they were just a couple of regulars here, yet they flanked the barmaid resolutely like hired security. The smaller one stood with his arms folded across his chest. The larger, older one let his arms swing casually at his sides, one fist hovering over a dagger strapped to his side.

As Ketz crawled around in the mud, the barmaid chirped, "Oh, look who's finally awake."

At first, Ketz couldn't tell if they presented an immediate threat. He got the sense that they hadn't quite decided either. "Hey, fellas," he groaned. "Miss. Y'all mind tellin' me how long I been lyin' out here?"

"Longer than I like on my watch," the barmaid said, pouting.

"Looks to me like you should move on along, son," said the larger, older man, "before the town watch comes along. You don't wanna be the outsider found lyin' in the mud when they get hold of you. No, sir. You got anywhere to stay, son? If you do, I suggest you get yourself there."

"Yeah. Sure. Sure." Ketz made it up onto both feet. He stumbled towards the porch. *Tia and Hallucia are back on the boat. Somethin' bad's about to happen there. I gotta get sharp, quick.* "Look, cool. Just give me my sword there, and I'll…"

"No way," said the barmaid. She stepped backwards, into the light of the doorway. "You really think we're gonna *re-arm* you, after what I just saw you try to pull in my bar?"

Ketz squeezed his eyes shut and shook his head. "I was…sittin' and playin' some cards with a gentleman. Then a couple of assholes we'd been playin' with earlier snuck up on me. I almost got 'em, but they –"

"Oh, don't even start with that," the barmaid shouted. "I saw the whole thing. You freaked out and pulled this sword on that well-paying gentleman. It's lucky for you one of his friends saw it happenin' in time to stop you! You'd managed to hurt that old man, you got any idea the trouble you'd be in right now?"

"More than you'd imagine," Ketz mumbled.

"*What?*" said the younger man, taking a step forward across the squeaky porch.

The older man stepped further forward, faster. He splayed a palm at Ketz. "Look, kid, just go and sleep it off somewhere, will you? You can come back tomorrow, when you got your mind right, and talk to the people here about your —"

"I ain't got time for that." Ketz took a lurching step up onto the porch. He tugged at the lapels of his uniform. "Look at me, will you? See these duds? I'm employed on an important vessel, downhill at your docks. I'm one of the rankin' bodyguards of the daughter of Orcris Brendi. Heard of him? Once his Excellency hears you've got in the way o' one o' his rankin' agents doin' his duty, he'll…he'll…man, I tell ya…" Damn, his skull hurt. So did his jaw. He usually knew how to work through pain. Why did this kind make it so hard to get full sentences out?

"Oh, son." The barmaid sneered and shook her head. "You can stop right there."

"See, here in Petrune," said the younger man, "you ought to have heard, we ain't ones for suckin' the cocks of…what do your bosses call 'emselves? The *highborns?* Yeah, boy, that ain't where we come from. Hey, come to think of it…now I get a better look at you, though, past that fancypants uniform…that ain't where you come from, neither, is it?"

Ketz lifted his shaky head and met the man's eyes. For a second, he thought he'd lucked out after all, found himself face to face with some sort of sympathizer to his cause…whatever the fuck his *cause* was.

The man's face twisted. "You make me sick. You're a disgrace to us all." The toe of his boot kicked mud from the edge of the porch, so it splattered like cold shit across Ketz's face and chest. "Go on, get out of here."

The barmaid added, "I don't care what fancypants vessel cut you loose on our little shores here." She stabbed her thumb at her heaving chest. "If you think that means you can walk into my place and start trouble with my good customers, you and your boss have the wrong idea about this town. You can tell him I said that, too."

Bright rage blazed through Ketz's brain…if not enough to clear away his muddled state, enough so he no longer gave a shit about it. With an explosion of maddened willpower, he lunged upwards and forward, between the two do-gooders. Their big hands swiped at him, then their tough, meaty arms buffeted across his back. He collided with the barmaid. Her crossed arms convulsed against her chest, pressing the Ghestru blade back from him. His fist crashed into her face. As her nose and jaw shattered, her hands spasmed open from the sword. Ketz's other hand shot out and caught the sword. He jerked it upwards. The barmaid screamed and yanked her arms back. Three little severed fingers sprinkled across the boards at her feet.

The local men went for their knives, all while Ketz's blade lashed about in a flashing rainbow arc. Flesh, muscle and bone split beneath the edge. A man's arm fell off at the elbow. The stump coughed a few times, then sprayed everywhere, including all over Ketz. He crouched and snarled, his eyes darting left and right. The other man clutched at his two slashed, spurting pectoral muscles, like a bashful girl trying to cover her bare breasts.

Ketz looked around in a daze and spotted the barmaid. She sank to her knees and let out a pitiful, high-pitched moan from her ruined mouth, all while staring in disbelief at her pruned hand.

Sword in hand, Ketz bounded across the muddy thoroughfare and vanished into the woods. From there, he made his way downhill towards the beach.

TWENTY-TWO

As he hurried through the woods, Ketz stripped down to his trousers, boots, and sword. Keeping his body moving wasn't the problem, even while working through this much pain. The problem was getting his mind clear and focused. He dashed down a steep ridge. Through the trees, he saw the fire lights rising from the beach. His head still stung and throbbed as he crept stealthily through the brush. He could already sense that something was wrong. The lights shown brighter than before. He darted along faster.

Finally, he saw the *Arlash* rocking in the surf. Flames blazed across the deck, licking upwards and climbing the sails. A wave of crewmen bustled down the gangplank, shoving against each other, then flooded out across the beach.

"Where's the captain?" someone shouted.

"The captain's dead," boomed the imperious voice of Orcris Brendi. He strode down the gangplank, his long robes and silky white hair flowing out behind him in the night. He stepped out between his men, all a-fluster, then gestured royally over his shoulder. "So soon shall be my three greatest mistakes. Look well on what you witness here tonight, men. See what becomes of those who betray the trust of the true bloodline."

Behind him, four more figures descended the gangplank. Two spearmen dragged a pair of small, squirming shapes between them. Both captives were female, one much shorter than the other. Ketz recognized the smaller one as Brili. Her slight, silken garments had been torn away, so she hobbled forward naked. Her red skin gleamed all over with redder blood, which wept freely from all the fresh gashes that covered her. Ketz couldn't tell in this light where all her injuries were, except for the swelling all over her face, especially beneath her eyes.

Ketz's breath caught in his throat as he peered at the other prisoner. Tia hung limp by the arms, her knees dragging in the sand. Her uniform was torn to shreds, glistening with fresh blood, some of it hers. The hanging flaps of cloth showed fresh weeping scrapes and lacerations. One of her cheeks swelled to the size of a plum, squeezing her left eye almost completely shut. Her hips twisted jerkily like someone had kicked her hard in one of them. When she breathed, her sides heaved and quivered, maybe from some broken ribs.

The spearmen dragged Tia and Brili out into the middle of the beach, then thrust them down onto their knees and held them there.

"Before we see about our business," shouted Orcris Brendi, "I want you all to witness this. My sweet daughter has been abducted by thieves in the night...degenerates of the same ilk as this hill-trash beast, one I trusted to safeguard my own daughter from our enemies!" He slapped Tia across the back of the head, then looked to Brili. "*This one*, though...one of our own race...well, more or less, I suppose...now, at this hour, it comes to my attention that she has spent her time colluding with the interlopers...*those who sought to undermine our rightful place in the order of things.*" He yanked the servant girl's hair back by the scalp. "Why did you do it, little Brili? Come now, tell us true. Why did you betray your own race...your own children? Do you now see what happens, to those who betray the trust of the true bloodline?"

"Do what you wish to the woman who kills people," Brili sobbed. "But please, first, show me my boopa! Let me know that my boopa will be safe, please!" She clawed and yanked at Orcis Brendi's robes. "*Please, your Excellency*, my boopa had nothing to do with what has —"

"Oh, you mean this *boopa?*" said Orcris Brendi. He gestured over his shoulder.

Two more retainers descended the gangplank. They crossed the dock, holding a squalling child dangling by the arms between them. They reached the sand, dropped the child, then spread out around it, giggling idly. They kicked it so it bounced across the sand between them, back and forth. It howled as its brittle little bones snapped with each kick. The men kept kicking it back and forth long after it stopped screaming, 'til it flopped limply like a jumbled sack with little limbs flopping here and there. The prostrate mother let out an ear-splitting shriek of disbelieving agony. Finally, the men left the dead child in the dirt. It twitched a few more times. One of the men wandered back over, giggled some more, and stomped on the head so the skull split like an eggshell. Brains squirted out all over his boots. Brili collapsed forward sobbing.

Orcris Brendi stalked back and forth, in front of Tia and Brili. "As you can see, my dear," he said to Tia, "you chose your secret confidants poorly. Now that you've seen how serious I am, why don't you tell us all why you and your brother really came to me, seeking work?"

Tia lifted her head, spat blood, and snarled, "You fuckin' perfumed prince moron! Them *thieves in the night* are already dead! Look around down there, you'll find what's left of 'em. Oh yeah, and that *sweet daughter* of yours? While you've had your head up your ass, she's gone and brought the wrath of a god down on you, a god who's gonna –"

"*Silence!*" Orcris Brendi backhanded Tia hard across the face. He rose back up, spreading his arms. "Hear me well, men! Our ship is lost, our cargo lost, but my daughter may yet be saved. She and her captors cannot have gotten far. But before you strike out, I want you all to watch this…to look upon the little barbarian bitch that has failed us all, betrayed my trust…she and her wretched brother, whose mind I still don't know."

Ketz crouched low and crept as close as he dared, through the brush, without revealing himself to any of these fools, just yet. One hand settled on his sword grip, while the other pointed as he tried to count how many of the Ghestru sailors were still alive. His throbbing head kept making him lose count, but it didn't really matter. There were way too many of them to take on alone. So what other options did he have? He felt around in the soil at his feet, 'til his fist closed around a heavy rock. He worked it free, ripping up clumps of dirt and sticky roots along with it. He found the right grip and lifted the rock. His aim with projectiles wasn't the best, as he'd been reminded nights ago at the town gates of Belcrasche.

Lands I love, he thought, *let this rock fly true now, for my sister's sake, please…*

Orcris Brendi stretched his upturned palm out to the side. One of his followers stepped up reverently and placed a wide, curved, heavy blade in his hand. Brendi took it in both hands and settled the edge against the back of Brili's neck. He did so almost delicately, then he lifted the blade high and let it fall, in a whistling chop. The little red head popped off, bounced, and rolled from side to side in the sand. The body slumped and sprawled. The stump let out one powerful jet of blood, then coughed out a spreading dark lake.

"That one's betrayal was inexcusable," said Orcris Brendi, "but it was a simple creature that had suffered enough." He said to Tia, "I regret that your death must be likewise swift."

He nodded to one of his men. The man yanked Tia forward by the hair and shoved her head down, baring her neck. Orcris Brendi leveled the heavy blade over her. Watching from the bushes, Ketz positioned himself better and took aim with the rock.

Far to Ketz's right, a man's voice boomed, "What crass show of lizardshit is this?"

Ketz recognized that voice from somewhere. With it, there came a fresh bloom of light and the click of approaching sleashkill feet. One by one, everyone on the beach looked. While they were distracted, Ketz crept out of the bushes. He edged out across the sand, keeping to the shadows, 'til he could see what everyone else was staring at. His eyes found their way to the hillside trail he'd followed up to the town earlier. A large group of local men now filled it with their descent. They all came on foot, except for the one in the lead riding atop a sleashkill…a man who wore a fancy long gray coat, brandishing a long-stemmed torch high above his head.

Orcris Brendi gaped at the procession. He absently lowered his blade, away from Tia's neck. "Sheriff," he cried out, trying to sound jovial and inviting. "Oh, thank the gods, here you've come. I'd not dared hope word would reach you so fast, even —"

"*Thank the gods* all you like, old man," said the sheriff of Petrune, "but don't thank me or these boys here just yet."

"What are you talking about?" said the merchant brazenly, as though he knew how to use that weapon in his hand on anything other than prostrate prisoners. "As you can see, we've suffered a terrible calamity, one you must —"

"Shut the fuck up," barked the sheriff. "Where's your captain?"

"Our captain is dead," said Orcris Brendi, who suddenly fought to subdue the tremble rippling through his voice. "As master of this voyage, anything you might have said to him, you may now say to me."

The sheriff looked around at the burning wreckage. His eyes paused on Tia on her knees next to Brili's headless corpse, then on the dead child lying in the sand behind them. "Yeah. Looks like you've really got your voyage mastered, meatskin."

Orcris Brendi blustered, unused to folks he saw as underlings talking to him like that. "Yes, well…we're busy getting the situation under control, so we don't have time for your interruptions right now."

"You should have thought of that before you let your thugs run wild in my town."

"What in the name of the gods are you blathering about,

Sheriff?"

The sheriff dismounted and strode towards Orcris Brendi. His men fanned out onto the sand behind him. "Was a troublemaker in the tavern just a little while ago. A bad'n. Everyone who saw what happened said he wore the uniform of one of your crew. He got a few drinks in him, then he went crazy and hurt some people. He cut up a bargirl. Sight of the state of that poor gal, it makes me sick." The sheriff shook his head solemnly. "While he was at it, he fucked up a couple of guys who tried to stick up for her. One of 'em lost an arm, doesn't look like he'll make it."

Crouched and listening, Ketz remembered how cute and sweet the bargirl had seemed at first. He felt a little guilty for slicing off her fingers. *Too bad the bitch threw in with Minquo.*

Orcris Brendi strode forward, smiling with his habitual self-assurance. "I'm terribly sorry to hear that, Sheriff. I've no doubt which ill-begotten member of my crew was responsible for this unfortunate outrage."

"That so? In that case, the sooner you hand his little punkass over to us, the sooner we can put all this quietly behind us."

"Good sirs, I'm afraid that's simply not possible as of yet. If you would merely –"

"*Not possible as of yet?*" The sheriff sneered, affecting a high-pitched prissy lisp, waving a hand overhead mockingly. "In case you forgot, Mister Orcris Brendi, you ain't in one of your fancypants Imperial ports. You're here on my terms, so you can shove all that *let's just pay off the locals* shit right up your fat pompous ass. Folks from my town, on my watch, have been attacked by your crewmen running amok. Me and these boys ain't leaving 'til we see justice done. So let's start over. How you wanna deal with this, huh?"

As Orcris Brendi and the sheriff stared each other down, the remaining fighting men from the former's crew – still torn and bloodied and dirtied from whatever they'd just endured on board – stepped out around their master. Their fingers twitched eagerly to draw blades and bloody them afresh. That included the ones who'd been holding Tia. They let go and stalked forward with the others. Tia slumped next to Brili's corpse, forgotten by everyone but Ketz, who still watched from the shadows, waiting for the right moment.

Tia groaned and pushed herself partway up. Ketz glanced back at the two groups facing off. He noticed the rock still clutched in his fist. The local sheriff's men numbered about half of Orcris Brendi's crew. The former still snarled at the latter, ready for anything, showing no fear. The night went deathly silent. The air crackled electrically with impending chaos and bloodshed.

One of the sheriff's men stepped to the fore and flung up his hands. "Everyone, wait a second! Cool down, fellas, let's just talk about this!"

"Stand down, deputy," the sheriff shouted.

"No, sir, really, I have to protest, by my sworn duty." He flung an arm out at the burning *Arlash*, at its already battered, dirty crew. "Just look at the sorry state of these men. Something don't add up. Maybe there's somethin' to the old man's tale, like maybe him and us got the same problems, like some kinda traitor in his midst."

Orcris Brendi stepped forward, pointed at the deputy, and said swiftly, "I'd listen to your man there, Sheriff, if I were you. I'm sure we can accomplish far more by looking at our common interests."

While the sheriff considered it, everyone in both groups looked at the other side, then at each other. The tension didn't exactly subside, though little by little, the strained passions cooled off.

Shit, Ketz thought, *that won't do at all.* He rose, stepped forward, and chucked the rock hurtling through the air with all his might. It arced down and bounced right off the head of the sheriff's would-be peacemaker.

The man stumbled left and right, eyes rolling, but he didn't fall over. Instead, he planted his feet soundly and shouted, "What the fuck was that?" He glared forward. "*Aw, you sonsofabitches!*"

Before his sheriff could check him, he lunged, whipped out his blade, and stabbed Orcris Brendi right in the throat. Brendi sank gurgling to his knees, coughing and spouting blood all over his immaculate chest. He was dead before his dick hit the dirt. Men on both sides roared, drew their blades, lunged, and crashed into each other with a cacophonous smack, hacking and gouging heedlessly, slicing and tearing chunks out of each other. The sheriff and his loyal outnumbered men fought like three for each of Brendi's indentured slave-fighters. Bodies on either side landed in the sand in increasingly rapid succession, turning the beach into a gory stew of corpses. Their brethren trampled and tripped over them, eager to kill and die.

While all those assholes were tied up in the fight, Ketz darted over to Tia. "Sis, *sis*, get up. Tia, it's me! C'mon!" He grabbed her by the shoulders and pulled her to her feet.

"Ketz! Aw, thank fuck, I thought I was – *Ow!* Hey, watch it!"

"You're welcome, sis."

"No, seriously." She hugged herself delicately with one arm, while pulling herself up on him by the other. "This shit hurts. They worked me over."

"You and me both," he said, even though he could already tell she'd had a worse night than him. "Can you run?"

"Yeah...*Ah!*" She clutched her side. "Yeah, I think so. Just..." She turned back to the little naked, headless corpse and moaned, "Aw, fuckin' hell, Brili..."

"I know," said Ketz. "Look, I'm sorry I couldn't –"

"*You're* sorry," said Tia, with something that might be either a sob or the strain of her injuries. "I'm the one got her mixed up in all this, her and her..." She glanced at the little bloody shape several yards away.

Ketz looked at the flames that spread through the *Arlash*, now belching from its lower windows. "Out of all the servants still trapped on that ship, looks like her and the brat probably got off easiest. C'mon let's get the fuck out of here before one side or other of those assholes wins."

As they darted for the trees, Tia panted, "You won't believe what just happened on that...that..."

"I got an idea," said Ketz. "It's worse than you think. C'mon, move it!"

They vanished into the trees. Behind them, the howls of slaughter rose higher and louder through the night.

TWENTY-THREE

They didn't know these woods, yet they fell into their usual rhythm just fine, darting up and down along the hillside that stretched out next to the river. Their lightly treading feet instinctively sensed out the bare spots between the foliage, navigating it as though taking a familiar, beaten trail. Ketz still held onto Tia, helping her along. Sometimes she winced and gasped, had to will herself to keep moving, to not fall into a lurching shamble. One of her hands still dug into his shoulder while the other clutched her side.

"Hang on, sis," Ketz kept whispering. "I got you. That's it, that's it, c'mon, girl, you're doin' great."

"Man, shut the – *Ah!* – shut the fuck up, *I am not doin' great.*"

They reached a sandy, secluded glade by the water. Ketz settled her to the ground and leaned her back against a fallen log. "Damn, girl, they really made a mess of you, huh?"

"No shit!" Her eyes rolled glassily. "You look like hell too. Wild night of shore leave?" She chuckled, then grimaced.

"You could say that. Look, we gotta figure out how to get you –"

"Fuck off," she said deliriously. "I…just need a few minutes to…Leave me be for a bit, will you?"

She lulled and swayed, on the verge of going into shock. Slowly, her breathing steadied. She went deep within herself, processing the pain, pulling herself together, not away from it, but through it. She'd taken a beating that might have killed a normal girl. Tia of the Nagga Mountains, however, was no normal girl, even by the measure of her tough, hill-dwelling upbringing. She was still gonna stand up, walk away and be done with all of this lizardshit, little worse off than when she had walked into it.

She opened her eyes, one of them anyway. The other one had swollen up worse by now, held almost entirely shut. The rest of her face was still pale and clammy. "Hey, let's make this the last time we take jobs from Ghestru, cool?"

"Cool by me," said Ketz. He crouched and squeezed her hand. "This wasn't their doing, though."

"Tell that to…" Something about how her mouth moved didn't feel right. She flexed her jaw. It popped in a way that felt unnatural, sending a jolt all through her. Once it subsided, she felt closer to one piece, like it had been dislocated and she'd just worked it back into place. "Tell that to Brili and her brats. Those bastards, I swear, I'll…"

"They ain't our problem no more, or anyone's," said Ketz. "What the hell happened on that boat back there?"

Tia rubbed her head. "It all happened really fast…It was…the Lady Hallucia herself, I think. Or that thing inside her. Weirdest damn thing…Brili came down to see me, said a couple messengers from town had come aboard, with a message for Lady Hallucia."

Ketz perked up. "What two messengers?"

"How the fuck should I know? I never saw 'em…not while they were still in one piece."

"Both with bad skin, wearin' yellow tunics, I'll bet," Ketz muttered.

"Huh? Y'know what, Brili mentioned somethin' like that. She said she didn't like 'em. I guess neither did the crew, 'cause they weren't allowed below deck, or anywhere close to Lady Hallucia. Anyway, they'd told Brili to tell me, and for me to tell Lady Hallucia…*that the moon had shifted from water to land.* I went into Hallucia's room and told her."

"Was it Hallucia you told?"

"Oh yeah, it was her, when I went in there."

"You're sure."

"Yeah, I'm sure. Will you shut up for a minute? It's hard

enough to piece it all together without you constantly interruptin' me. Anyway, I made sure to look into her eyes and everything, before I said a word about it to her. She said that didn't make a damn bit of sense. I believed her, mostly. Like, when I repeated the words, she looked surprised and confused like anyone, 'cept then the words sank in, and she looked mighty scared and haunted, like somethin' was comin' to get her. Ketz, I swear, I...I never seen anyone look so scared or helpless. It was awful.

"Whatever that was about, I couldn't get it out of her just then, so I went out and told Brili to go tell the captain to detain those messengers. Once Brili left, I went back into Hallucia's room. I was fixin' to pry more answers out of her, one way or another. 'Cept when I opened the door, she wasn't Hallucia anymore. She...that thing...Trosola...*it* came flyin' out at me, from all the way across the room, before I had time to pull my blade. She slammed into me so hard, I went backwards through the doorway and hit my head on the wall." Tia rubbed at the back of her scalp. "I don't know how long I was out. Must not have been that long, since no one found me like that, or if they did, they didn't bother over me. Soon as I came out of it, I ran up top as fast as I could. 'Cept whatever happened up there, it had already happened. She – *it* – was gone. All those sailors – the ones who weren't dead – had had enough time to get their shit together and start beatin' on Brili. I think they was gettin' ready to take turns with her, but they stopped when they saw me burst out onto the deck." She laughed bitterly. "Lots of good that did her in the end."

Ketz reached out slowly and placed a gentle hand on his sister's shoulder.

She shrugged him off. The longer she spoke, the less riled she sounded, more dull and distant. "They shoved her down on her knees, so she looked right at me. I'll never forget that look on her face. She kept screamin' at me, *I'm sorry, I'm sorry, woman who kills people! Please don't let them hurt my boopa.* Then one of 'em punched her in the face so she shut up. By then, the rest of 'em were comin' at me. I was still woozy from gettin' knocked out. Right then, I didn't have any more of a chance than Brili. Next thing I know, they all had hold of me, draggin' me up next to her, and there was that perfumed prince cocksucker, prancin' back an' forth, spoutin' all that same lizardshit like I guess you showed up in time to hear."

"Shit, this is worse than I thought," said Ketz. "Sis, we been played."

"You think?"

"There's more than you know." He told her what had happened at the tavern, with Minquo. "The fucker says he's *in business with a god.* Him and Trosola, I think they been workin' together this whole time. I don't know how they been keepin' in touch, but somehow, they coordinated all this."

"For what?" said Tia.

"For the perfect moment for her to fly the coop, through a bunch of chaos, so it'd look like somethin' no one would trace to him."

"Sounds crazy to me…but I guess he's gotta be crazy, workin' knowingly with a Spirelight god…'cept why hire us in the first place, as her bodyguards *or* her kidnappers?"

Ketz glowered. "We were hired to *look* like bodyguards and kidnappers, so we could take the fall."

Tia rubbed her bruised head. "I think we just did."

"Not quite," Ketz snarled. "We're still alive. I don't think Minquo expected that to happen."

"Oh well, fuck it," said Tia. "Either way, I had my fill of this shitshow. Just…give me another minute. I almost got this pain under control. Then we can figure out how to slip out of this shithole town, through all the patrolmen probably lookin' for us, so we can find our way home."

Ketz shook his head. "No way. I ain't done with this business yet."

Tia sat up sharply. *"Are you fuckin' shittin' me?* Look, Brendi already got what was comin' to him. We'll figure out how to get Minquo later. He's famous, remember? He won't be hard to catch, when we're ready."

"It ain't Minquo I'm worried about. It's that god in his pocket, or more likely he's in hers. She's loose in our realm of physical existence, in humanoid form. We seen what she can already do. Who the hell knows what those two got planned together? Whatever they mean to unleash, it ain't okay with me. Is that okay with you?"

"No, it ain't," said Tia. "Shit, I hate it when you're right."

"Look, sis, you're in bad shape, I can see that. You can get goin' home. I'll go do what I gotta do, then I'll catch up."

Tia stood up. "Fuck that. You think I'm gonna leave somethin' this big to you, see how badly you'd fuck it up on your own?"

"Fair enough."

"Guess now, the question is, where are they headed?"

Ketz stared out across the river as it glistened in the moonlight. It was peaceful and quieted his mind. What had Minquo called those boxes of rancid dirt? *The soil of the homeland of a dejected god, placed in proximity to her so she may grow strong in advance, on her way home to those lands.* "They're headed to Tatelle," he said. "Minquo seemed mighty concerned about gettin' Hallucia to a specific place there, at a specific time...where'd he say for us to meet, again?"

"Some tavern outside of town...the Spine-Rat. Before the sun rose, on the night the *Arlash* was supposed to dock there."

"All that specific timin's gotta mean somethin'. They're fixin' to kick somethin' off."

"Shit," said Tia, "that gives us less than four days." She caught Ketz by the arm. "When we *do* find them, you're gonna remember that they're both our enemies, right?"

Ketz sighed. "I'll tell you when we get there."

"If you'd said anything else, I'd'a called you a liar and slapped you silly. Okay, let's find the quickest way by land to Tatelle.

TWENTY-FOUR

They crouched in the brush, alongside the road that ran out of town, down the coast. Eventually, there sounded the clicking gallop of sleashkill hooves. A pair of riders rounded the bend, donning the same rough spun uniforms as the rest of the local law around here. The men rode at a slow canter, out on patrol, likely with the twins' descriptions at the top of their shit list. As they drew nearer, Tia peeled off the remains of her ruined top, then squirmed out of her trousers.

"What the hell you doin'?" Ketz hissed.

"Quiet," she said. "Be ready to do your part."

With that, she stood up naked, wiping gobs of congealing gore onto her hands from her discarded uniform, before casting it aside. She smeared the mess all over herself, caking it particularly thick around her inner thighs. As the riders drew near, she shambled out of the brush into the middle of the road, where she fell to her knees and let out a blood-curdling scream that sent birds into a frenzy through the surrounding trees. The riders yanked their beasts to a halt.

"Now what the hell…?" said one of them.

"Some damn naked girl…" The other patrolman dismounted and approached. When he reached out, Tia flinched away, hugged herself, and sobbed louder. "Shit!"

His companion also dismounted. "Hey, naked girl out here on this road at this hour? Our lucky night!"

The closer patrolman sneered over his shoulder. "Shut up, asshole. Look at her! She's been done dirty like…Holy shit…Hey girl, we ain't gonna hurt you. What happened?"

Tia looked up timidly. "Those…those two renegade hill-folk Schomite kids…the ones everyone's lookin' for…I was walkin' home with some milk for mama…*just some milk for mama*…they came out of the bushes and grabbed at me. I ran. They chased me. They…they…"

"Take it easy, kid. We get it. Look, we're here to help."

The other patrolman stepped up beside his companion, looked Tia over, and shook his head. "Fucking hill-tribe savages…"

That's when Ketz sprang from the brush behind the patrolmen. He grabbed them both by the hair, one in either fist, and slammed their skulls together with an echoing clap. They both dropped to the ground senseless.

Tia stood up and brushed off her terrified-victim act like dust from her shoulders. She put her hands on her hips, looked at the unconscious men, then back up at Ketz. "Oh good, you got the idea." She started dragging one of the patrolmen into the bushes. "Go make friends with their sleashkills."

While Tia got the patrolmen stowed, Ketz turned back to the startled, agitated animals. He eased in close, caught them by the bridles, and guided them off to the other side of the road. He tethered them to a low-hanging branch, then went back to assist Tia with the patrolmen. She'd already dragged both of them off the roadside. He found her stripping one of them naked.

"What you doin' now?"

"We need new clothes." She sniffed inside the trousers she'd just removed. "Okay, good, these ain't *too* nasty." She wiped away the worst of the gory mess away with her old ruined clothes, then pulled on the pants, cinched the belt as tight as it would go, then pulled on the fresh shirt, vest, and jacket, the last of which hung way too large over her slight frame. "Well, the top fits better, at least. We can't ride all the way to Tatelle lookin' like…well…us."

Ketz still had on his boots and trousers from the Ghestru uniform. He peered down dubiously at the unstripped patrolman. His own boots and trousers were dark enough that all the splatter wouldn't show much come daylight, once it dried, so long as no one looked too closely.

Tia was right, though. They'd reach their destination quickest by the open road. That would go smoothest if they looked more like law local enforcement.

Ketz rolled the heavy, unconscious man around, working him out of his shirt, vest and coat. The guy groaned and squirmed sometimes, so Ketz worried he was about to come around already. He drew and examined the thin, curved sword the guy wore. It was carved from the same river-monster scale as those pirates had used, though more elegantly sculpted. So maybe take that with him too? Nah, he liked how the Ghestru blade had worked out for him. He cast the newer weapon aside.

Tia's Ghestru sword had been taken from her, so she strapped on the curved scale blade from her unconscious man. She drew it and shifted about, testing the weight and action. She was still smarting from the beating she'd taken earlier, which hitched up her footwork a little, but not much.

"Oh, quit lookin' at me like that," she said. "I'd almost think you fell for my act back there."

He frowned at the unconscious men. "These guys sure did. One of 'em even wanted to do the right thing, from the sound of it."

"Wanna wake him up and apologize?"

"Fuck that." Ketz strode out, across the road, back to the two tethered sleashkills. On his way, he shook his shoulders, better feeling out how the new shirt and jacket fit him. "We'd best ride hard and hope like hell these beasts hold out. Got a feelin' these disguises won't hold up so well in broad daylight."

He took one beast by the bridle, led it out into the middle of the road, and climbed up into the saddle. The beast was still shivery and scared, but it accepted him soon enough as its new rider. Tia drew her beast out and climbed into the saddle. They kicked their steeds into motion and galloped down the road through the night.

TWENTY-FIVE

They made camp only once during the journey, sleeping just three hours each. One slept while the other kept watch and hunted for food and fresh water. They lost enough time catching up with their prey, just locating the quickest route to Tatelle that the beasts could take. Their best hope was still to reach the Spine-Rat just ahead of Minquo and Trosola, to catch them in an ambush.

The town rolled into view over the last sloping hill, as the first glimmers of dawn crept across the waters beyond the distant harbor.

Tia sniffed the salty, fishy air, from downhill where the river met the ocean's morning tide. "Yeah, sure smells like we're in another harbor town."

As they trotted down the winding road, a crooked line of swaying, stilted shanty-shacks rose up to meet them. The ground grew muddier, so they had to make their beasts go slower. Out front of one of the shacks, light burned from a small cooking fire. A bundled-up toad-like figure sat hunched over it, stirring slowly. The wooden spoon extended from a withered, bluish, long-fingered hand. Ketz reined his sleashkill to a halt near the fire.

The hunched, ancient figure looked up drowsily, as though just now noticing them. "Safe travels, I trust, on this brisk morning," said a crackly old-lady voice, "…Officers."

"Indeed, ma'am." Ketz had listened to enough policemen talk to know how to adopt their diction, projecting that steady mix of imposing authority, smug neutrality, and condescending friendliness. "We don't wish to take up much of your time. We've ridden far from our point of call, in

THE RENEGADE GOD ~ 201

search of some fugitives. We hear tell their hideout is someplace in your area."

"There's no fugitives here…lad and lass," the old crone droned, returning her attention to her kettle.

Tia guided her mount up alongside Ketz's. "We ain't suspicious of you, lady, relax. We just have a name of a place where…our sources say they might be headed. Maybe you could point us in the right direction."

"If you truly seek the right direction within this township, young lad and lass, I might offer guidance. Stop to rest a while. Enjoy a cup of morning stew."

Ketz smelled it from the saddle. The aroma sure was tempting, after the past days' diet of roots and rodents. "That's nice, but we really don't have –"

Tia swung down out of her saddle and stormed forward. "Look, lady, we just need to ask directions. Now can you do that or not?"

The old woman kept stirring. "But of course, young lass."

Ketz's sharp ears caught small, whispering movements up and down the string of shacks. He looked around furtively. One by one, through the gloom, gangly, lurching figures shuffled out onto the narrow porches. They didn't move like day-laborers coming out to stretch and breathe the morning air before setting off to their day's toils. Ketz's hand drifted silently over the saddle-horn, towards his sword. In the old woman's tiny firelight, he saw his sister's lean arms tensing, her fingertips curling and quivering impatiently at her sides.

"We just need to get to the Spine-Rat Tavern, ma'am," said Ketz. "You know the way there or not?"

"Ah yes, the Spine-Rat…*yes, oh how I know that place well*, of old…Many a memory from my youth, I still hold, dancing to the songs of a wilder, more permissive time. But you're a good, upright lad and lass, aren't you, I can see, wouldn't like to hear all about those old follies…*dancing to the song of Trosola, how she once let us all know ourselves for the first time.*" Her eyes flashed like spinning coins in firelight. "You wish to know the way there, do you, brave policemen?"

Ketz slid from his saddle and edged towards his sister's side, hand on his pommel. In his peripheral vision, the creeping shapes of the neighbors edged down off their narrow plank porches, filling the muddy thoroughfare in either direction. The thickening mob closed in. Dull, hungry eyes gleamed in the gloom like a swarm of fireflies.

He kept pretending not to notice. "Yes, ma'am, we do. Just go ahead and point us in the right direction."

"Yes, of course," the old woman hissed. She pointed off down the road. "Just follow this little street down past the next four shacks, then take the winding road through the woods to your left...there, down and down and down the way, through the dark of the Trosolmarsh swamp, you will find the Spine-Rat. Tell me, though, these fugitives you seek...do they go to threaten our Lady of the Light and Dark?"

"Lady of what?" said Tia.

"Our Lady of the Light and the Dark lives in the Trosolmarsh swamp. If you go that way, you may learn to see her there, in those vines and trees. If she likes you, she will grant you safe passage through her marshes."

Tia smacked her forehead. "You gotta be shittin' me."

"Oh. I see." The old woman's face drooped, as though disappointed in a pair of naughty children. She leaned forward so the firelight fell across her dried-nut face...across the symbol, freshly carved into her forehead, the scabs still sticky and smeared. "You thought that we who dwell by Her forest have not always known that it was Her rightful home...that the time for her return is at hand...that it's She whom we serve, and not Their sea, out there?" She flung a hand idly over her shoulder in the direction of the harbor. "Oh no, children. We have long sensed the time coming when all will see Her, and She has shown herself truly, to reward us with Her kiss upon our foreheads."

"Fuck this." Tia turned back to their mounts. "C'mon, Ketz, let's —"

"I see you, young travelers, oh yes, as I saw in my dreams after she kissed my forehead. You have come to hinder Her designs. I am sorry, young travelers, so sorry."

The old lady sprang to her feet, quicker than such a withered frame should have allowed. Tia cursed and jumped back. As she went for her blade, the woman fell on her like a striking snake. The slimy, rotting mouth gaped wide and sank jagged, yellow teeth into Tia's forearm. Tia jolted, snarled, and yanked back. The old bitch held on, digging in faster. Her feet and skirt dragged through the tiny fire, spilling the steaming pot. The flames caught her and licked quickly upwards through her skirt, brighter and higher. The old lady didn't seem to notice, even as the stench of roasting humanoid flesh fumed off her through the smoke.

That was Tia's sword-arm with the old lady hanging off, to. Tia backfisted the old bitch in the forehead repeatedly, in a rapid tattoo of dull thuds. The lady still wouldn't let go. This was becoming worrisome fast.

Ketz's sword was out by now. As he stepped up alongside them and lifted the blade, his eyes played a ghastly trick on him. In the rising flames, it looked like the whole body dragged limply, as though already dead. One of Tia's blows had broken the neck, so the jaws stayed clamped on in some final death-spasm. No, that old gray-blue head still snarled and worried and gurgled from side to side, no matter how many times Tia slammed her knuckles into it. There was no getting a clean swipe at the neck, not with Tia shrieking and jerking and dancing around as the heat of the flames climbed closer to her. Ketz shifted his feet and chopped lower. Ancient bones split beneath the edge like soggy twigs. An arm fell off in the mud. The upper torso hung at two angles, split partway in half. A cascade of sickly-smelling blood spilled out like dirty water from a ripped sack. That swipe must have cut the heart in two, but those jaws still clung to Tia's arm.

To their left, the sleashkills shrieked and reared.

Ketz's second swipe lopped the body the rest of the way

204 ~ MATT SPENCER

in half. The flaming lower quarters landed with a heavy splash, the feet still in the cooking fire. Tia staggered as the head and shoulders still dangled from her arm, lively as ever. Ketz started towards her, then glanced around. The other creeping shapes were closer now, on either side in two thick, shambling waves. The first bunch got between the twins and their braying mounts. In the firelight, scythes, pitchforks, and other crude weaponry glimmered in their pocked, boil-infested hands.

Tia got up next to one of the porch beams and bashed the thing on her arm against it 'til the bloody, shattered jaws loosened and fell away. The head splashed in the mud, the broken jaw still whining silently as it flexed open and shut. Tia jumped when she saw the hoard closing in. She shook her smarting sword-arm and reached again for her blade. Blood dripped from her hand and sleeve, making her grip slippery, so she fought for a proper hold as the first of them reached her.

"Blasphemous interlopers," hissed a man, "can't let you get near our Lady of –"

Tia's blade whipped out about and crashed down on his crown, splitting his skull to the teeth. When she wrenched the blade free, the man dropped, his brains running down his face like muddy shit. At least something seemed to put these fuckers down for good!

Another of them swung a scythe at Ketz. He sprang over it and sliced the guy across the belly. The man's legs crumpled beneath him, his guts spilled out, and he sat in his own red puddle, like someone who'd just shit and pissed themselves. The man marveled dully at his own entrails in his lap and lifted the slippery loops on his fingers.

Whatever these folks had been turned into, at least they were sort of slow. None of them seemed to have been trained fighters to begin with. Still, there were lots of them, most of them were swinging sharp objects around, and the two opposing blades at the center could only deflect so many strikes, so quickly, for so long. On each of their foreheads, the mark of Trosola had been freshly carved.

No sooner had Ketz dropped the first guy then the next one came gouging at his shoulder. He pivoted away, his blade dipping beneath the attacker's. The attacker's blade still nicked his sternum, so the moment froze, flashing in and out of existence. Then he felt his blade sink through a throat and split a spine. Only as his blade slid free did he realize he'd just stabbed a girl at least three years younger than him. She sank to her knees, gasping and spurting, right as another set of hands yanked him backwards by the shoulder. The grip spasmed away. Ketz spun in time to see Tia's blade jutting out of a spreading red patch in an old man's chest. When the man kept squirming, she yanked her blade free, flung him to the ground, and brought her boot heel down on his head in one stomp that shattered his skull.

The twins hacked and gouged in a rising frenzy. Limbs fell and flew from spurting stumps, on bodies that kept coming, silently and obliviously, 'til they had nothing left of themselves with which to attack, so they fell to be trampled into the mud by their companions.

Yards away, the two sleashkills shrieked louder. Both beasts reared up one last time, above the heads of the mob, before many hands and pinions pulled their massive bulks down. The bleating rose to the agonized pitch of creatures getting ripped to shreds, before going abruptly silent.

Meanwhile, the upset cooking fire had spread and caught the front step of the old lady's shack. As it spread across the porch, Ketz felt its heat at his back. He looked around quickly, hacked his way free of the tangle, then retreated backwards and caught a rung of the porch beam. He tore it loose with a furious, nail-popping wrench, spun back, and fanned the flaming end in the face of the next ghoulish townsman to come at him. The creature tried to press aside the flaming wood. The hands touched the flame and recoiled. Ketz shoved the flaming end right into the man's ragged clothes.

The flames caught and climbed the body. The man didn't scream, just squirmed and hopped around, as though trying to shake it off like a swarm of insects. Ketz kicked the blazing man hard in the gut, sending him careening back into the rest of them. For a moment, the man fell and vanished within their onslaught, flames and all...then the flicker of yellow and orange rose up one body, then another, 'til ever more of them hopped and squirmed, igniting each other left and right.

Tia and Ketz fought their way back to each other's side as the mob dispersed around them, through the vile, roasting stench. From there, it wasn't hard to dash downhill, putting plenty of ground between themselves and the slow creatures. A few of them still tried to follow. The twins turned back long enough to cut them down with relative ease, then broke into a run down the road.

Before long, the mob was a distant heap of grotesquely milling silhouettes, from which a golden bonfire bloomed ever wider and higher, belching black smoke against the brightening sky. Tia and Ketz trotted to a halt, panting, clutching, and leaning on each other. Their stolen uniforms were now cut and torn to hanging shreds. Ketz let the remains of his jacket slide from his shoulders. None of their fresh wounds seemed serious, but then again, their adrenaline hadn't subsided.

Tia clutched her still-tender ribs. "This shit," she panted, "I'm fuckin' done with it. Let's go finish it, quick, before it's us who's done. I don't care how. Just so those two fuckers responsible are dead."

Ketz caught his breath. "Figure that ain't far, at least." He pointed to the lonely road that cut off to their left, through the Trosolmarsh swamp.

"You sure that's the right one?" said Tia. "That the old bitch wasn't lyin'?"

"Looks like the best shot we got," said Ketz. "Unless you wanna go back to ask around among those kindly townsfolk."

TWENTY-SIX

True to its name, the Trosolmarsh swamp spread out gloomy, silent, and soggy, even on the narrow road. The sky shimmered ever paler through the high, mossy treetops, like some great silver beast's long, spiky trail. Yet so little light leaked down between those trees, as though this forest shunned it, along with all sounds of life. Only a soft, moaning wind sent skittering whispers through the surrounding wet brush and reeds. In such black stillness, the twins' soft footsteps echoed deafeningly. Their ears perked keenly, for any further traps their prey might have set.

As the adrenaline cooled from all the hard riding and fighting, their aches and pains and weariness crashed ever heavier on their bodies. Still, they kept on at a steady clip, walking faster than many people ran. Tia's limp had come back. Several times, she started lagging behind. Then with a defiant snort and snarl, she redoubled her pace 'til she strode ahead of Ketz so he had to work his own cramping legs harder to catch up.

"Hey, whoa, there, sis. Stop and rest a spell, or you're gonna fall flat on your face."

"Can't," she growled. "We're too short on time as it is."

Ketz looked around and agreed. The further they walked, the more familiar this all looked, like if he stepped off the trail into the marshes, he'd know the slimy sludge and pulp around his feet like he'd been born here. All that was missing was the flame-spouts...and the other dancers.

"Ketz...?" said Tia.

"I know this place," he sighed.

"Okay, but...hey, hold up, now you're the one goin' too

fast!"

"She's waitin'," he said. "We gotta hurry."

Finally, the woods got brighter around them…not quite like the trees finally let in the dawn or like something glowed through the thinning branches ahead…more like an eerie combination of the two, yet something else altogether. Even the air tasted different…something electric to it, invigorating…magnetic. Before they knew it, they both found themselves moving forward quicker and easier. Their injuries smarted just as sharply, yet the crushing weight lifted from their shoulders. At the same time, they both felt more intensely aware than ever of their hunger…no, this felt more like a *thirst*. Whatever awaited them at the Spine-Rat, it wouldn't be a hot breakfast with some chicory. Some preternatural balm radiated from nearby, *wanting* them to reach it. It wanted to meet them at their best, or as close to it as possible. They sniffed towards it eagerly.

A burning smell floated through the trees ahead…someone's campfire, maybe? No, this smoke was muskier, full of exotic incense and perfume, of a specific kind. *The smell of Spirelight sorcery, of Spirelight gods.*

They edged off the roadside and through the marshes. A long, strangely shaped wooden building came into view. Clean white smoke billowed from a tall brick chimney near the back. The architecture was unlike anything they'd seen lately, certainly not this far inland. Just enough sun spilled down across it to show the marks on the swinging sign above the front door.

Tia swatted Ketz's shoulder. "You read those marks?" she whispered.

"Yeah."

"They say what I think they say?"

He nodded. *"The Spine-Rat."*

It sure fit the bill for *a lonely roadside establishment*, as Minquo had put it. The name was written in Schomite marks, but the building stood in accordance with the Spirelight's

Sacred Architectural Geometry – octagonal, with sharp arches jutting up from each corner, with perfectly centered, oval-shaped windows of smoky glass, running between them like a chain of beads. Even the broad, grassy yard seemed to match the structure's symmetry, like the natural extension of some breathing organism, with edges that still crawled outward, wanting to keep growing, to consume the rest of the surrounding environment. No one went in or out, though red lights glowed from within the smoky windows.

"I don't get it," whispered Tia. "There ain't even a guard."

Ketz's eyes gleamed in that strange way. "Maybe they don't need one. Whatever's makin' that red light inside, it's the only guard the place needs."

"How you figure that?"

"Can't you smell it on the air...*taste* it?"

"I'd slap you upside the head, but you're talkin' like you already been hit there more than plenty." Still, she'd be lying if she claimed her mouth didn't water with that same primordial awareness. She gritted her teeth against it, managed to keep her head about her, and said, "So let's *not* go right in through the front door, then."

They crept around through the trees, peering out at the structure from all sides. Around back, beneath the tall chimney, they spotted a sheltered stone dugout leading down to a shadowed basement door. None of the red windows faced them from here, but they still surveyed the whole scene minutely. They broke cover and darted across the back yard through wet grass, to the steps leading down to the basement. They reached it and got down the stairs without trouble. Crouched at the bottom, they went deathly still, pressed their ears to the door, and sniffed the air that leaked through the seams. Above, the weird perfume had been overwhelming. Down here, a fresh stench leaked out at them, over fetid basement dirt and refuse.

Tia turned away, wrinkled her face, and hissed, "Oh, fuckin' hell!"

"Yeah," Ketz whispered. "Whoever's behind this door, they're pretty ripe."

"Pretty dead, you mean," she said, then went stiller than ever. "For a while, too."

Ketz listened for anyone who wasn't dead, then tried the knob. The door creaked open with a rusty whine. The twins froze pensively. The death-choked air flooded out and hit them in the face, but no solid attackers met them. A faint, steady drumbeat echoed down from above.

"I know that drumbeat," Ketz whispered.

When it continued undisturbed, they edged inside, choking down their gorge against the stench. At the other end of the bare-dirt floor, the red light spilled downstairs through a narrow, twisting stone stairwell. Ketz closed the door slowly, doubly sure to make no noise. As their eyes adjusted to the faint red gloom, they noticed three motionless humanoid shapes, that had been shoved or tossed up against the walls at odd angles like discarded rag dolls. Flies buzzed around them.

As Tia and Ketz darted towards the stairs, something shifted to their left. They pivoted towards the noise, their blades sliding out quietly. No mad subterranean beast sprang forth at them, though.

"It seems to me, you kids are just too stubborn to die," rasped a choked, pained voice. It came from one of the bodies, the odd one out, to their right. "Everyone else…continues to be far more reasonable, or so I hear. Perhaps I was…hasty, to cast you aside as I did."

They stared through the gloom in disbelief. Ketz followed Minquo's voice across the floor. "You got that right, asshole," he hissed, lifting his sword to strike. As he closed the distance, though, his boot struck something — two more boots, outstretched, pressed tightly together. He stooped, reached out, and felt tight cords binding Minquo's legs. "The fuck…?" Through the dim light, he beckoned Tia to his side.

She knelt, discovered the same thing, and smirked grimly. "Let your *Lady of the Light and the Dark* down, huh?"

"The…what…? Oh. Yes. Of course." Minquo hacked out bitter laughter. "That is…what they know *her* as, in these parts. It seems they have for quite some time."

"Guess that includes whoever used to own this place," muttered Ketz.

"You could ask them yourself," said Minquo, "but they don't seem to be the talkative sorts." He cocked his head at the other two bodies that lay across from him. "If your guess is correct, it seems I have something in common with them, besides these festive accommodations. As to our mutual friend, the renegade god, I believed until recently that she and I worked together, towards mutual ends. It would seem…"

Minquo coughed, then groaned and squirmed in the dirt. It sounded like he had a few busted ribs in there, maybe a collapsed lung. Credit where credit was due, that would make him one tough bastard, holding it together and talking as well as he did. In this darkness, it was impossible to tell how bad the damage was. Apparently not bad enough for Trosola to leave him unrestrained.

"It would seem she has used me, all along," he finished saying.

"Oh, you mean like you used us?" said Ketz.

"Well, now that you mention it…" Minquo grinned through bloody lips.

"Oh, you think that's funny, huh?" growled Tia. She leaned in on the dark, bound shape. The tip of her long knife tickled his bristly, leathery cheek.

"Sometimes one must take a good laugh where one can find it," said Minquo. "I would offer that as sagely advice for your trails ahead, kids, but I doubt you've any to look forward to…future trails, that is."

"Oh yeah? So just tell us *why*, would you? What the fuck did you think was in for you, betrayin' all our kind, hell, the whole world, to a creature like that?"

"Is it not simplicity itself, young lady?" He coughed again, harsher and wetter this time. "No, I don't guess it would be.

You're far too young. As my years have passed, I've just gotten better and better at my work, unconcerned with glory or any other higher purpose, taking whatever work I found from the finest bidders who'd have me. I can't even tell you how many years it's been, since I met anyone even close to my equal...and I never once realized how boring it had become...not until I had the opportunity to serve a god. What more exalted thrill...could there be...than that? I just...expected my services to be retained for longer, throughout her coming reign."

Ketz shared his sister's boiling desire to kill Minquo slowly and painfully. Still, he eased her back and whispered calmly, "How many of them are up there?"

Minquo hacked out another agonized chuckle. "Stupid kids. You're both as dead as I am."

"Oh, who said anything about killing any of you?" said a crystal, sprightly voice from the stairwell. "You're all far too cute for that."

Tia and Ketz stood up sharply. They pivoted and pointed their blades at the stairwell, *en garde*. Trosola strode easily down the steps. There was no need to guess which one they were looking at. Her yellow eyes glowed at them, as she held her back and shoulders straighter and prouder than ever. She now wore a light, flowing gown of some otherworldly fabric that shimmered orange and blue and gold, dancing with light that wasn't there. Not just the dress, but everything surrounding her was...*wrong* like that. Every inch of her stood out crisp and clear, like she glowed in the dark, except she cast no illumination into the surrounding shadows. It was like she stood in full daylight somewhere else, superimposed on these surroundings like a projected illusion. Even when she stepped off the bottom stair and across the earthen floor, she appeared weightless, like she probably wasn't even leaving tracks in the dirt, except they couldn't see the dirt well enough to tell.

She approached them like she was oblivious to the

immediate threat they presented…or assuming her mere magnificence would awe them into compliance. Tia and Ketz had stood within the presence of Spirelight divinity before, though. They weren't impressed. They'd also seen what she could do physically, but that had been against degenerate, undisciplined river pirates and broken-spirited indentured Ghestru slaves with no idea what hit them. Last time, she'd caught Tia off guard. Tia and Ketz were spry, sharp bandits of the Nagga Mountains, veterans of Trescha, and they weren't off guard now.

As they lunged at her, she smiled serenely, threw back her head and stretched out her arms. Her strange glow no longer confined itself to her. It lit up the whole room, as though from a thousand clear, pure candle flames. Tia and Ketz froze in their tracks, less than three feet away from her. They recovered from the initial shock and continued forward…except they didn't. They couldn't. They'd frozen mid-strike, immobilized from head to toe, as though the air itself – this light of Trosola – had become solid crystal, holding them like fish trapped in ice. They could still breathe, their nerves and muscles still quivered murderously, and their snarling lips still rippled back from their sharp teeth, salivating for her.

Trosola lowered her arms, folded her hands behind her back, and strode between them casually. She looked them over like someone gazing on sculptures in a museum. The drumbeats overhead had stopped.

Everything was deathly quiet, 'til she spoke "Ah, sweet Tia….and *sweet, sweet* Ketz." Her voice lowered huskily as she stroked his cheek. "I'm so glad you've both made it. I so look forward to having you with me, to share in everything that's about to happen. Yes, you, Ketz, my sweet, ravaging plaything, I look forward to your companionship most of all."

"*Hallucia…*" Ketz managed to say through his teeth. He was surprised how easily he could still get words out.

She frowned, almost crestfallen. "Oh, Ketz, I thought you

understood! You're not talking to that little Ghestru bitch. We don't have to worry about her anymore."

"Yes," he spat. "Yes, I am. Fuck you, whatever you are. Hallucia. I know you're in there, you hear me? Remember what I said…about…"

"Of course she is, and of course she does." Trosola patted Ketz's cheek. "For all the eternity that is me, though, I just don't understand why you care. She had nothing to do with all the fun we had. All she did was quaver and cling to you, blubbering about how unfair her fate was, as though it wasn't all her own doing." She stroked the tattoo across her chest.

"This place ain't her doin'," said Ketz. "Neither is whatever infernal catastrophe you've cooked up here, with…hey, seriously, what the fuck *are* you cookin' up, anyhow?"

"This, sweet Ketz, has been *cookin'* for a long, long time before poor, pathetic little Lady Hallucia ever invited me in…before she or any of you in this room were born. Before the rest of that ungrateful Pantheon cast me out, I was one of their most visionary, architectural minds, seeing how this lovely little planet of yours could be remapped, reformed, in our divine, collective image. This swampy riverside province here was to be *my* keystone of it, where *my* grand city-state should have been built, with *my* shining temple looking out from on high, across our lands.

"When the rest of the Pantheon decided on another vision, they thought they could discard me and be done with it. They meant to leave my lands to rot into a forgotten little swamp, neglected to wither in the dark. You both saw the architecture of this place, from without, didn't you? You met some of my local terrestrial acolytes, too, it looks like. Did you think it was the Spirelights – those who serve the rest of them – who made the local people build it like this? No, no, my sweet ones, *my* spirit has been so strong within these lands that their builders are born to my spirit, breathing it in their very cribs as babes.

"What the others didn't realize was that I was far from the first outcast spirit to dwell out here. Within the marshes around us, there dwell the Devils of the Dark Lands, who the Pantheon long ago ceased to traffic with. Here, those devils rose to meet me, so their powers blended with mine as we fed each other. In time, I brought them in line, under my control, as well. Ever since, my essence has bubbled and churned beneath the surface, pressurizing within confinement, waiting for the day when all aligned for me to burst forth. Oh, Deschemb *shall* be reshaped in a new divine image…just not the one the rest of the Pantheon expected."

"Speakin' of all that *bubblin'* and *pressurizin'* and *burstin'*," said Tia, speaking for the first time since this ethereal paralysis had taken hold, "it sure does sound like you've spent plenty of all this time just diddlin' yourself."

Trosola clapped twice, loudly. A moment later, one set of feet echoed on the stairs above. Then another. Both descended unhurriedly, before a pair of stately figures entered the room behind her. The men wore uniforms of black and deep gray, black capes flowing out behind them, with pale, purplish skin and swept-back, ice-white hair. They strode out to either side of Trosola, before their eyes settled on Tia and Ketz. That's when their faces twisted with steely hatred. They drew straight, thin acid-etched short-swords from their hips. Their pristine dress, weapons, bearing, and lean, stalwart presence marked them as high-ranking officers of the Spirelight International Police. One of them looked quite a bit older than the other, more scarred and craggy in the face, with easier, suppler, more seasoned movements. But for the hypnotized reverence in his eyes, he looked almost bored. He spotted the twins' immobility before his younger companion did. The latter's whole frame blazed with more youthful fire, which made the perpetually hypnotized glaze on his eyes even creepier. He almost kept lunging, but his companion grabbed him by the shoulder in a powerful grip that yanked him to a halt. Their mistress smiled over her shoulder at them.

"As you can see," said Trosola, "these two handsome gentlemen move unhindered within my radiance. Soon so shall you, once you've learned to accept me."

"Great," Tia sighed. For the first time in her life, her voice withered in utter, bitter defeat. "So all this time, we've been workin' for the damn Spirah Empire. Now we're all fucked. How you like that?"

Trosola blanched. "*Their* Empire? Oh no, sweet Tia. Haven't you been listening? Yes, these warriors once served that same enemy that has plagued your people, the one you've spent your whole life fighting. They once served Trescha, no less, but found the mandates of their new Priest King too blasphemous in the face of everything they'd been brought up to serve, to believe in. This older one couldn't keep his mouth shut, and his little brother followed him blindly and idolizing as ever. They'd have been executed for treason and blasphemy themselves, except they managed to escape and…how do you terrestrial creatures put it…*went rogue*. Not unlike your old friend Captain Gris, am I right? These two, however, found their new divine purpose within my special light." She approached Ketz, her eyes never leaving his, 'til they stood nose to nose. She gave him a quick peck on the cheek, in a gesture obscenely like that of a true, caring friend and lover. "Such divine purpose can still be yours, Ketz. Isn't that the real reason you've come? We can all be honest with each other."

"Yeah," he said, "thought about it. I've decided you can go fuck yourself."

"Have you really? I'm still not so sure."

Over her shoulder, he saw the younger Spirelight officer's eyes blazing a little hotter than before, like the guy was jealous. He felt his own paralysis more torturously than ever. His blood raced hotter and faster, so his limbs tensed and his veins bulged. Fresh sweat broke out all over him, and he could tell that she saw it and smelled it.

Still nuzzling close, she reached up and pried his sword from his fingers, fitting her own awkwardly around the grip. No sooner had she done so than she gasped, took several paces backwards, and held the pretty Ghestru blade out in front of her, in wonder. She beamed with a new kind of self-satisfied astonishment, almost alarmed, mostly delighted to find that she could still surprise herself. She swung the blade wildly and clumsily, giggling at the *whooshing* noises it made, like a little kid playing warrior with a stick. Her two Spirelight Policeman retainers edged backwards so she wouldn't absently hit one of them with it. They exchanged nervous sidelong glances, obviously not daring to voice objections. That was weird to spot. Ketz had assumed they must be too deeply mesmerized to worry about self-preservation, let alone show such traces of doubt.

"You know, I once thought you humanoid creatures were so pathetic, how you so passionately and elegantly forge these...crude tools with such ornate, reverent craftsmanship, all to just go running around chopping each other to bits over petty disagreements. It always seemed silly. But now that I finally hold one in my own hand...*my own hand*...Yes, there's a *horrible beauty* to it, isn't there...this skill of yours, this artistry? In your days of service ahead, you'll have to teach me all about it. Ketz, I bet it will be the...*second most fun* we've had between us, within these frail skins. Oh, don't worry, there'll be plenty more of the other, too. I look forward to trying you out, too, Tia...maybe even both of you at once. You know, Ketz, of all the terrestrial humanoids I've tried in that way, you've been my favorite, by far. Oh, don't look so wounded, Minquo! You did your best. It's not your fault you didn't find your way into my services 'til you were well past your prime."

Amidst all this, Ketz had almost forgotten Minquo was back there, still tied up. When he figured out what Trosola meant, his stomach rolled over a few times.

"I think everyone here is on the same branch of the tale-leaf with me by now," said Trosola. She gestured over her shoulder at her Spirelight retainers. "Boys, take our three honored guests upstairs and situate them properly. It's almost time for the End and the Beginning."

With that, she strode between the retainers and walked upstairs with Ketz's sword still bobbing and fanning at her side like a toy.

TWENTY-SEVEN

The Spirelight retainers grabbed Tia and Ketz by the scruffs of their necks and marched them up the stairs in single file. The twins still couldn't move of their own volition, yet their legs worked just fine when the Spirelights pushed them along. The older one shoved Ketz into the lead, so he marched up the staircase first. Ketz didn't like any of this, but he liked that part least of all, not being able to look back and see Tia, especially with that younger, less predictable retainer in charge of her.

Nah, these boys seemed as stoically fixated on their god as any Spirelight policemen, and this god seemed intent on saving Tia and Ketz for herself – now *there* was some cold comfort, of a sort. All he heard back there were Tia and the younger policeman's footsteps.

They came out into the main upstairs room. The red candles still burned in every window, though it was Trosola's light that filled the tavern. The room was one large oval shape, the rear quarter cut off by the bar. No decorations hung on the walls. Ketz felt the hard boards of the floor through his boots, saw the clay texture of the walls, the whalebone-sculpted counter, the bottles on the shelves behind it…but none of the hues, shades or dimensional depth that should have gone with them. All those surfaces looked like etchings on glass. The divine shades pulsed through them, in rolling clouds of green and gold, purple and silver.

Halfway across the room, the policemen shoved the twins roughly down onto their knees, facing the bar. Whatever Ketz's eyes told him, that was definitely a rough-grained wooden floor under his stinging knees. He heard the man behind him turn, walk away, and march back downstairs. Moments later, the guy returned and shoved someone else down on their knees. That must be Minquo. The accompanying groan said yes. Ketz couldn't see anyone else, but he heard the boots of the two Spirelights walking away, one to the left, the other to the right. A moment later, the sounds of drums rose again, softly at first, then louder and louder.

From outside and downstairs, the drumbeat had seemed to echo from somewhere far beyond the gulf of dreams. Now that it rose thunderously all around him, he felt like the sound had swallowed him, so he floated in a womb of its cacophony. The strange light of the place pulsed and danced to the sound, shooting back and forth like living lightning, inside and outside Ketz's brain. In it, he felt the heat of the night-flames from the swamp, the churning, slithering life of it, the frenzied, pulverizing gyrations of its dance. Ketz's vision swam, and he saw the swamp within the walls...not the sleepy swamp through which he and Tia had just walked, but as it had been in the ancient, forgotten nights when Trosola had ruled it openly, as it would be again soon...

Such divine purpose can still be yours, Ketz, said the rhythm of the drums in Trosola's voice. *Isn't that real reason you've come? We can all be honest with each other.*

Hallucia, his brainwaves screamed into the thundering firmament, *you're still in there, I know it! Wake up, please!*

Out strode Trosola. Her ethereal gown blended so with the translucent surroundings that she looked like a floating, disembodied head, shoulders, arms and chest, atop one more flowing cloud among many. She went behind the bar and sprang nimbly up onto it. There she stood, tall and proud, arms splayed. Ketz's sword still jutted out from her left fist, one thin bar of pure, razor-sharp, murderous light amidst this dizzying kaleidoscope.

"Lands of Deschemb, Lands of the province called Tatelle. I am Trosola, Highest of Gods of the Spirah

Pantheon. Here I stand before these witnesses, within this innermost chamber of the Great Sacred Heart, at the Eye of Your Great Eternal Storm." She pointed the blade forward and downward, then spun herself in a perfect circle like a dancer. The blade's tip punctured the air itself, like some invisible gelatinous surface, so a geyser of balefire spurted into the air around her like blood from an artery. She glowered triumphantly through the blaze. "With my sword in hand, I enter you, to take into myself all your ancient, primordial power, to be made one with eternal divine wisdom and vision!" She pointed the blade skyward. "Spirah, Spirah, SpiiiiiiiiiiIIIIIIIIIIIIII…" She quivered ecstatically, as though absorbing it already, all in one great gulp, and then she kept quivering, then shaking, then gyrating…No, it wasn't something filling her. Rather, something within her boiled to the surface. The sustained note singing from her mouth cracked, but kept spilling out, weaker now but still steadfast. "*IIIIIIIIIIII…am…Hallucia Brendi, and I do not…*"

A single violent undulation rolled through the whole body, like a snake gone mad, cracking itself like a whip. Something black rolled up through the flame-spout around her, then pulsed out through the room. Everyone shook with her, down to their core. Everything darkened, within a deep purple storm cloud. Once it passed, there stood the god in a woman's body, proud and pure as ever. Now she held the sword by the blade in both hands, the point turned downward.

"I am Trosola, God of the Spirah Pantheon and of these lands, and I hereby…

In her other voice, the girl's voice, "With my sword in hand…

In the voice of the god, "…With my sword in hand, I cut from me all that has…

Her grip tightened 'til her knuckles bulged white. Blood ran in rivulets down over the smooth sheen of metal.

Hallucia said, "I cut from myself *all that I am not…*

The arms shook spasmodically. The hands gripped the

blade so tight, it seemed at any second, the edges would split through the bones and slice both in half. Even from out across the floor, one thing looked damn sure: god or woman, those fingers would never work right again.

"…And what I am *not* is the Lady Hallucia Brendi! For I am…

"…Nothing but a silly little girl's mistake…" The arms rose. The quivering blade turned inward, 'til it hovered right above her heart.

"*Oh, cute,*" roared Trosola. "Really? What the fuck do you expect that to do? Go ahead. Run us right through on it! You think that'll kill us here, like this? Sure, right, a silly little girl who made a mistake. Your shit luck! Now be a dear and go drown in flames within your mistake, while a god is reborn, rising to be…

"…While a woman now cuts a god away and casts it from herself!" The tip of the sword pressed deep into Hallucia's flesh, above the center of the tattoo on her chest. She jerked it downward, sideways, let out a gasping cry, folded partway forward, and pulled the tip away reflexively. Her bloody, quivering hands almost dropped the sword, but she willed her numbing grip to tighten. Blood welled and spurted from the slice in her chest, painting the front of her dress red, all the way to her feet.

Trosola twisted the panting lips back into a defiant sneer. "Now look what you've done. Oh well, what would your little Schomite pals out there say again? *Scars are just…*"

Hallucia gritted her teeth and pressed the point back into the wound. She sliced down again, this time inward, beneath the mark. With a piercing scream, she jerked one last time, outward and upwards. Her arms spasmed outward. Her bloody fingers flew open, casting the sword away so it clattered across the boards, somewhere on the floor in front of her. The translucent swirl had become a pulsing, cacophonous maelstrom, wracking the spectators, body and soul, threatening to fry their brains and boil their guts to sludge that would leak out of their every orifice.

Trosola pulled the shaking, swaying body erect once more, with some effort. "See?" she panted, scowled in surprise, then forced it out stronger, "*See?* Now what…did you hope…to accomplish…with that little stunt?" God or no god, she was still anchored within a humanoid body, so she felt the natural effects of sudden, copious blood loss. She still lifted her hands, which opened and closed, every digit curling and wiggling just fine, even as the severed tendons poked from beneath the flesh and scraped against each other. "Ah, look at that! All those rules don't apply to us anymore." The fingers of one hand came to rest on the slices in her chest. "Just like this little stunt didn't do you a squirt of piss worth of –

Suddenly the jaws clenched. Hallucia's eyes blazed out blackly. "You're nothing but a failed god, who now falls back to the Devils of the Dark Lands who you thought you could enslave…*Devils of the Dark Lands, come take this bitch from me, from all of us!*" Her fingers fastened deep through the sundered tissue. Her nails burrowed deeper 'til they touched bone. With one last great wrench, she tore the circle of flesh straight out of her chest and flung it away. It landed somewhere with a wet plop.

Trosola screamed…not the scream of a woman, but of a shattered god…and not from Hallucia's mouth. The spectral firmament went inky black with the infernal, slavering shapes that rose up around the god. Their teeth and claws sank into the glowing specter and clung fast as it thrashed its way out of Hallucia. They dragged the shape downward 'til it split in many directions, into the fiery circle she'd cut in the air around her. Once the final fluttering shreds of her disappeared into the rift, so did the Devils of the Dark Lands. The rift whispered shut behind them.

Then there was nothing but an empty tavern, with red candles guttering on the windowsills. No one stood atop the bar but a young Ghestru woman soaked in blood. Her eyes rolled, she swayed from side to side, then she toppled backwards and crashed behind the bar.

TWENTY-EIGHT

Ketz blinked and plunged into an eternity of spinning blackness. When he opened his eyes, only a few seconds had passed. He tumbled forward onto his hands, then pulled himself up and looked around blearily. Everyone else still crawled and lurched around, coming to their senses at their own pace. His eyes settled on the distant countertop, where the explosion of cosmic theater had just played out. He scrambled forward, sprang up onto the bar, jumped down on the other side, and landed in a crouch.

Hallucia lay on her back in a spreading pool. Her chest heaved as she breathed in deep, laboring gasps. Her breastbone and ribs gleamed whitely from the ragged hole she'd made in herself. Ketz looked around 'til he spotted a pile of bar rags. He snatched a clump of them, knelt, and pressed it hard against the wound.

"Hallucia? *Hallucia!*"

Her eyes fluttered up at him. "Hi, Ketz." She sounded sleepy.

"*Hot damn, girl!* Way to stick it to a fuckin' god…literally. It's okay, the bitch is gone. See, what I tell ya? Knew you had it in you. Shit, girl, you're a mess! Hang in there. You're doin' fine. I seen way worse. Seriously, though, that's gotta be the most hardcore shit I ever saw someone pull in my whole damn life!"

"Thanks, Ketz." Her slick, red hands quivered up towards his face. Nerveless fingertips touched his cheek, leaving a dark smear. "I…was somewhere far away, drowning somewhere deep and dark, where she always sent me when she…Then, you know what? I heard your voice, shouting to me, and followed it out, back into myself…while she was there. And I realized you were right. I could fight back. And I did. You wanna know something really funny?" She chuckled deliriously.

"What's that, darlin'?"

"Once I…found my way out…tried…she wasn't even that tough! Some god, right? You know what's really too bad, Ketz? You only —" Then she just stopped.

The compress turned red beneath his hands. He still held it there, against her still chest, even after the pulse went away. A moment later, a warm, slender, familiar hand settled on his shoulder. He hadn't heard Tia approach. She knelt beside him and pressed something into his palm. He recognized the grip of the Ghestru sword. His fingers convulsed around it, and he rose quietly to his feet. His eyes cleared as he and Tia walked out from behind the bar.

A few yards away, there stood two more figures, side by side…Trosola's two Spirelight policeman retainers. They stood poised with their blades drawn, yet their fists shook around the grips. Their eyes trembled, looking as blasted and dispirited as Ketz felt. He glanced over at Tia, who also stood with her blade ready. She was the only one with anything close to earnest bloodlust left in her eyes.

Ketz met one man's gaze, then the other. No one moved. Finally, he said, "So what do you think, boys?"

The younger one said, "You…you guys…Holy shit, you're Tia and Ketz of the Nagga Mountains, aren't you?"

"That's us," said Tia bemusedly. "What about you boys?"

The older one's face relaxed, so he suddenly looked almost like a different person, like he'd been holding that scowl of grim resolution in place for years. He said, "I think…we're nothing but a couple of disgraced former policemen, forsaken by Priest King Kalesha like she forsook the gods." He turned his head to the side and spat. "Worst part was, after Kalesha came to power, it wasn't just her blasphemy I could feel in my bones. I *couldn't* feel the gods anywhere anymore, through her or otherwise. I didn't even recognize this world around me anymore, like the gods had deserted it – deserted us – all because of her…at least she's the one I used to blame. So I took my brother and we ran off…and then we found a god who was still here, one who'd still speak to us. And she was beautiful. And powerful. Now look how all that worked out for everyone." He sighed, shook his head, but still didn't lower his blade. Neither did his little brother.

Ketz looked them over. "Sounds to me like we're all just a bunch of tired fugitives who got suckered into a big damn ugly worthless mess, where a lot of people died, all 'cause of some damn god." He sheathed his blade.

The two Spirelights looked at each other, then sheathed theirs. Ketz shot Tia a sidelong look and cleared his throat.

She shrugged, rolled her eyes and sheathed hers. "Figures, we didn't even get paid."

Right then, Ketz's arm brushed his belt and he noticed something still dangling from it other than his sword…that shore leave coin purse Orcris Brendi had given him. It still hung mostly full. He hadn't had a chance to spend most of it, after all, other than that one crystal chip he'd lost at Octospheres. He almost mentioned it to Tia, then remembered their two new companions and decided not to for now.

A loud groan sounded somewhere behind them. They all turned to look. Off near the center of the floor, there lay Minquo on his stomach, his swollen cheek pressed against the floor, his hands still tied behind his back, his bound feet sticking up in the air pitifully.

Tia walked over, knelt next to Minquo and drew her long knife. With a few quick slashes, she cut away his bonds. He sprawled out, panting in agonized relief. "Thank you, young lady…Thank you so very much."

"Don't mention it. Really. All right, c'mon, up with you." She got one of his arms around her shoulder and hauled him to his feet.

"*Ow!* Easy there, now, young lady!" He sagged against her, struggling to plant his wobbly legs.

"Of course." She walked him over to the bar, pulled out a stool, set him on it, and held on 'til he steadied himself. "So how you doin', old man?"

"I feel...very fucked up." He looked around. "I could certainly use a drink."

"You know what?" said Tia. "That might be the best idea I ever heard out of you. Since we're all here, still catchin' our wind and such, I think we could all use one. On me, boys!"

Without waiting for anyone's opinion, she went behind the bar and grabbed a tall bottle of fine, strong spirits, along with five glasses. Ketz winced and lowered his eyes, recalling who else was still back there on the floor. By now, he felt more numb and tired than anything else. Tia grabbed more bar rags and wiped the crimson puddle from the countertop. She came back around, lined up the glasses and filled them, then sat on the stool next to Minquo. Minquo lifted his drink with shaky fingers and sipped.

Tia raised her glass. "Well, here's to one hell of a mornin', am I right, fellas?"

Ketz raised his glass. "I say to Hallucia."

Everyone looked at each other. Tia's eyes settled softly on her brother. "Yeah. To Hallucia and Brili." Everyone toasted and drank, then refilled their glasses.

Minquo sipped, groaned, then slouched forward. "This sure is fine...even if I am still in so much pain, I can barely move. You know...I must admit, it's funny when I think about it...Tia and Ketz...Here we sit, in a tavern, after quite a fight...much like we first met, yes?"

Tia grinned. "Hey, what do you know, you're right!" She spun him on his stool, so they faced each other. The sudden movement made him moan pitifully. "You just reminded me of somethin' else, too. Minquo, ol' buddy, when we first made our little business arrangement, you remember what I said would happen, if you dealt us dirty on this job?"

He peered at her quizzically. She reached for his belt buckle, undid his trousers with one hand while she unsheathed her blade with the other. He drew up, went pale, and shook his head frantically.

The two Spirelights exchanged looks. The younger one said, "What is she talking about?"

Ketz cleared his throat, rose and grabbed the bottle. "Nothin' we wanna watch, boys. Trust me. C'mon, let's the three of us step outside a while, pass this booze around out there. Hell, sounds like we've got quite a few stories to tell between us. Anyhow, I could use the fresh air."

He urged them to their feet, stepped between them, threw his arms around their shoulders, and walked them to the front door. They stepped out into the cool morning air. Behind them, back at the bar, Minquo started shrieking.

Matt Spencer is the author of five novels, two collections, and numerous novellas and short stories. He's been a journalist, New Orleans restaurant cook, factory worker, radio DJ, and a no-good ramblin' bum. He's also a song lyricist, playwright, actor, and martial artist. He lives in Vermont with his girlfriend and two cats. Check him out online at http://mattspencerauthor.wordpress.com, on Twitter at @MattSpencerFSFH, and on Facebook at Books by Matt Spencer.

Thanks for reading, folks. Hope you enjoyed the ride. Now don't forget to go to let everyone else know what you thought! Be sure to pop over to Amazon, Goodreads, your blog, and whatever social media you frequent, and drop a short review (or a long one, if you feel like it).